PR...

ILL-GOT...

"Jennifer McAndrews's *Ill-...* ....g about mystery full of small-town .... ..y, charming characters, and a plot that kept me guessing. Georgia Kelly is an adorable heroine whose clever wit and humor made me laugh out loud!"

—Jenn McKinlay, *New York Times* bestselling
author of *The Drop of a Hat*

"Georgia Kelly is a plucky heroine whose love of stained glass, kittens, and her grandfather will draw you in and keep you turning pages. *Ill-Gotten Panes* is filled with small-town characters, intelligent cops, and a heroine who feels like a dear friend—one you want to sit down and spend time with, as she figures out who is who in Wenwood and how she fits into her new home."

—Nancy J. Parra, author of the Baker's Treat mysteries

"A stunning mystery . . . a great whodunit . . . cleverly crafted . . . kept me on the edge of my seat."

—*Cozy Mystery Book Review*

"Georgia makes an appealing lead character . . . Cozy fans may want to watch how this series develops." —*Booklist*

"[A] sweet debut . . . This cozy will snag those intrigued by the stained-glass side of the story and a gorgeous cover (can't go wrong with Tiffany)." —*Library Journal*

"A wonderful debut . . . I loved this book."

—Mochas, Mysteries & Meows

"Fun . . . . ppealing."

...Book Musing

Books by Jennifer McAndrews

ILL-GOTTEN PANES
DEATH UNDER GLASS

DEATH UNDER GLASS

Jennifer
McAndrews

BERKLEY PRIME CRIME, NEW YORK

BERKLEY PRIME CRIME

An imprint of Penguin Random House LLC
375 Hudson Street, New York, New York 10014

A Berkley Prime Crime Book / published by arrangement with the author

ISBN: 978-0-425-26796-7

PUBLISHING HISTORY
Berkley Prime Crime mass-market edition / July 2015

PRINTED IN THE UNITED STATES OF AMERICA

10 9 8 7 6 5 4 3 2 1

Cover design by George Long.
Cover art by Stephan Gardner (Lott Reps).
Interior text design by Kelly Lipovich.

Penguin
Random
House

For Mom

ACKNOWLEDGMENTS

Anyone who has ever written a book, or attempted to write one, will tell you there's more to the story than you see. More to its creation than coming up with a plot and getting the words down in the right order. These acknowledgments are about that unseen story, about the people in my world to whom I owe thanks for making the writing possible.

First and foremost to my daughters Tracy and Christine for keeping me company and keeping me laughing, and to my husband Bob for walking my path with me. Thanks to my mom and my sisters for lending their shoulders (and singing "Soft Kitty") and to Petra Durnin for her friendship, guidance, and our champagne afternoons. Deepest gratitude to Susan Faggiani for being there and for being family, to Doreen Orsini for being a partner in crime and laughter, and to my writer besties Julie O'Connell, Ginger Calem, and Linda Gerber, as always, for being my pillars.

Big thanks to the wonderful people at Berkley: Robin Barletta, Danielle Dill, Stephan Gardner, Ian Hodder, and Pam Barricklow.

And finally—and I cannot believe I failed to do this last time—thanks to the super folks at Stained Glass Workshop, especially Jerry and Elizabeth, who taught me how to work with glass, and more, how to appreciate the effort and skill it takes to create even the simplest pieces of this beautiful art. I hope that someday I may create something worthy of their teaching.

In the meantime, Wenwood awaits . . .

1

"It was not my idea," I said.

"Yes, Georgia, it was." As Carrie removed the keys from the ignition, I pushed open the passenger door and stepped out onto the curb. Creeping past the midpoint of August, the sunny, dry days and warm nights of early summer had progressed to rainy nights, hazy mornings, and steamy afternoons. We had arrived at the large blue pseudo-Victorian home during that atmospheric sweet spot between clear sky and muggy, with patches of ground still damp and soft after an overnight storm.

"You said," Carrie continued, slamming the driver's door behind her, "that I shouldn't be spending all my time at the antiques store."

I waited for her to join me on the newly poured sidewalk. Mud pooled in the gullies on either side of the pristine concrete, spicing the air with a sweet, moist-earth fragrance. Near the apron of a neighbor's driveway, a trio of chickadees splashed in a curbside puddle. "I never said that. Why would I tell you that you were spending too much time in the shop you *own*? That's crazy. When did I allegedly utter this craziness?"

Carrie sighed and resettled her purse on her shoulder, careful to avoid catching her soft brown curls beneath the strap. "I don't remember exactly. It was during that whole to-do with Pete."

"Ohhh." While the whole town of Wenwood called my grandfather Pete, to me he would always be Grandy. A couple of weeks after I'd moved back to town and into Grandy's spare bedroom, we'd suffered a little misfortune that Carrie was being kind in downplaying as a "to-do." The whole story involved Grandy being unfairly accused of murdering the owner of the local hardware store. In all the anxiety and heartache of those days, I could have said any number of crazy things before the real murderer was locked up. "That explains why I don't remember. But I still don't think I should be held responsible for anything I said during that time. I was under duress."

Carrie stifled a chuckle. "Duress or no, you said it and it got me thinking and now here we are."

She gestured toward the old Victorian, and I gazed up at the sprawling house at the end of the long, straight walkway. Like so many homes in Wenwood, this one had seen better days. Missing balusters gaped like lost teeth on the porch, and gutters hung low in places beneath a much-patched roof. As with very few homes, the owner of this one was investing in bringing the house back to its original beauty, what with the new sidewalks and unpainted patches framing newly installed windows. Revitalization and renewal. The new battle cry of Wenwood.

Carrie took in a deep breath and started up the walk. "The reality is, there's no reason for me to be in the shop every day. Weekends, sure, but Tuesdays? Wednesdays? They're just not big days for antiques hunters. Not really worth the cost of air-conditioning, you know?"

As I trailed along behind her, the front edge of my flip-flop scooped up a wet mimosa blossom, its delicate pink stamens slipping under my toes like bubble-gum-colored seaweed. Funny how even the simple act of walking up a path proved problematic for me. "What about all the online sales?" I asked, wriggling my toes and tapping my foot in a foolish attempt to dislodge the blossom. "I thought that was a big piece of the business."

She shrugged, tossed me a too-bright smile. "Nothing wrong with expanding. This could be a whole new revenue stream for me, working with renovations, finding just the right luminaire or even a fainting couch."

Though she sounded much like she was trying to convince herself, I couldn't argue her reasoning. In fact, she was probably onto something. The town of Wenwood had steadily grown smaller and older after its main industry—the riverside plant that had churned out building and paving bricks for nearly a century—had closed. For years residents had moved out and moved on, leaving crumbling roads, empty houses, and shuttered businesses behind.

But nearly a year ago, the Stone Mountain Construction

group had bought up the property on which the old brickworks sat and started building a marina in its place. Many
remaining residents were hoping a marina would generate
tourism sufficient to reenergize the town. A number of
folks, in fact, were banking on it, including the woman on
whose property we stood. In their quest to bring homes
back to their former glory—or, perhaps more accurately,
back to their turn-of-the-century roots—who better to
advise owners on their decorating or to acquire those
hard-to-find pieces than the local antiques expert?

As we climbed the steps to the porch, Carrie pointed
to the transom above the door. "That's the window Trudy
and I thought you could do something special with."

By "something special," Carrie meant a custom stained
glass piece. I gazed up at the window, at the beams of wood
keeping the sun off the porch and keeping the heat from
our heads. Stained glass was at its most brilliant when
sunshine streaked through bringing the spectrum of color
to life. Here, where the sun's rays were blocked, artificial
light would be needed to make the glass burst with color.
But once the lighting was in place, the effect might possibly
be stunning.

"Custom glass was your idea?" I asked.

Carrie nodded and rang the bell. Before I could count
one Mississippi, a furious barking erupted on the other side
of the door. Neither the yap of a small dog nor the deep
timbre of a large dog, the mid-range noise was filled nonetheless with ferocity.

Heart rate instantly increasing, I slid backward a step.

"Don't worry," Carrie said. She smiled reassuringly, but I decided the safest place was behind her.

"I'll wait here," I said, as a woman's voice carried through the door, saying *hush, hush*. The dog did no such thing.

The knob rattled moments before the door swung inward, and a flash of tan and white flew at us.

"Fifi, no," the woman shouted.

The bulldog ignored her command. With her jaws gaping and her weight vibrating the porch boards, she rushed straight for Carrie. Before Carrie could grab the dog's collar, Fifi skirted around her and mashed her muzzle against my shin.

I skittered sideways, half fearful, half shocked by the cold nose. But Fifi backed and came at me again, hindquarters rolling side to side in doggie glee while she snuffled at my feet.

"She's quite harmless, I assure you," the woman said. "Fifi!" She clapped her hands twice, but Fifi ignored her, preferring instead to drool all over my bare feet.

"She smells that creature," Carrie told me.

"Friday is a kitten," I said, defending the now four-month bundle of mischief I'd found behind Carrie's store. "She's not a spawn of the underworld."

"Your opinion," Carrie muttered.

"I'm so sorry." The woman—slender and tall with gray hair and a somewhat pinched expression—advanced, crouching and reaching for the dog's collar. "She's not accustomed to heeding my commands."

The dog had settled into sniffing my feet, and I reached down to pat her head. "She's fine, actually," I managed to mutter. My heart rate slowed and I could once again draw full breath as I stroked a hand across the silky fur of the dog's head. Thus alerted to my attention, Fifi gazed up at me with huge brown eyes that would put a stuffed animal to shame. I might have mumbled something about her being a good girl but not loud enough for Carrie to hold against me in the future.

Presumably seeing that the dog was no threat to me nor me to it, the woman abandoned her quest for the dog's collar and straightened.

Her gaze scraped me head to toe, her lips tightening at the sight of my unruly red hair, kitten-holed T-shirt, and dog-slobbered plastic flip-flops. "Have we met?" she asked, blinking.

I couldn't find words to answer. Seeing her that still, that formally posed, made me pretty sure I'd seen her play the evil stepmother in a Disney cartoon.

Carrie stepped into the breach. "Trudy, you remember I told you about my friend who does stained glass, right? This is Georgia." As she introduced me, she turned in my direction and held both palms to the heavens in the manner of a spokesmodel presenting a car.

"Georgia Kelly," I said, reaching a hand toward the woman.

Trudy laid the tips of her fingers against mine, and I ended up clutching her hand as though I were about to kiss it rather than shake it. She repeated my name, a deep furrow forming between her eyebrows, emphasizing the wrinkles she'd earned in her lifetime. "You seem so familiar and yet I don't recall your name at all."

"But I told you," Carrie said, a note of patience coloring her voice.

The older woman waved dismissively. "Yes, yes, I mean aside from that, dear. Well, no matter." She stepped backward into the house, sweeping her arm toward the interior in invitation. "Please come in. Fifi, you come inside, too."

Fifi trotted along beside me as I followed Carrie inside. My flip-flops smacked against the worn wood floor, Carrie's low heels clicked, and the dog betrayed us both by padding along soundlessly. As Trudy tended to the door, we waited in the small entry foyer, cool air washing over us and the scent of lemon cleaner tickling my nose.

The front door clicked shut, and Trudy strode between Carrie and me, with a simple, "This way" as she passed.

She led us out of the foyer to our right, through an arched doorway and into the sort of space I'd only ever seen in magazines . . . or hotel lobbies. Three tall and narrow windows faced the front of the house, bathing the room in light, while the yellow painted walls helped create the illusion the room sat directly at the end of a sunbeam. I walked slowly through the slanted rays to the couch Trudy pointed us to, and sat on the low-backed ivory couch with the sun warming my back. Ahead, French doors with floor-to-ceiling windows on either side provided a view of an abundance of roses in the backyard.

Fifi jumped up onto the couch beside me, eliciting a "Fifi, no!" from Trudy. But Fifi ignored her, stretching out, and Trudy sighed. "I just can't make that dog listen."

"Try giving orders to a cat," I said.

She gave no indication of hearing me. "It would be different, I suppose, if I had raised her from a pup," Trudy said. "But her original owner was a bit more—how should I put it?—indulgent." She lowered herself into one of the striped damask wingback chairs facing the couch, her spine straight and her head tipped to the side. "Georgia Kelly," she said again, that same pinch across her brow announcing that she was forcing her mind to a question.

I shot a look at Carrie, who leaned forward and smoothly drew Trudy's attention. "Georgia repaired a Tiffany lamp for me," she said.

"Tiffany-style," I said, "not the genuine article." Repair a real Tiffany piece? I did that in the same dreams in which I was independently wealthy and had a glass workshop in the south of France.

"Still beautiful," Carrie said, while Trudy gazed appraisingly at me. "And of course I've sold several of her other pieces. Stunning, really. So naturally when we talked about that window over your door I thought of her *and* those roses you have out back. I thought it might be a nice idea to carry that motif into the transom."

Afraid I might start squirming if Trudy kept staring at me like I was some sort of specimen prepared for dissection, I sprang from my seat and crossed to the French doors. In the center of the little slate patio ringed by roses sat a wrought iron table and a pair of chairs I recognized from the back room of Carrie's antiques shop.

"And would the name of my business be incorporated into this *motif*?" Trudy asked.

I looked over my shoulder and met Carrie's eye, certain she would share my bemusement over *motif*, but she only raised her brows in question. "What do you think?" she asked. "Can you work it in?"

"Depends on what exactly the name is going to be," I said, wandering away from the doors and toward the fireplace yawning along the western wall. "Whether you're going to go with simply *Trudy's* or *Trudy's B&B* or—"

"Oh, my dear," Trudy said, managing to get a shudder into her words. "There will be no *B&B*, thank you very much."

I bit my lip to keep back a giggle. For someone who didn't get too distraught by a dog on the furniture, Trudy seemed to be working awfully hard at being classy.

Carrie shifted forward in her seat. "Did you have another name in mind?"

Trudy's chin lifted a notch and her tone carried a melody of pride. "I've registered the business as Magnolia Bed and Breakfast."

From where I stood I tried to peer through the white sheers on the windows to see if there was, in fact, a magnolia tree on the property that I had failed to notice. But all that was visible was the fronds and blossoms of the mimosa, all pink and green and looking like the nineties exploded on the lawn.

"What do you think, Georgia? Can you do magnolias in stained glass?" Carrie asked.

Pausing to admire the collection of china knickknacks above the fireplace, I caught sight of myself in the mirror hung above the mantel, heartlessly reflecting an image of my hair. The humidity was not being kind. I looked like *I Love Lucy*'s home perm episode.

I turned my back on my image. Out of sight, out of mind, right? "Magnolias are one of the classic flowers in stained glass," I said. "Tiffany frequently featured magnolias in their windows and lamps because they're so lovely. I could bring some designs by and some examples."

"Tiffany's did?" Trudy didn't sit up straighter as much as her neck sort of elongated. I supposed Tiffany was the perfect antidote to *B&B*.

I smiled and nodded, not bothering to educate Trudy on the difference between jewelry store founder Charles Tiffany and the stained glass innovations of his son Louis. It was all in the family as far as I was concerned. A Tiffany was a Tiffany. And it seemed to please Trudy.

"That sounds marvelous," she announced. "What color can you make the blossoms?" She shifted her attention to Carrie. "Can we bring the color into this room? Drapes? Pillows? Throw rugs?"

As Carrie and Trudy batted ideas back and forth, I reclaimed my seat next to Fifi. The pooch had rolled onto her back and let out a grumbling whimper as I sat. She stretched and pushed her nose against my thigh. Hoping it was attention she wanted and not some flesh to nibble on, I reached out and carefully rubbed her exposed belly while admiring the rhinestone-ringed name tag hanging from her collar. The sparkle stirred my mind, and I belatedly wondered where Trudy was getting the money for the renovations to the house. Of course it wouldn't be impossible that she simply had a good deal of money socked away somewhere. And perhaps the hints of neglect outside and in were the result of frugality rather than financial limitations. But Wenwood had been known more for its work ethic than its wealth, and yet there Trudy sat, spine straight in her wingback chair, gold watch heavy on her wrist and precious gems winking over her fingers.

The theme song from *Mission Impossible* blared from Carrie's purse, making her flinch, wide-eyed, and bringing me back from my contemplation of Trudy's bank balance. Carrie and I spent a fair amount of time together, and I recognized that particular tune as her default ringtone for calls from people outside her contact list.

"I'm so sorry," Carrie said, glancing back and forth between me and Trudy. "I thought I switched it off . . . I . . ." She tugged open her purse, dug frantically for the phone. "I'm sure it's nothing. I'll just—" Her eyes fell on the display screen and the number appearing there. The pink flush of embarrassment drained as quickly as it had bloomed, leaving her skin magnolia pale. "I'm sorry," she said softly, standing. "I need to take this."

While Carrie ducked into the foyer, I smiled at Trudy, searching my brain for the right question to engage her with while I worried over who or what might have caused such a reaction in Carrie. "So, um, Fifi had a different owner. How did she end up with you? Did you adopt her from a shelter?"

Trudy peered closely at me as though looking for an answer to a question only she knew. "Georgia Kelly," she said again.

"Why do you keep saying that?" I asked.

She shook her head slowly, the movement barely disturbing her drop earrings. "There's something about you, dear. Something not right with you being a Kelly."

I fought to keep the surprise and hint of offense from showing on my face. I had no idea what she was talking about, but I didn't figure it was anything good, or possibly, you know, sane. I opened my mouth to ask her what she meant by such a remark in the same moment Carrie rushed back into the room.

"We have to go," she said, reaching over me to grab her purse. I froze in response to her sudden haste; Fifi scrambled to her feet, alert to the new charge in the air.

"What is it? What's wrong?" I jumped to my feet, steeling myself for whatever news she might hurl my way.

Swinging her purse over her shoulder, she said, "My husband's business is burning. I have to go."

2

"**D**o you want me to drive?" I asked, rushing down the path away from Trudy's house.

"It's fine. I'm not upset." Carrie fumbled the keys and they hit the sidewalk with a heavy metallic thud. She hissed a curse, grabbed the keys, and continued stomping her way to the car.

"Are you sure? I only ask because you seem a little, um, wound up." And I didn't want either one of us to die in a motor vehicle accident. I stood beside the car, waiting for her to reach the driver's side, waiting for her to change her mind and hand me the keys.

Instead, she took the time to meet my eyes over the top of the sedan. "Why would you say that? I'm fine."

Once she was in the car with the door shut behind her,

I climbed into the passenger seat. "I say that because we're speeding off to a fire at your ex-husband's business."

"And?"

"Your *ex*-husband. This is Russ you're rushing to help. The guy you divorced. And you're going off with lights and sirens and a death grip on the wheel. Any reason?" I pulled my seat belt into place without taking my gaze off of Carrie. I had never had the pleasure/experience/bad luck of meeting her ex; they were divorced before I even met Carrie. But over the past couple of months, she and I had shared a good number of tales of woe featuring our former flames. As could be expected, she had little good to say about Russ, though I knew—even though I could be faulted for the same behavior—she was hardly being unbiased in her complaints.

She maneuvered the car into a smooth U-turn, and we sped up the block of grand old houses, centennial trees shading lawns and road alike. I sat in silence for a while, giving Carrie the time she needed to gather her thoughts and answer my question. I did not want to prompt her, or pressure her, and in any case had learned from the beginning that she wasn't one to stay quiet for long.

"It's hard, you know?" she asked as she signaled a turn onto the highway. "Well, you do know. You go for so long thinking of someone as your husband"—she shot me a glance—"or your fiancé, your *partner*, and when everything's calm and normal you remember they're not that person anymore. But when things get stressy and crazy . . ."

I did know, she was right. There had been more than a few times in the past eight-plus months after our engagement ended when life events had gone pear-shaped and the first person I thought of was Eric. When things got tough, my addled mind still prompted me to seek his shoulder for comfort. It always took a few tough moments to remember no, he was no longer the person I ran to, no longer the rock in my life—for better or worse. Luckily, that breath-stealing moment of realization was getting shorter and shorter.

Still, I folded my arms across my chest and gave Carrie a stern stare. "I just think it's best you remember there was a time you might have derived a little guilt-ridden satisfaction from seeing his business burn to the ground, so there's no need to risk a speeding ticket, or our necks for that matter. You said no one was hurt, right?"

"Right."

"Then maybe slow down, huh?"

Carrie gave the steering wheel one long last white-knuckle grip, then softened her hold and let up on the gas. "Okay." She nodded. "Okay. Good point."

We settled into a legal speed, cruising past trees in full green and wild flowers in full bloom. A general fragrance of flowers snuck into the car with the air-conditioning. Or maybe that was the candle-scented air freshener dangling from the glove box.

"Why did you get the call, anyway?" I asked. "Doesn't he have anyone else he could call? You said he got all the friends in the divorce. Couldn't he beg one of them for help?"

"It wasn't Russ who called. It was the police department." She kept her gaze fixed on the road ahead. "I'm still part owner of the building."

We cruised past half a dozen ancient oak trees while I attempted to process that information. "'Part' as in equitably divided during the divorce?"

Her grip on the steering wheel tightened again. "As in purchased when we were married. After the divorce, he wanted to buy my half but he didn't want to go into any more bank debt. And I'm embarrassed to say I wasn't kindhearted enough to offer him any kind of private loan."

"Doesn't he have anyone who could front him the money? What about family?" I shifted in my seat, making a futile attempt to lean my arm up against the window ledge all casual-like but my elbow kept slipping down the curve of the door. "Brothers, sisters, aunts, uncles?"

"His brother Gabe . . ." She shrugged and shook her head as if she were shaking away a memory not worth revisiting. "Well . . ." She let the statement fade and I opted not to push.

"What about his folks?" I asked. "Are they still around to help out Russ?"

Carrie tipped her head from side to side, lips pressed tight as she considered my question—or how best to answer. "They don't have the best relationship."

"No?"

"No, they . . ." She took a bracing breath. "They helped me pay for the divorce."

My mouth dropped open but no words fell out; I had none. Maybe the reason Carrie didn't speak much about her marriage to Russ—other than to inform me he was a talentless slacker with a ready smile, a quick promise, and nothing to back up either—was because its dissolution had divided his family.

She peeked at me from the corner of her eye, then shrank a little in the driver's seat, looking abashed. "I know. I know. You don't have to say it."

I almost laughed, my belly clenching in discomfort at the awkwardness of it all. "I can't say anything. I don't know what *to* say." Or think. All I seemed capable of doing was picturing the special joy of dinner with Russ's family. Holidays were undoubtedly the stuff of Tim Burton's nightmares.

I kept silent for the rest of the ride, leaving Carrie the opportunity to share more surprises with me or not. Uncharacteristically, she chose not, so that in the relative quiet of the car, my thoughts bounced from those of Russ's family to my own. My mother had been home from her honeymoon with husband number five for nearly a month and I'd yet to visit them. I really had nothing against new husband Ben, the latest in a line of men Mom married in a peculiar effort to fill the shoes of my late father—Mom's "one true love." Since Dad had passed before I turned two, I had no true memory of him, only memories I created around the stories my mother told, so I never saw the subsequent husbands as trying to fill my father's shoes. To me they were just a series of guys I got accustomed to thinking of as stepdad du jour before my mother moved on.

To the best of my knowledge, though, none of my family members had ever felt opposed enough to any of my mom's husbands to pay for a divorce. Given the way Grandy had taken to referring to my former fiancé as "that swine," I reasoned he would happily fork over any money it took to end a bad situation. I deeply wanted to ask Carrie for more details about her former in-laws but I risked only one more inquiry into whether she would prefer I drove, before maintaining silence until, finally, after a twenty-five minute ride, we turned onto the town of Newbridge's main commercial road. Small businesses with gold-lettered windows and retail shops with colorful awnings edged the road on either side, its full length blocked by a police cruiser.

Unable to proceed any farther by car, Carrie steered onto a side street. Little more than a wide alley divided the commercial strip from residential property. Single family homes with narrow lawns and empty driveways flanked the street where Carrie eased the car to a stop alongside the curb. As calm and cool as she was pretending to be, her choice of vacant spot betrayed the true tumult within. I climbed out of the vehicle after her, calling over the roof of the car, "Are you sure you want to leave this here?"

She stutter-stepped to a stop. "Why? Is there a sign? Can we not park?"

I pointed upward, toward the unimpeded view of a wide blue sky. "There's no shade."

Carrie moved to reopen the car then shook her head. "It'll be fine," she said. "Let's just go."

Slinging my purse strap over my shoulder, I rounded the car and joined Carrie in the middle of the side street, quiet save the occasional *woof* of a dog and the shouts of a couple of boys on bicycles.

We walked diagonally across the road to the corner from which we could once again see the squad car blocking access. Clusters of people stood along the sidewalk, talking quietly, shaking their heads. I followed the angle of their quick glances. Eyes on the scene beyond the squad car, I walked full stride into a gutter puddle.

I huffed out a sigh. It was going to be one of those days.

Water swept over my foot and splashed against my ankles. I had just enough sense to keep my other foot dry, and hopped over the remainder of the puddle to join Carrie on the sidewalk.

Side by side, we walked toward the center of the area cordoned off by police with a combination of caution tape, vehicles, and cruisers. My footsteps squeaked from the water coating the sole of my flip-flops and droplets of water splashing up the back of my calf, handily undermining the aura of High Noon that hung over the street.

A Pace County police officer climbed out of the squad car at our approach. "Excuse me, ladies," he called. "This road's closed to non-business owners."

Carrie stopped short. She fluttered a hand against her throat, looked left and right as though searching for someone to give her stage directions. "I—I was asked to come," she said.

The officer moved toward us, one hand on the butt of his gun in classic patrolman style. "Sorry, can you speak up?" Not to say that I didn't respect the Pace County PD, but the officer's toes-out stride, gangly frame, and peach fuzz goatee made him look like a boy scout who'd donned the wrong uniform. And I had never been able to consider a boy scout any manner of authority. It might have been the neckerchief.

I touched my fingers against Carrie's arm, silently encouraging her to move forward. "It's okay," I called. "She is a business owner." Waving to a vague spot up the street, I edged behind Carrie, just enough to force her to pick up the pace so I didn't catch the back of her foot with the front of mine

"Georgia," Carrie whispered as I hustled her along. "We can't lie to the police. It's wrong."

"It's not a lie. You own your own business, right? And half of an office building. You qualify." I guided her past a Laundromat with a sandwich board sign out front, big letters advising patrons to enter through the back.

"I don't own a business *here*," she said, but the tension had gone from her voice.

"Someone here wanted to speak to you but I doubt it was the rookie in the squad car. He didn't look like he was expecting anyone." I glanced around, looking for some sign of other police officers but finding none. "We'll find whoever is looking for you."

A stout man in a gold shirt and a kitchen apron stood in the doorway of a coffee shop, arms folded and eyes on the scene across the road. Even his presence did little to shatter the feeling of walking into a ghost town.

"I don't suppose you've remembered the name of the cop who called you yet?" I asked.

"Officer Reinhart or Reinbach or—" Carrie shook her head. "Something with an *R*. Once he told me why he was calling, all I could remember of his name was *Officer*."

She stopped again and turned to face the other side of the road. After keeping the sight in the corner of my eye, the full-on view of what had, until yesterday, been Russ Stanford's law office should have been less shocking. But the cream-colored stone façade was streaked black around the windows and door, as though something evil had gripped the jambs and sashes in its violent escape from within. Broken glass glittered, jagged and deadly, across the sidewalk, while police tape cordoned off the entirety of the ruins.

I looked to Carrie, tried to discern from her expression what emotions might be overtaking her, whether any memories—fond or otherwise—may have been awakened by the evidence of fire in her former husband's place of business. Her face remained unchanged, eyes clear and wide open. Only a hint of resignation tugged down the corners of her mouth.

"All right," she said. "Let's see what they want."

With the squad car blocking vehicular access to the road, we safely crossed the street without looking both ways first. The only thing we might have been struck by was a stray pigeon, or maybe a mosquito.

As we drew nearer the building, a trio of men emerged from behind it, their steps slow and measured, their eyes on the scorched façade. Two of them were unknown to me. The third I previously had tangled with . . . as it were.

He looked our way in the same moment I extended my

elbow to nudge Carrie. His eyes narrowed, and I tried to tell myself the action was the result of sun glare and not something personal.

"Miss Kelly," he said as he and his cohorts ambled toward us.

I nodded, either acknowledging his greeting or agreeing that was indeed my name. "Detective Nolan."

"I can hardly wait to find out what brings you here," he said, the barest hint of a smile tugging on his lips.

A scant two months earlier it had been Detective Nolan who had turned up on my doorstep, waking me from a dead sleep and hauling my grandfather—Grandy—into the police station for questioning in relation to the murder of a Wenwood shop owner. Following the ordeal I felt a dozen years older; Nolan, annoyingly, looked the same as he had that morning on Grandy's doorstep. The same dark hair softly graying at the temple, the same watchful brown eyes, the same tough jaw clenched above a somewhat askew tie—the somewhat askew tie terminating in the gold detective's badge clipped to Nolan's belt.

I tipped my head to my left. "This is my good friend Carrie Stanford. She was summoned. I came with her."

The detective left off his perusal of my muddy foot and shifted his attention to Carrie. "Mrs. Stanford," he said. "Sorry to have to ask you to come down here."

Carrie stiffened marginally. "That's Ms. Stanford, please. Russ and I are divorced."

Nolan was too much of a professional to flinch at Carrie's sharp tone. "I'll remember that." He introduced the two men with him—one, another gold badge member of the Pace County PD. The other, Chief Fire Marshal Barker, extended a hand to both Carrie and me.

"Thanks for making the trip," he said in a rasping voice that perfectly complemented his lined face and thick silver hair. "Easier if you see the damage for yourself."

"Easier how? Why?" Carrie's brows dived toward the bridge of her nose, and anxiety raised the pitch of her voice. "I was told no one was hurt. Is that not true? Is that why I need to be here in person?"

Nolan rushed to reassure her. "Nothing like that. There's no evidence of anyone being inside. According to neighbors, the fire was started somewhere around four this morning, not within business hours."

"Wait." I put up a hand to pause the information. "You said 'was started.' Does that mean—"

"Oh, yah," Chief Barker ground out. "This here's the most suspicious fire I've seen in a long time."

3

Chief Barker stood with us, inches from the threshold of what had once been Russ Stanford's law office, and swept the beam of a flashlight around the interior. He bounced the light against three distinct spots in the fire-damaged space—a blackened desk ahead and to the left, a corner deep to the right, and a doorway straight ahead at the other end of the room. "There, there, and there," he said as he shifted the light. "See how they look worse than some of the other spots?"

Carrie and I nodded in vague unison. Where the walls enclosing the open-plan office appeared slick with soot or bubbled from heat, the areas Barker indicated were shrouded in almost unfathomable blackness. A piece of furniture that might once have been a desk was slumped one-sided to the floor, waiting for the beat of a butterfly's wing to bring the rest of it down.

"Those are your likely acceleration points," Barker said. "We got some testing to do so we can bring the science to the judge, but even just lookin' at this, this was most likely a set fire, starting in three separate points. Probably garbage pails, a little gasoline thrown in there."

Following the thought, I murmured, "And three pails at the same time couldn't be an accident."

"Exactly." Barker swung back in our direction, where the sunbeams pushing through the blown-out windows washed away the gleam of the flashlight. "We'll do all the tests, of course. Check everything out. Meantime, you're gonna want to get some fencing put up around this place, keep folks from wandering in and getting hurt."

"Put up fencing?" Carrie asked. "How do I—?"

"There must be a business, a company or something." I looked to the fire marshal. "Right? Would they need some kind of certification or something?"

Barker's mouth softened into a kind smile. "You give me a way to get in touch with you, I'll make sure you get the names of some of the folks we know who do this sort of thing—the fences and cleanup and such."

We stood in a silent huddle in which I waited for Carrie to say something and Barker waited for one of us to say something.

"After, we'll let you know when we can turn the property back over to you," he said slowly, gaze locked on Carrie.

Her eyes widened and she nodded in understanding. "Oh, I'm done? That's it, right? I can go and you'll contact me?"

26

Barker smiled again. "Well I got nothin' else for you. But the detectives will have some questions."

We thanked the fire marshal, and I did my best to shake off the sense of incongruity created by thanking a man who had shown us destruction. After Carrie gave him her business card with her contact information on it, she and I shuffled back across the sidewalk to where Detective Nolan stood, arms crossed, watching the other detective stroll away.

His gaze slid sideways as Carrie and I neared. "Let's get some coffee," he said. He tipped his head in the direction of the coffee shop and, without waiting for us to agree or decline, started walking.

After a quick, wordless check with one another, Carrie shrugged, I grimaced, and we were off.

"I don't understand," Carrie said as we hurried to catch up. "Why do I need to answer questions? It's Russ's business. For that matter, where is Russ? Why isn't he here?"

He slipped pinched fingers along the lapel of his suit, straightening what had never been out of place. "We're still trying to locate Mr. Stanford."

"He's missing?" My question ended in an embarrassing squeak.

I thought Detective Nolan might have grinned, but the unusual tug of muscles around his mouth didn't last long enough for me to be certain.

"I wouldn't go that far just yet," he replied, voice distinctly mirthless. "He's not answering his phone or his door. Just makes him out of reach, not missing." He turned back to Carrie. "So it's up to you. You're a part owner and his ex-wife," he said. "You need to answer questions."

"Yes, ex-wife." Carrie skitter-stepped and drew level with him. "Ex. What would I know?"

A little breeze of déjà vu stirred the hair on the back of my neck. The temperature may have been rising steadily toward steamy, but I didn't welcome the chill. "Please tell me you don't think Carrie had something to do with the fire."

He glanced over his shoulder at me, his mouth a firm line accustomed to holding in secrets. "If that were the case, *you* would be waiting in your car."

"Oh, you think so?" I said. I might have added a smirk, which might have been unwise.

"Still a possibility," he said.

"As if you—" I began. But Carrie put a hand on my arm, and the quelling look she shot me made the protest slip away.

Carrie may not have spoken a word, but the caution in her gaze reminded me of the wisdom of keeping my mouth shut and smirk-free in the presence of detectives. I walked quietly beside her, all too aware of my capacity for letting my mouth get ahead of my brain. Or, more to the point, letting my default trust in people's good nature lead me into self-incrimination.

"Go ahead inside," the detective said, lifting his chin to indicate the coffee shop before veering away. "I'll be right with you."

Without a backward look in our direction, he crossed to the squad car blocking the street.

"Quick, while he's not looking. Let's make a run for it," I said, trying to lighten the mood.

Carrie kept her voice a fraction above a whisper. "We didn't do anything."

"You sure? You're not lying to me about sneaking up here last night and torching your ex-husband's livelihood? Sounds like great revenge to me."

"Except I still own half the property that livelihood sits on," she said. "Or used to sit on, anyway. Setting fire to it would be a little like cutting off my nose, wouldn't it?"

She was right, of course. And the fact of her ownership would, I hoped, keep her from being dragged down to the Pace County Police Department station house for further questioning or—heaven forbid—arrest, and would keep that shine of innocence around her.

Unless of course there was a great insurance payout to be had if—

I stopped in my tracks and shut my eyes tight to banish the idea of Carrie having anything to do with the fire. Insurance payouts or no, Carrie would never do such a thing. She wasn't the arson type. She didn't even go in for decorative candles.

Before ducking into the coffee shop behind Carrie, I looked to see what was more important to Detective Nolan than starting his immediate semi-interrogation of her. He stood beside the squad car that blocked the street, talking with the uniformed officer. Clouds slid over the sun, momentarily softening the glare of the morning, so that when the light reasserted itself, it was easier to spot the sun's rays picking up streaks of gray and surprising hints of gold in the detective's hair and splaying a shadow of his broad shoulders across the pavement.

Nolan pointed to the opposite end of the street, the rookie officer nodded and tugged open the door of the car, and I became aware of the hazardous road my mind was about to wander down while gazing at the back of Detective Nolan's pale gray suit. I mentally smacked myself. The good detective did not merit my attention—not that sort of attention, anyway. What was wrong with me?

The rich, edgily bitter scent of coffee sneaked past me on a breeze.

"Are you coming?" Carrie asked from behind me.

I turned to find her hovering in the open doorway of the coffee shop. The same shop from which the aroma of coffee wafted. My taste buds awoke and my stomach rumbled. Hunger. Low blood sugar. That explained my new perspective on Detective Nolan.

"I think I have to eat something," I said when I reached Carrie.

"How is that possible?" She held the door open to allow me to precede her into the coffee shop. "How can you think of food when I'm about to be questioned by the police?"

Telling her I wasn't the one about to be questioned would have been bad form. I smiled at a dark-haired girl wearing black slacks and a waiter's apron. "Anywhere?" I asked, waving toward the dozen or so booths stretching the length of the left side of the establishment. A dining counter stretched the length of the right. At its end stood the stout man with the apron who'd been standing outside the door earlier.

The waitress nodded. "Two?"

"Three, actually." Carrie led the way to a booth in

front of the windows. She tossed her purse onto the seat and sat down with a thud of butt on vinyl. "I can't believe I have to talk to the police because they can't find my ex-husband. Russ and I have been divorced for almost a year and still he manages to ruin my day."

I eased onto the bench seat opposite her, leaned my elbows on the table. "Carrie, you might still think Russ is a pain in the butt who makes your life miserable, but I don't think you want Detective Nolan to know that. Don't give him any cause to suspect you might be carrying a grudge. Or a torch, for that matter."

She let out a breath, shoulders sagging as she exhaled. "Okay. You're right. Okay. I can do that."

The waitress dropped a few menu folders on the edge of the table in the same moment Detective Nolan strode through the door of the coffee shop. "Can I get you something to start?" she asked.

Carrie ordered tea while Nolan echoed my request for coffee and slid into the seat beside me. Prior to his arrival I'd been mainly sitting in the middle of the bench. Now I would have to shift over to avoid his thigh pressing against mine for the duration. With the path my mind continued to threaten to wander, the last thing I needed was proximity.

"Here." I tapped his arm, the bulk of his suit jacket preventing me from touching the man beneath. "Scoot out and I'll sit next to Carrie."

"This won't take long." He pulled a pen from his breast pocket and dropped his notepad on the table.

I huffed to cover my discomfort and reached for a menu.

Detective Nolan laid a hand atop the menu, stopping me from pulling it close. "I said it won't take long."

"I'm hungry," I said, doing my best to scowl at him.

At this, he turned his head, held my gaze. "Would you please not order until I've gone?"

Strange. Most professional-type people I knew were accustomed to doing business over a meal. Had that particular multitasking brilliance not yet reached the police department? How could that be? And yet there we were, Nolan's brown eyes locked on mine.

He slid the menu toward me. "Decide, but don't order."

It wasn't a command, but a request, and not an unkind one.

I did a combination nod and shrug, and when the waitress dropped off our coffees and tea, told her I wouldn't be ordering just yet.

Cup of java in front of him, Detective Nolan opened his notebook and flipped to a clean page. Try as I might, I couldn't catch the contents of the pages previous to the blank he stopped on. It would have been nice to see, say, a list of suspects, with Carrie's name absent. But no such luck. She'd have to keep her name off any such list by excelling at the detective's game of twenty questions.

"You say you're divorced from Russ Stanford, is that correct?" he began.

With steady hands and perfect posture, Carrie prepared her tea. She confirmed she and Russ were divorced for just over nine months.

"Cause of divorce?" He didn't take his eyes off Carrie.

"Infidelity," she said, lifting her teacup. "His."

I wanted to reach across and pat her hand. The best I could do in the moment was catch her gaze and give her a sympathetic smile.

"You were awarded partial ownership of the property at 832 Broad Street as part of the settlement."

She shook her head, keeping the teacup close but not yet taking a sip. "We bought it together after we got married. It wasn't awarded to me like some kind of consolation prize."

Nolan made some marks in his notebook—the notebook he cleverly kept beside his coffee cup, blocking my view of its contents. I grabbed my own coffee and took a sip, followed by a gulp. My eyes popped wide, my taste buds rejoiced. It was the best cup of coffee I'd had since leaving the city. Sure, the coffee at Grace's luncheonette in Wenwood village tasted better than the brew Grandy's old drip coffeemaker produced, but this . . . this was smooth and strong, no undertones of burnt beans, no hidden staleness, all flavor. I closed my eyes and savored another swallow.

"I take it you're aware of the current value of the property." He covered his notebook with a loose fist while he took a gulp of coffee. I watched, but he showed no sign of recognizing the amazingness of the coffee. Some detective.

Nolan continued, "Can you tell me how much the building is insured for?"

Carrie set down her cup, catching the edge of the spoon resting in the saucer. The clatter sounded deafening in the quiet of the coffee shop. "I believe it's no more than current market estimate."

"You believe?"

She let out a little huff. "We were just starting out. We barely had the money to make loan payments. To insure the property for more than the bank required . . . we couldn't afford that."

The waitress snuck up to us, order pad at the ready. I cut a glance at the detective who had been adamant I not eat until he left and gave the waitress what I hoped was an apologetic smile. "I need a few more minutes."

Expression neutral, she wandered off, and I shifted my attention back to the policeman's version of twenty questions.

Nolan made a note, then looked to Carrie. "Is it likely given current market decline that the property is insured for more than its value?"

Carrie made a flustered little noise, her cheeks going faintly pink. "I suppose. I don't really know."

"Any chance your ex-husband might have taken out additional insurance, say, for the business?"

Fueled by caffeine, my mental calculator put two and two together and flashed a sum. "You want to know if it's possible Russ set fire to his own building?" I asked.

He gave me a subtle nod, but kept his gaze on Carrie.

She shrugged dismissively. "Anything's possible, isn't it? If you're asking me if I think he would do something like that, then no."

Again, she gave a subtle shrug. Nolan may not have known Carrie well enough to recognize the motion as something telling, but I did. The double shrug meant she was unsure, doubting herself.

"Are you aware of any enemies he might have? Anyone who might want to put him out of business for a while?"

Something skittered across Carrie's face, something sour with an aftertaste of dark humor. "I really don't know."

A check to my right showed Nolan, pen poised above his notepad, eyes on Carrie. I supposed his hesitation made sense. She wasn't listing names for him to write down. Easy enough to remember a "no." But his perfectly still, perfectly somber consideration of her spooled out a tendril of uneasiness in my belly.

"Do you have any idea where Russ is now?" He lifted his cup and drank down coffee like it was water.

Her bitter expression morphed into a grimace. "If past experience is any indicator, he's found himself a bed other than his own to sleep in, preferably one belonging to a blonde."

And there was the anger she shouldn't have showed. Under the table, I swung my foot out, hoping to connect with her shin. Instead, I merely scraped the side of her calf with the edge of my flip-flop. She looked to me and I widened my eyes and pursed my lips.

She grabbed for her teacup, rattling it and the spoon against the saucer in her haste. "Which is of course his prerogative," she mumbled, then raised the cup and took a series of delicate sips.

I did the same with my coffee while Detective Nolan scratched out a few more notes.

The waitress sauntered over to the table, pulling an

order pad out of her apron along the way. "Ready to order?" She used the pad as a brace to click her pen against.

"No, I need—" I began.

"Go ahead and order." Detective Nolan flipped his notebook closed. "That's all I have for now." Coffee cup in one hand, notebook in the other, he pushed to his feet.

"For now?" Carrie asked in a voice made even smaller from being blocked by a teacup.

At last, he forced a tight, polite smile. He presented Carrie with a business card he pulled from the breast pocket of his suit jacket. "Call me if you think of anything about Russ that might be useful."

After one last slug of coffee, he set the mug down. He took one step away from the table before turning back. His expression opened from stern, professional police detective to warm, concerned gentleman. "How's your grandfather?" he asked.

His question caught me by surprise, and I mentally scrambled for an answer. "I, um, he's good. He's good," I stammered. "Why do you ask?"

"I wondered if he was . . ." He paused, searched the ceiling for the right word. "Unwell. And that his health was what was keeping you in Wenwood."

I shook my head. "No, Grandy's fine. Same old stubborn teddy bear."

Detective Nolan stood motionless, as though waiting for more, as though expecting me to give him the reason I remained in Wenwood. But that was something I had yet to fully discover myself, much less voice.

He sighed slightly. "Glad to hear it," he said then turned to Carrie. "If I have any more questions, I'll let you know."

Without further hesitation, he strode out of the coffee shop.

While the waitress hovered beside the table I pushed aside the stray thoughts the detective's unspoken question had awoken, the why I stayed and if I would leave and what's next either way. Those thoughts only ever led me in circles.

Carrie practically dropped her cup into its saucer. "What does that mean, if he has any more questions?"

"What can I get you?" the waitress prompted.

"I . . . ugh." I held up a "one-minute" finger to Carrie and ordered up an egg and onion omelet and handed back the menu I never opened. When I'm in the mood for eggs, the variety of options present in a menu serves only to confuse.

The waitress swept up the remaining menus and left us alone.

I took a quick sip of coffee before addressing Carrie. "I think it just means he might think of more questions. I don't think there's anything sinister there."

She sighed and sank against the vinyl cushioned back-rest. "You warned me to stay calm and I blew it."

"You didn't blow it." Firmly shutting away thoughts of my own life issues, I softened my posture, smiled a little. "Probably if you didn't get a little cranky talking about your ex, *that* would be suspicious."

She let out a reluctant half laugh. "I almost lost it when

he asked if Russ had any enemies. I'd be shocked if Russ hadn't cheated on some other woman who could give me a run for number one enemy by now."

That little wisp of worry stirred once more, but I mentally stomped it down. Carrie may wish Russ hives in uncomfortable and embarrassing places, but she wouldn't actually put itching powder in anyone's shorts. I knew that, and I was certain Detective Nolan knew that, too.

Mostly certain.

Hopeful.

I swallowed down the last of my delicious coffee and looked around for the waitress. It was then, as I turned full around in my seat, that I noticed traffic moving along the main drag and pedestrians strolling by the coffee shop's plate glass window. Business had resumed in downtown Newbridge.

"Funny thing is," Carrie said, sitting up again and leaning into the table, "Russ is a pain in the ass, but I really don't think he does have any enemies. He's not the type. He's more the laid-back, everyone-loves-him type."

Catching the eye of the waitress, I lifted my coffee cup into view—a silent request for a refill. "Maybe he's changed since you guys split. Maybe his latest conquest has a jealous ex who's a bodybuilder or a boxer."

"Or an arsonist."

I grinned. "And Russ is in hiding from this guy because he's afraid to have his nose broken. Or his knees."

Carrie chuckled. "That's it exactly. He's hiding out in his brother's hunting cabin, hoping—" Her jaw dropped and her eyes popped wide. "The hunting cabin. I should have told

Detective Nolan about the hunting cabin." She huffed and put a hand to her forehead. "Russ is probably there."

An older woman holding the hand of a smiling little girl pushed open the entrance door and cheerfully announced, "Here we are. Waffle time."

The waitress greeted them like old friends, all the while sliding my omelet onto the table and holding a carafe of coffee. She refilled my mug and checked if Carrie wanted to order anything more.

"Why don't you have another cup of tea?" I suggested.

Carrie agreed and I waited until the waitress walked off before resuming our conversation.

"Isn't hunting usually done in cold weather?" I asked, laying a napkin across my lap. "I don't remember ever seeing advertisements for hunting shorts or tank tops."

"In summer they fish." She rolled her eyes and huffed again. "I should call Detective Nolan and tell him. Is his cell number on here?" She picked up the card he'd left. "Maybe I can get him back here before he's gone too far."

I shoveled a forkful of eggs into my mouth and threw good etiquette to the wind by speaking with my mouth full. Anything to avoid more contact with the good detective until I understood why I had become so fascinated with the confidence of his stance or the forthrightness of his gaze. "You don't know for sure Russ is at the cabin," I said. "I don't think there's any need to rush to talk to the detective. Besides, you shouldn't tempt him to take a cell call while he's driving." Yes, I was babbling. I would have said anything to stop Carrie calling and convincing him it would be a good idea to change direction and return to the coffee shop.

"No, you're right." Carrie considered this while the waitress delivered a fresh cup of tea and went through the usual "How is everything?" Once I'd assured her the eggs were fine and she sauntered off, Carrie continued. "I bet his staff knows if Russ is fishing, and they should be arriving soon. I could ask them." She sat up straighter in her seat, peered over my shoulder.

I turned and followed her gaze. From where we sat, though, we had no view of the blackened building.

She dug in her purse and pulled out her phone. "Already after ten, though. Someone should have turned up already."

Shaking my head, I traded my fork for my coffee cup. "You never worked in an office, did you?" I sipped while Carrie confirmed my suspicion. She had spent her career years to date working at the antiques shop that her family had handed down through generations and visiting estate sales in search of rare and sometimes beautiful objects. I had spent my career years manning a desk and suffering through some seriously bad coffee and high-profile financial scandals. This disparity made me qualified to educate my new best friend on the way the corporate world worked. "Number one rule—no, wait. Number one rule is avoid office politics. Number two rule is if the boss is away fishing, nine o'clock is overachieving. Give them time."

Carrie slid to the farthest edge of her bench seat so she could watch for arriving employees without craning her neck while I enjoyed yet another refill of delicious coffee.

By the time I finished my omelet, I was well into the third cup of coffee. My stomach was beginning a protest when a dark-haired young woman dashed past the window and slammed open the door. The older woman and little girl enjoying waffles at the counter jumped at the noise. Okay, I did, too. The only one unaffected was Carrie, who had no doubt seen the woman coming all along.

"Susie," she shouted. "Susie, are you here? What the hell happened?"

Our waitress spoke as she hurried out of the kitchen, more animated than she'd been all morning. "I've been trying to call you. Is your cell off? There was a fire," she said.

"Obviously," the dark-haired girl snapped.

"Firemen and cops were in and out most of the morning," waitress Susie said, joining the newcomer by the door. "You just missed them."

"What about Russ? Did anyone get hold of him?"

Carrie abandoned all pretense of not listening to strangers' business and slid from the booth. "Russ wasn't answering his phone and he wasn't at home. Do you have any idea where he is?" she asked.

The girl turned, annoyance bunching her brow. "Who are you?"

As Carrie reached the middle of the café, she extended a hand. "I'm Carrie Stanford, Russ's ex-wife. The police called me when they couldn't reach him. You are?"

Go, Carrie. Cool and calm and a little bit snippy. Not a guaranteed method of grabbing the upper hand but fairly reliable and masterfully executed.

Pink flushed across the dark-haired girl's cheeks. "I'm Melanie, Russ's administrative assistant." She took

Carrie's hand, but from where I sat, her grip looked a little tentative.

"Melanie, would you be able to tell me where Russ is, please?"

But Melanie narrowed her eyes, calculating. "Hold it. You're Russ's ex?"

"Yes, now can you tell me—"

"He's mentioned you. You guys are on pretty good terms, right?"

"Well, we—"

"Great." Melanie's grin was wide and somewhat alarming in its sudden appearance. "Wait here. I'll be right back."

I had just wedged myself out from behind the table by the time she exited the restaurant. I climbed, with one knee, back upon the bench and leaned to watch her out the window.

"Where's she going?" Carried asked waitress Susie. When Susie only shrugged, Carrie directed the question to me. "Where is she going?"

I shook my head, no idea. Wherever she was going, she was going in a hurry. If she kept up that speed, she'd be covered in sweat in no time. "She said she'll be back," I muttered, then turned back to face Carrie. "You'll just need to find out where Russ is and then we can get out of here." I didn't have anywhere I needed to be until the evening, but the back of my mind, the quiet place that foments ideas while I'm not paying attention, was urging me to get started designing a window for Trudy's bed and breakfast.

"I'll get your check," Susie said.

It took her only moments to present us with the bill, at which point I realized Carrie and I were paying for Detective Nolan's coffee. Not that the cost of a cup of coffee was going to overdraw me at the bank, but the very idea that he left without throwing so much as a couple of singles down on the table was irksome.

Carrie and I were quibbling over how much we should tip our waitress when Melanie returned to the café, shuffling gracelessly under the weight of the large cardboard carton emblazoned with U-Move-It's diamond-shaped logo that she held before her. A yellow plastic grocery bag hung heavily from her wrist.

She backed her way through the door, stumble-spun to the lunch counter, and dropped the carton on the counter's shiny blue surface. "There," she said, prying the plastic bag from her wrist and plunking the bag atop the carton. "Your problem now."

Carrie side-stepped toward the counter, eyes on the carton, face scrunched in apprehension, as though the box might contain an assortment of spring-loaded snakes. "What is all this?"

"This"—Melanie flapped her hand toward the box—"is what's left of the Heaney estate. Russ asked me to pick these up from Hudson Estate Sales and bring them to the office. But seeing as there is no office and Russ said you might be interested in this stuff, I'm giving it to you. No way am I storing that musty crap in my apartment."

Cautiously, I slid the bag to the side of the carton and attempted to peer inside the carton. "What's in there?" I asked.

Melanie sounded annoyed by the question. "Junk. Trinkets and letters and old pictures and . . . crap Russ thought

43

you"—she lifted a chin in Carrie's direction—"might want to have in your shop. You're into antiques or something, right?"

"Exactly where is Russ?" Carrie asked.

Melanie huffed, placed a hand on her waist, and cocked out a hip. "Fishing trip."

Carrie flashed me a smug smile. "Fishing. Up at Gabe's cabin?"

It was Melanie's turn to look smug. "Mmm, you haven't talked to Russ in a while, have you?" she asked, and Carrie's smile fell. "Let's just say I doubt he's at Gabe's cabin, okay? Look, I gotta run. Now that I know I don't have to work today, I'm way behind."

"Hold it." Carrie jerked a thumb at the U-Move-It carton on the counter. "What am I supposed to do with all this?"

Melanie tugged a set of keys from her purse. "I guess go through it and talk to Russ about it when he gets back?" She shrugged. "Okay then. Bye all."

"Bye!" The little girl waved her fork.

"Call me, okay?" Susie called out.

She waved a farewell as Melanie dashed through the door.

Carrie turned and gaped at me. "Now what?" she asked.

A seed of an idea took root. "I guess we're loading this stuff into your car," I said. "And then . . ."

"And then what?"

"Well, if you're not in any rush to get back home . . ." I said.

She put a hand on her hip. "Spit it out."

"Do you know where Gabe lives? Or, I guess, where he works?"

"Of course but—" Her eyes widened in unhappy understanding. "No. Absolutely not. We are not going to go see Gabe."

"Yes. Absolutely yes," I said just as firmly. "Look, Russ might not be at Gabe's cabin, but Gabe still might know where he is. Mutual friends? Neighbors? That kind of thing."

Shaking her head, Carrie lifted the yellow plastic bag Melanie had left behind and passed it to me. "Let the police do it."

"I'm sure the police will, but I suspect you might be in a bigger hurry to find Russ than they are." I paused while she hefted the carton off the counter, then held open the door for her to pass through.

"They're going to be more interested in finding out whether or not that fire was an accident, and if not, who-dunit." We ambled down the sidewalk, heading for the car that had been baking in the sun. "You're the one who'll end up fielding all the questions and talking to the fencing people and dealing with insurance and the gas company and the phone company and if we can find Russ . . ."

"Georgia." Carrie came to a stop and turned to face me. "Did you get some kind of Miss Marple disease when you were figuring out who killed Bill Harper? And now you need to feed the sickness?"

"Um. No." I resumed walking, slowly, considering how best to answer the question. "That's not it," I said at last.

"In fact, I only have a vague idea who Miss Marple is." I was wise enough on the walk back to give the gutter puddle wide berth. "I think that helping figure out who killed Mr. Harper and getting Grandy out of jail, that made me feel—I don't know—useful somehow? Like I'm contributing?"

At the car, Carrie balanced the carton against the rear fender. She dropped her purse on the trunk and fished around inside the bag. "I don't understand. How could you not feel useful?"

"Maybe unwelcome is more like it. I don't get the warmest reception from the good people of Wenwood," I said on a sigh. "If I can help, then maybe I could be, you know, less of an outsider?"

Her brows drew together across the bridge of her nose. "So sticking your nose into crime is your way of sucking up to the townspeople?"

I opened my mouth, waited vainly for a coherent noise to come out. In the end, I shrugged. Oftentimes things sounded less crazy in my head than they did out loud.

Lifting a set a keys from her purse, Carrie shook her head in a manner that made me think she'd make a good mom. "Fine. Let's go look at cars."

4

Carrie had the good sense to call the dealership before we took the ride and make sure Gabe was working. "I can't believe I'm doing this," she said, as we headed south on the highway. "Really. I could just ask him over the phone if he knows where Russ might be."

"Phones are nowhere near as much fun as road trips." I flipped down the sun visor and perused the collection of CDs Carrie kept there. "Besides, I really do need to start thinking about buying my own car. May as well get my research going."

She checked the rearview mirror and smoothly changed lanes. "You could research online."

"Blind shopping on the Internet inevitably ends with two hours lost to YouTube. I need a place to start." I selected classic Alanis Morissette and popped the disk into the CD player.

"Buying a car, worrying about fitting in . . . Does this mean your trial period is over and you're going to commit to staying in Wenwood permanently?"

Settling back in my seat, letting the air-conditioning blow the frizz of my hair away from my face, I sighed. "I think so. But I go back and forth. I like it here, you know?" I gazed out the window, where even the highways were surrounded with thick green trees and cheerful wildflowers. "But this wasn't exactly the way I pictured my future. I pictured big city, power lunches, and mass transit, not front porches and the luncheonette."

Carrie chuckled. "What we picture our future to be and what it turns out to be isn't always the same thing. But we adjust."

"When everything fell apart for me, I came here to rest and figure out how to start over. I figured the starting over itself would be elsewhere. If the starting over happens here, is that adjusting? Or giving up?"

She shot me a sidelong glance, one filled with compassion but empty of an answer.

We rode the final miles to the dealership in silence. What ran through Carrie's mind along the way I couldn't guess at; what ran through my mind was the same old circular indecision about whether to fully commit to Wenwood or move on. By the time the enormous U.S. flag flying over the dealership came into view, all I had concluded was that, stay or go, I was going to need money and I was keeping my cat.

Carrie parked her car along the street in front of the dealership, and I stepped out onto the curb and faced a gleaming row of new cars. Sedans, pickups, SUVs all waiting for the perfect owner to arrive. Alternating vehicles sported cheery blue or red balloons; every vehicle sported a ticket price I knew without even looking at that I couldn't afford.

"Any idea where they keep the clunker trade-ins?" I asked as Carrie came around to meet me. "They're more in my price range."

She shook her head, eyes and mouth pinched. "I was only here once," she said tightly.

I reached a hand to her elbow, stopping her progress. "Why don't you wait in the car or . . . ?" I glanced up and down the road, searching for a likely spot. "Or go grab a donut and some coffee? This was my idea. You don't need to see Gabe."

"More food?" Carrie forced a smile. "It'll be fine."

Marching on ahead, Carrie smoothed the hair away from her forehead and flicked the curls over her shoulder. With each step she stood a little straighter, her chin a little higher. Meanwhile, the tension across my shoulders grew tighter and seemed to stretch into my belly. I swept my fingers across my stomach, trying to brush away the nerves and the guilt lurking behind, but I feared nothing short of turning and running would help.

Carrie tugged open the door to the showroom, and I followed her inside. More shiny cars mocked my bank account and employment status.

We crossed polished floors and passed shoppers and

salespeople alike, Carrie pointing to the back of the show-room anytime anyone with a salesman's smile came near. "Service," she announced, and they melted away.

The cross from showroom to service meant stepping off gleaming marble and onto dull linoleum tile. Dusty letters affixed to the wall read PARTS AND SERVICE. Beneath it, a sign informing patrons about labor rates made me rethink the idea that buying a clunker would save money.

Ahead of us at the service counter a heavyset man wearing socks with his sandals muttered profanity as he settled his bill. For that brief moment, I decided buying any car at all would be a bad plan.

When the muttering man walked away, Carrie and I stepped into his place.

"Afternoon, ladies." The man behind the service counter couldn't have been any taller than I was, but he had a friendly smile and a surprisingly clean work shirt for someone who worked in the service department. "What can I help you with today?"

"I was hoping to, um . . ." Carrie took a deep breath. "To see Gabe Stanford, please."

"Is this about a repair? Are you a customer?" the man asked.

"Sister-in-law," I said.

"Former," Carrie added.

Counter guy raised his eyebrows, looked back and forth between us.

"It's about his brother," she said.

His face paled and jaw fell. "Oh, God."

"Oh no, no, not that. He's fine!" Carrie rushed to say.

"We presume," I put in. No need to remove any incentive the guy had for moving quickly.

"Can you just . . . is he here? Can we talk to him?"

Counter Guy's sandy hair bounced as he nodded. "I'll go see if he can take a break," he said, already moving away from his register.

"Oh look," Carrie said after Counter Guy disappeared through a doorway. "There's coffee."

I followed her gaze to a cup-at-a-time coffeemaker stored below a wall-mounted television playing a midday talk show. Once again I rubbed a hand against my stomach, three cups of coffee shop brew swirling within. "Pass."

"If you can't drink any more coffee, how could you expect me to eat more food?" Carrie asked.

Turning my attention back to her, I said, "I was just trying to spare you . . . the . . ."

"Carrie. What are you doing here?"

She spun to look at the man who had crept up behind us and robbed me of speech. I hadn't held an image in my head of what Gabe Stanford would look like. Carrie had never shared a picture of Russ with me, leaving me uninformed on any family traits. But even if I had been expecting the dark hair and blue eyes, I never would have anticipated the apparent reincarnation of Paul Bunyan. Granted, rather than a red and black checkered flannel, he wore a grease-streaked shirt with GABRIEL stitched over the breast pocket, and fortunately he wasn't carrying an ax because that would have utterly freaked me out. Gabe was easily six-foot-eight, with the barrel chest of a pro football player and hands the size of watermelons. I fought the conflicting urges of backing away from him and ducking under him for protection.

While Counter Guy squeezed behind Gabe and took a seat on a stool behind the register, Carrie introduced me to her former brother-in-law. My hand vanished in his as we shook hands in greeting.

That was the extent of any pleasantness.

"I'll ask again. What are you doing here?" Gabe repeated, his voice the growl of boulders grinding one against the other.

"I just . . ." Carrie faltered. "Just . . ."

Rather than take that step back, I edged forward, moving that little bit closer to Gabe than Carrie stood. "I asked her to bring me. We were hoping you would know where Russ is," I said.

His lips quirked in a bitter smile. "Why would I know?"

"Because you're his brother? He might have mentioned something to you?" Being an only child myself, I could only speculate at sibling attachment based on observations. Most of those observations of Wenwood and its Hudson Valley environs told me family around here stuck together. I should have kept in mind the brief glimpse Carrie had given me of the Stanford family.

"Russ is a grown man. He doesn't need to check with me for permission on anything. Just ask him, he'll tell you."

"I would very much like to ask him," I said. "But according to his administrative assistant, he's gone away fishing and didn't tell anyone where he was going."

"And we were hoping since you guys usually go fishing

together, you might have some idea where Russ might go on his own," Carrie added.

The big man scoffed. "Wherever he is, he's probably with Brittany. You might try asking her friends."

"Brittany?" Carrie practically spat the name.

"Yeah, you know, his next wife."

In that moment I didn't know what Carrie was feeling about this new bombshell. All I knew was my stomach was churning on her behalf. The twisted truth of it is, you might have made the best decision ever in getting out of a relationship, you might have been emotionally betrayed, but hearing the other party has moved on before you still stings.

"He's getting married again?" Carrie asked in a tiny voice.

Gabe shuffled his feet, turning to face her fully. "He wouldn't be getting married *again* if you'd have stayed with him."

"Russ cheated on her," I said.

He spread his arms wide, palms up. "That's what men do. Men are not meant to be monogamous. It's against our biology. If you'd have just understood that, then you two would still be together and my stupid-ass brother wouldn't be planning to sign a prenup for wife number two."

All I could do was blink, buying time while I waited to see if his words would make sense or, at the very least, not infuriate me. "I'm sorry, I want to be clear on this. Did you say 'not meant to be monogamous' because of biology? So simply being men gives men permission to ignore their vows?"

"All's I'm saying is a man can't be expected to spend the rest of his life with just one woman. It's why I told Russ, if he signs that prenup, he's going to lose everything he has left to that girl and all because of natural urges that can't be ignored."

"Natural urges?" Carrie echoed, disbelief apparently overwhelming any lingering distress she felt over hearing of Russ's upcoming marriage. "Natural? Your brother met that girl online. How is that natural?"

I shot her a look, shook my head. "So there's a prenup." I folded my arms, gave Gabe my shrewdest look. "And you don't think your brother, or any man ever, should have to pay any sort of price for being unfaithful to his wife?"

Gabe shrugged in a manner to indicate he didn't make the rules, he only played by them. Meanwhile, behind him, where only Carrie and I could see, Counter Guy rolled his eyes.

I glanced at Carrie. "Now I know why you don't like this guy."

"Come on, let's just go," she said. "He doesn't know where Russ is."

I narrowed my gaze at him. "Don't you even want to know why we need to find your brother?"

He pursed his lips for a moment, looked upward as though considering the question. "No. Don't need to know that. So I can go back to work now?" He gave us a great big false smile. "Thanks for stopping by."

As he lumbered back through the doorway that presumably led to the repair bays, I let out a disgusted huff. "He honestly believes . . ." I said. "Natural urges?"

Carrie stood with arms wrapped around her belly and eyes on the floor. "He's not the nice brother," she murmured.

A *no kidding* or *you don't say* was waiting on my tongue. Common sense and compassion prevailed.

I reached out and rubbed a hand against her upper arm. "I'm sorry for making you come here," I said.

She lifted a shoulder, tilted her head momentarily to the side. "It's okay. Usually I can handle him. I guess the day's been harder than I realized."

Putting an arm over her shoulder, I turned her back toward the showroom. "Come on," I said. "Let's go look at cars I can't afford. Then we'll call Detective Nolan and let him know where to find the Neanderthal with the answers."

"See?" she said, giving me a shaky smile. "Some things are best left to the police."

5

With the haze of the early morning burned away
and the heat of the day not yet hitting its potential,
I set a pitcher of tea on the front porch steps to steep in
the sun then headed downstairs to my workshop.

Windows on two sides—one facing north, the other
east—provided ample natural light by which to work. I
had been slacking off a bit in the prior couple of weeks,
spending a good deal of time pulling weeds, fertilizing,
and otherwise tending to the small garden I had planted
along the back fence of Grandy's yard. The herbs took
root and flourished almost immediately. And while the
vegetables had rooted well, they were only just beginning
to offer up their bounty. Fresh cucumber and green beans,
a smattering of onions and summer squash. Some very
pathetic tomatoes hung on their vine, but I held on to hope

for improvement, while the strawberry patch continued to defy any efforts I made at encouraging it to produce fruit. I loved fresh produce, and gardening was a worthy project but it was time to pick up my stained glass tools and get back to work. Especially if I was going to pull off something as ambitious as a window for a local business.

The worktable centered in the corner of the room stood empty with the exception of a stack of old newspapers I had allowed to pile at one end. I grabbed a dust brush from the shelf hung below the table and swept the dust away from the surface.

At the first *hish* of the brush, a white ball of fluff flew down the stairs, raced across the linoleum floor, and slid into my ankle.

"Easy there." I paused in the brushing to reach down with my opposite hand and scoop up the kitten. She was still a mite too small to jump onto the table by herself. If I didn't grab her up in time, she would attempt to claw her way up my leg to reach her goal. I had learned this lesson the painful way and still feared permanent scarring.

I deposited Friday the kitten beside the stack of newspapers, where I foolishly thought she would remain. But the *hish-swish* had beckoned her for a reason, and the moment I resumed brushing, I had her wide-eyed attention. Forelegs nearly resting on the table, butt in the air, she followed the motion of the brush for two swipes before she pounced.

Of course, she was no match for anything longer and heavier than she was, but I moved the brush back and forth slowly and gently a few extra times, allowing her to catch the wood back beneath her paw and feel triumphant.

Yes, I was letting her win. If someday she needed therapy to recover from my indulgence, so be it.

I slid the brush back under the table, pulled a newspaper from atop the pile and laid out a few sheets. Friday "helpfully" swatted at the pages so that the newsprint rubbed onto the tips of her bright white paws, matching the natural patch of gray between her ears.

Once the papers were in place I made quick work of lifting my basic toolbox onto the table, setting out the Homasote board—a two-foot square of pressed fiberboard that made an ideal surface for cutting glass and soldering—and retrieving a vinyl accordion folder in which I kept an assortment of patterns that had caught my eye at one time or another.

With the folder splayed open, I flipped through folded papers, sought a pattern that would reinforce some skills and test others. I wanted to create a decorative pane, the sort that would hang in a window rather than be one. I had yet to complete a design for Trudy Villiers's window, but trusted images and ideas would come to me while I took another project from pattern to patina.

The folder's sections held patterns with flowers and fish and birds, art deco and classic and European-inspired abstract designs. I had a precious few patterns for Celtic knots that tempted me, but in the end I withdrew a pattern of a sailboat at sunset.

The image reminded me of the construction going on down at the old brickworks, the construction that promised to take an abandoned, tumbledown factory and give it new life as a boat shop and restaurant overlooking the piers. More, it made me think of the man at the helm of the renovation: Anton Himmel.

I sighed. Friday blinked big blue eyes at me. It had been weeks since I met Tony for an event best described as a business dinner. He had been kind enough to answer my questions about the deal he'd struck with the Wenwood town council that allowed his construction project to take place. At the time, despite his good looks and easy demeanor, I had been intent on keeping the dinner businesslike, telling myself I wasn't ready for anything else. But now . . .

Now maybe I was. Maybe that readiness to let someone else close again accounted for my new awareness of Detective Nolan. Maybe my subconscious was trying to tell me something. Maybe it was time to stop being alone.

Moving to the corner of the room, I switched on the radio I kept there, always tuned to the greatest hits of decades past. An old Pearl Jam tune dispelled the quiet of the room and helped me force my thoughts away from Chip Nolan and Tony Himmel.

But no sooner had I relegated the men to the back of my mind than memories of Russ Stanford's burned-out building took over the front spot. Despite his careful use of "probably" and "likely," the fire marshal had seemed certain the blaze was purposefully set. What would anyone gain from burning down a law office? "Who would do that?" I asked Friday.

The kitten yawned.

"Pay attention. This could be important," I told her. I stooped down to locate some poster board and carbon paper. Noting I was running low on both, I set the supplies on top of the table while I dug a three-quarter-inch-thick piece of wood from an untidy stack I kept propped against the wall. Last up, a hammer. "What reason would someone have to burn down a building, huh?" I asked.

Friday hopped up onto the stack of newspapers. I reached over to her and scratched the bunny-soft fur atop her head. She squinched her eyes closed in kitty bliss and a quiet purr rumbled through her.

"Do lawyers keep evidence? No, the police keep the evidence, right?" Sadly, I knew that from having marathon-watched Court TV during a particularly long battle with the flu. I smoothed Friday's fur flat and went back to my project.

With the pattern on top of the carbon paper, poster board below, I pinned the assemblage to the piece of wood with tacks and gently tapped the tacks with the hammer—hard enough to hold, loose enough I'd be able to remove them.

"So there's probably nothing incriminating in the office. Nothing I can imagine, anyway."

One more yawn and Friday curled herself into a circle the size of a honeydew melon and closed her eyes.

"Fine," I said, eyeing the kitten. "Have a nap. I'm the crazy person talking to a cat anyway."

Though I kept quiet while tracing a pen across the pattern, the pressure and the presence of carbon paper transferring the design to the poster board below, my mind continued to ask the same questions I had no answer to, until I hit the point where I reminded myself I was focused on the wrong thing.

Trudy Villiers wanted a window. A custom-made, custom-designed window. I should be worrying about that.

My pen traced over horizontal lines that curved to resemble waves, over the gentle slope of the sailboat's hull and the swell of the sail. But the images in my mind were swirls of pinks and lavenders, the cluster of a blossom, the turn of a petal. Magnolias. There were a few varieties, I thought. Weren't there?

I forced myself to finish tracing over every line in the pattern on the table before giving in to my mental wandering. As I had expected, even hoped, I was suddenly eager for a sketchbook and pencils.

After tucking the pen into my toolbox, I crossed to a little bookcase underneath the north-facing window. My grandmother—who had used this same space for painting when she was alive—had a collection of field guides and encyclopedias of flowers. They may have been outdated, with the glue along the spine dried and the pages pulling away, but the appearance of the blooms hadn't changed.

I selected two of the flower books, grabbed my sketchbook, and scrounged around the bottom of my toolbox until I came up with a pencil.

Toolbox closed and locked, I said to the sleeping kitten, "I'm going outside. Stay here."

Friday did just as she was told. Nothing short of a wrecking ball had a chance at waking her.

Heading up from the basement the *thunk* of a pipe startled me, a pipe that banged only when a water spigot was turned off. Grandy was up and had just finished a shower.

Though he had finally given in and reduced the number

of nights he spent working at the Downtown Dine-In theater he owned, he had yet to retire completely. As a result, he often slept long into the morning after locking up the theater then driving home the night before.

I detoured to the kitchen to grab a pair of tea glasses, then doubled back through the circa 1960 living room and out onto the front porch. One look told me the iced tea was ready. After dropping my books and pencil on the little rickety wooden table, I made a quick run back into the house for a bowl of ice, then took the pitcher from the steps before settling into one of the two Adirondack chairs and pouring myself a glass of fresh-brewed sun tea.

On most days, the tall old trees thriving on the property kept the house cool. But sometimes the stillness of summer days meant the leaves served only to cocoon the house in damp and heat. I hadn't realized how hot and stuffy the inside had become until I felt the difference in temperature from the basement to the porch.

Encyclopedia open to an image of a saucer magnolia blossom, I lost myself in attempting to re-create its subtle beauty in my sketchbook. I was no artist, but enjoyed the experience of moving my pencil across the page and I could approximate the shape of the flowers in the space where I thought they might look best in the overall window design.

I had briefly switched my sketching to the lettering of *Magnolia Bed and Breakfast* when the front door opened.

"Georgia, is it really so hard for you to remember to write a note when you take the Jeep?"

Grandy strode across the porch that stretched to the right of the front door and dropped into the other chair.

Even in the open air the scent of his soap tickled my nose. His tanned and faintly wrinkled skin shined from the fresh scrubbing, and his deeply receding hairline terminated in damp, silver hair.

"I wrote the note. It said I went to pick up tea bags and eggs," I said. "I left it on the dining room table. I didn't think to put the note where you were guaranteed to see it, like, next to the strudel you think I don't know about." I looked over and up at him from below my brows. In other words, I gave him my "stern" look.

He snorted and settled back in his chair. "I don't know what you're talking about."

"Of course you don't." I looked back to the sketchbook opened across my lap. "There's iced tea there if you want."

Grandy lifted the pitcher free of the ring of condensation marking its place on the table. "I don't suppose you put any sugar in this tea?"

"You don't suppose correctly."

He grumbled but poured a glass all the same. "What are you working on there?"

Mostly I preferred to keep my novice attempts at sketching to myself. After all, they were only ideas, concepts, beginnings. Down the line I would refine the sketch as best I could, trace images from the encyclopedias, magazines, or photographs to piece together the vision in my head—a picture that I would transform into Trudy's stained glass window. Grandy understood my sketches were baby basic, but he had that grandparent's knack for seeing the intention on the page and not judging the skill.

I tipped the sketchbook in his direction.

"Are those pansies?" he asked.

Anyone else, I would have been mortified. But like I said, he didn't judge skill. Plus, I didn't know how much knowledge he had of flowers, if any. "Magnolias. I may be doing a window for a new bed and breakfast if I can come up with a decent design."

The tone of Grandy's voice equaled a verbal eye roll. "A new bed and breakfast. What will they think of next?"

Smiling, I picked up my pencil. "Gotta get with the program, Grandy. Once the marina's complete this little hamlet could become quite the getaway destination."

"Lord save us."

Glass in hand, ice clattering, he sat back in his chair and closed his eyes. Grandy wasn't opposed to the marina project; he understood its importance to the future of Wenwood and supported any efforts to restore the town to its earlier vitality. But as someone who had been employed by the brickworks for years on end, supporting progress didn't make it easy for him—or others like him—to see the old building torn apart and reshaped into something new.

In its heyday, the brickworks had set the pace of life in Wenwood. The residents were either employed directly by Wenwood Brick or worked in a supportive capacity for those who were—doctors, grocers, pharmacists, mechanics. After the low cost of imported brick slowly put the Wenwood works out of business, the town began a gradual decline that drove most of its youth to relocate and most of its older residents to sell and take early retirement in southern states.

But since Stone Mountain Construction had begun

work on the new marina, the faintest air of hope had settled over Wenwood. Though residents were sad to the point of heartbroken to see the old brickworks building transformed into a tourist-targeted landmark, little by little, folks had accepted the inevitable and some even warmed to the project, and now . . .

"Who's going to run this bed and breakfast?" Grandy asked.

"Trudy Villiers? Do you know her?"

He hmmed, head tilted back, eyes still closed. "Can't say as I do. May have known her husband, back in the old days."

"The old days," I repeated on a chuckle. "I don't even know if she is, was, or was ever married." She had had too many rings on her fingers for me to guess if one represented marriage. "I'll try and find out next time."

Grandy stirred himself enough to gulp down the rest of his tea. He pulled a sour face and set the glass on the table. "Needs sugar."

"Nothing needs sugar." I paused in my sketching to give him a sidelong glare. "Least of all you."

"Hmmph."

"Which reminds me, the garbage goes out tonight and the strudel's going with it. Don't bother looking for it in the morning."

He peered back at me, all eighty years of experience adding a shrewd glint to his eye. "You throw away my strudel, Georgia, and I'll have your car keys back."

It was an idle threat and I knew it. Grandy knew it, too. But it raised the specter of guilt and failure I felt at being an adult reliant on her grandfather. "It's not a car," I said, attempting to ignore that pesky guilt. "It's an SUV. And you're supposed to avoid sugar because of doctor's orders. Don't punish me for trying to keep you healthy."

"Healthy? You talk on your cell phone while you're driving," he countered. "That's not only unhealthy for you but for the rest of the people on the road."

"Grandy." Surrendering, I dropped my pencil into the gutter of the sketchbook and smacked the cover closed. "I'd have my own car if I could afford one. But as it is . . ."

I'd been without steady work for nearly a year now. No matter how much I tried to ignore the obnoxious little voice inside me that reminded me I was driving my *grandfather's* SUV, the voice persisted. And the voice embarrassed me. A well-paying, full-time job would put an end to my borrowing. But neither well-paying nor full-time were readily available in Wenwood. Especially for an accountant. The few pieces of stained glass that Carrie had sold on my behalf allowed me to purchase supplies for further pieces and help Grandy with utility costs. I'd begun working Friday nights at Grandy's dine-in where the minimal pay and conservative tips allowed me to have what passed for a social life: girl's night out with Carrie and Diana. If I wanted the kind of money and lifestyle I used to enjoy, I'd have to head back to New York City. I loved the city, I did. Moving back or taking a chance on another big city was definitely an appealing option but . . .

I filled my lungs with a breath of soft, clean air. The kind of breath you rarely experienced in a big city. In Wenwood, I smelled the ever present aroma of flowers on the air. Felt the sun peeking onto the porch and warming my toes . . .

Surely Wenwood had been a better place to spend the summer than Manhattan's odorous steam bath. And surely there were a few more weeks before autumn arrived and the end of the antiques hunter traffic forced me to make a decision.

"Fine," I relented as I stood. "Keep the strudel. Just try and eat more vegetables or something, okay?"

"Have you spoken to Drew?"

I paused in my reach for the pitcher of tea I had planned to carry into the house. "Drew Able? Your lawyer?"

I hadn't seen or spoken to Drew since the charges against Grandy were dropped. That Grandy thought I should speak with him now instantly resulted in sweaty palms and strained breath.

"Of course my lawyer," Grandy said. "I believe he could use someone to help out with his bookkeeping. You might want to stop into his office next time you go to town."

Oh, mercy. Next thing I know Grandy will be trying to set me up on dates. "Thanks, Grandy, but—"

"I'm not doing you any favors," he grumbled. "He can't keep up with his own billing. I haven't seen a single notice for the work he did for me, and you need to keep your skills sharp. Talk to him."

Talk to him. Drew Able, Esquire. The lawyer.

Grabbing the pitcher with my free hand, I nodded. "Okay," I agreed. "I'll talk to him tomorrow."

Maybe not about a job. But definitely about why someone stood to gain by burning down a law office.

6

"And I ended up agreeing to talk to Drew tomorrow," I concluded. I sat back in my chair and finally took a bite from the slice of sharp cheddar I'd been holding since I started the story.

Sunset had done little to ease the heat of the day, and Carrie, Diana, and I gathered gratefully in Carrie's air-conditioned apartment, sprawled on mismatched but cleverly coordinated furniture from bygone days, and snacking on cheese and crackers until it was time to leave for the monthly town meeting.

Diana shook her head in mock amazement, her long dark hair scraping the back of her Pace County PD T-shirt. "Your granddad's a hoot," she said. "Was he always like that? I can't remember."

By some measurements, Diana and I had known one

another our whole lives. By other, more accurate measurements, we had been childhood friends turned enemies during one of my years in Wenwood and had happily lost touch until adulthood and maturity and Grandy being accused of murder brought us back together. As neither Diana nor I had any immediate plans to try out for a cheerleading squad or become part of a chicky clique, this time around our friendship stood a better chance of lasting.

"I'm pretty sure Grandy has always been the same," I said.

"Somewhere at the crossroads of stern and sweet and scary and teddy bear," Carrie put in, pushing to her feet. "Can I get anyone a refill?"

Diana asked for a little more water and I declined. "You sure? No more tea?" Eyes on me, she circled around the back of her chair.

My "I'm sure" was cut short by Carrie's "Yeouch!"

"What happened?" Diana asked.

"You okay?" I asked.

I pushed to the edge of my chair, ready to leap up and assist. Diana, police officer's reflexes clearly sharper honed than mine, was already on her feet and moving toward Carrie.

"This stupid box." With the side of her foot, Carrie kicked a large carton out from behind her chair and turned it so the carton tucked beside the chair, a toe-sized dent showing beneath the diamond-shaped U-Move-It logo. She looked over her shoulder at Diana. "I can't wait until you guys find my ex-husband and I can get rid of this stuff. I spent enough years tripping over that man's junk."

She continued on through the living room and into the galley kitchen.

"What's in the box?" Diana asked.

I sighed. "Who knows? Some stuff Russ's admin had. She said she didn't have room in her apartment for it." I waved a hand to encompass Carrie's supply-closet-sized space. "Because this is palatial."

Eyebrows lowered, Diana edged toward the carton. "This is Russ's? Russ Stanford's? The guy whose business got torched? And you didn't look?"

I searched for words, suddenly tongue-tied by my own foolishness. We hadn't looked inside the box, nor the shopping bag. We'd taken Melanie on faith that the contents consisted of useless scraps from a deceased individual's estate.

"Carrie," I called, standing. "Did you look inside this box?"

From the kitchen came the clatter of ice hitting the bottom of an empty glass. "What do I care what's in the box?"

Now Diana raised her brows. A shift in her stance and a squaring of her shoulders was all it took for her to complete the transformation into cop mode. She held up a hand, palm out, in my direction. "Stay back," she said.

"Seriously?"

Diana glowered, and I folded my arms and waited.

As Carrie appeared in the doorway leading from kitchen to living room, Diana popped open the box with the toe of her canvas sneaker. The speed of the motion and the pop of the box top startled me into flinching.

Recovering myself, I leaned forward and peered into the box.

Diana sat on the edge of Carrie's chair, and Carrie stood watching over her shoulder. With deft fingers, Diana flipped past framed photographs and knitting magazines until she reached a series of photo albums standing on their ends. "This does look like junk," she said.

"There's a bag, too, but that's all old dry cleaning receipts and old bridge scores or something," Carrie said. She grimaced and handed Diana a glass of ice water. "I accidentally dropped the bag and it spilled all over the kitchen."

"You don't think this has anything to do with the fire, do you?" I directed the question to Diana.

"Don't know." Reaching into the box, she withdrew a pair of photo albums and handed them up to me. "Take a look through these."

"I'll get the bag," Carrie said.

With Diana perched on the chair Carrie had vacated and Carrie curled in the chair I had moved away from, I settled on the horsehair couch with the photo albums across my lap. Covers of worn leather felt like they might crumble beneath my fingers, the paper pages like they might disintegrate at my touch. Carefully, I turned to the first page. Black paper photo corners held the pictures in place and gave stark contrast to the faded shades of gray in the images. I peered closely at the first picture, squinting to make out the figures in their rigid poses. A stiff-looking couple, he standing, she sitting. In the woman's lap, acres and acres of lace presumably wrapped a baby.

The same couple appeared in nearly all the photos, the number of children pictured with them increasing, the black-

and-white images giving way to bleached color. Outdoors, indoors, picnics and Christmases, a family chronology captured in images. Now and again there were clusters of women gathered around card tables, grinning beneath identical hairstyles. And here and there, groups of men stood smiling next to pallets of red brick. These were the good old days of Wenwood.

"You know, if I knew how to knit, this would be a really great hat for winter." Diana held out an open magazine for Carrie and me to see.

"You don't know how to knit?" Carrie's voice cracked with disbelief.

Diana leveled a look at Carrie that would reduce a less cheerful soul to dust. "Do you know how to field strip a nine-millimeter Sig?"

"Are we done looking through this stuff?" I asked loudly. "Isn't it time to head over to town hall? Don't we want to get good seats . . . or something?"

Diana left off glaring at Carrie and turned to me. "You find anything interesting?" she asked.

I held up the photo album. "I think this woman only owned two dresses."

She huffed and looked to Carrie. "How about you? Did you find anything?"

"Nothing."

Diana sighed. "Nothing here either." She stood, brushing dust off her palms. "That's too bad."

"*That's too bad?*" I echoed.

She shrugged. "So I was thinking of becoming a

detective. Getting a lead on the arsonist who blazed that office might look good in my file. Maybe. And plus I'd get to help you out," she told Carrie.

"Win-win," I commented, fighting to keep a straight face.

Carrie fought valiantly, pressing her lips tight and avoiding eye contact. But she couldn't hide the humor lighting her eyes.

It was only moments before Diana huffed and shook her head. "Fine, fine. Let's just go to this town mudfest then. Maybe there'll be something worth investigating there."

7

Wenwood Town Hall was a stately building com-
prised of Wenwood brick and hometown pride. It
sat like a sentry atop a gentle hill, keeping the town safe
since the time of its founding, strong enough to do so for
many years to come.

By the time we arrived, the sun had set in my rearview
mirror and was sinking below the horizon ahead. Lamps
blinked to life at strategic points across the front lawn,
their spotlights on the half-dozen marble steps and double
set of tall white columns.

I cruised past the flagpole where both the U.S. and the
New York State flag, brightly lit from below, hung limp in
the still air and turned into the parking lot that ran alongside town hall. The lot was crowded with cars, leaving me
to take a spot toward the back, where the streetlamps were

buzzing their way to illumination. Diana and Carrie piled out of the SUV before I'd even pulled the keys from the ignition.

"Why are we in such a rush?" I asked, hurrying to catch up with them. "I was only kidding about the whole getting-a-good-seat thing."

"Maybe you were kidding, but it's not really a joke." Diana lifted her hair up off the back of her neck. Tugging a coated elastic band free from her wrist, she wrapped her hair in a casual ponytail. "Tonight's the announcement."

"What announcement?" Something tickled the back of my mind, something trying to tell me I knew all about the announcement. The knowledge, though, was too deeply buried for a little tickling to bring it to the surface.

Carrie looked over her shoulder at me. "Of which new merchant application the town council has approved?"

Two more steps and I was walking level with them and resisting the urge to smack my forehead. "That's right. The merchants."

After the untimely death of Andy Edgers, his son had slowly but thoroughly removed all stock from the hardware store Andy had owned and left the space vacant. For a while Carrie—among other residents, I had no doubt—had tried to convince young Edgers to take over the business and keep the hardware store in Wenwood. But he was among those who had grown up and left town for better opportunity and wasn't eager to move back.

Now, the town council, with recommendations from the merchants' association, would cast their votes to determine which business would be allowed to take over the space once filled with spackle, screwdrivers, and sandpaper.

Though we walked quickly, we were overtaken by two laughing, rushing women. "Stella. Regina," Carrie called.

The women stopped and turned. Dressed in soft blouses and denim skirts, with fashionable ropes of jewelry adding sparkle, both ladies smiled. "Carrie," the short-haired brunette said. "I suppose I shouldn't be surprised to see you here."

"You're here to celebrate with us, right?" The other, a thin woman whose red hair I would have bet was mixed in a salon, grinned and offered a hand to me. "I'm Regina Henry."

"Georgia Kelly." I shook her hand, nodded to my right. "This is Diana Davis."

They said their hellos then the handshakes repeated as Stella Mason introduced herself.

"What is it we're supposed to be celebrating?" Diana asked.

Regina held up crossed fingers. "The announcement that the town council approved Sweets—"

"Hush," Stella said on a laugh. "You'll jinx it."

Together we resumed the walk, heading to the end of the cement sidewalk and shuffling up the steps. Moving quicker than the rest of us, Diana raised a hand to acknowledge a man coming down the steps as we went up.

"Hey, Curtis," she said.

He stutter-stepped to a stop, then paired a brief nod with an "Evening" that seemed a feat of ventriloquism. A heavy,

77

dark moustache hung so low I never saw his lips move. "Here for the meeting?" he asked, pulling a pack of cigarettes from the breast pocket of his polo shirt.

"No," Diana said as we passed him. "I'm here to apply for docking privileges for my mega-yacht."

He gave a smile so slight I couldn't tell if he thought Diana's sarcasm was amusing or if he didn't understand her statement as sarcasm at all. "Yeah, uh, good luck."

Lifting the cigarette pack in a strange sort of salute, he continued down the remainder of the steps.

Stella spluttered a laugh. "Does that man have no sense of humor at all?"

Diana paused at the top step, waiting for the rest of us to catch up. "One of the volunteer firemen," she told Stella. "Takes himself a little too seriously."

"You mean you were kidding about the mega-yacht?" I jogged up the last few steps. "Rats. I guess that means I can't catch a ride with you to Fiji."

We walked as a group through the grand double doors and down the stairs to the basement auditorium, where rows of folding chairs filled the floor and town residents filled the room. Standing, sitting, laughing, or chatting, there were enough people gathered in that relatively small space to fill Grandy's theater.

"Front? Back? Anywhere?" Diana asked.

Regina and Stella excused themselves to go check in with the meeting organizers while Carrie and I scanned the room.

"I don't think we'll have many choices," Carrie said. "Not if we want to sit together."

Diana tipped her chin toward the far side of the room. "Seats over there by my Aunt Grace."

The only way to get to the other side of the room was to take the long way around the rows of chairs. I followed behind Diana and Carrie as we weaved our way through the clusters of people gathered at the back of the room before we could walk up the side aisle to the vacant seats Diana had spotted. Along the way I tested myself putting faces to names, waving to some, exchanging hellos with others, trying to gauge how familiar I was with the long-time residents of Wenwood. There was Rozelle—a petite woman with tight gray curls—who owned the bakery and was sweet on Grandy; Maura, the bleached-blond music lover who worked at the grocery; Theresa, the vet; and Hector, the barber; and a dozen or more people I had become acquainted with. I had that sudden, warm sense of belonging that comforted me down to my toes and grinned all the way to my folding metal seat.

"Hey, Aunt Grace," Diana said as we filed into the row behind her.

"Hiya, girls." Still dressed in the robin's egg blue cotton dress she wore for her workday behind the counter at the luncheonette, ash blond hair in a low tight bun, Grace turned in her chair and grinned. "Diana, I'm glad you're here. I was just telling Marjorie about that nice fella you're seeing but I can't remember his name. What is it? Gary? Gregory?"

Diana's eyes went wide, and the muscles in her jaw bulged. "Aunt Grace," she ground out through clenched teeth.

"Nice fella?" I asked.

"Gregory?" Carrie added. "Why haven't we heard about this?"

"Yeah, why haven't we heard?" I echoed.

Diana took a breath so deep her nostrils flared. "His name is Nick and I was hoping to keep things quiet."

"But why haven't *we* heard?" Carrie asked. "You're supposed to tell your friends these things."

"Not after you graduate high school you're not," Diana snapped. Her cheeks flushed red, and the hands that had rested loosely on her knees closed into fists.

Catching Carrie's eye, I shook my head as minimally as possible. Only recently Diana had been taken off the desk duty she'd been briefly relegated to while she addressed her "anger management issues" and restored to regular duty. No need for us to risk waking the sleeping cranky pants.

"Oh, Diana, relax," Grace said. "We all know a few good dates do not a happily-ever-after make. It's just nice to know you're seeing someone. No one's going to ask you when the big day is."

Diana took in a very visible, very audible deep breath and blew it out in a slow stream. "Sorry, Aunt Grace. I should not have overreacted. I will try to work on that in the future."

Sure, it was easy enough for Diana to cling to the mantras of her anti-anger training. But I didn't know how deeply the words had sunk in for her, and wasn't eager to test their efficacy.

Turning back to face the front of the auditorium, Grace

said to the woman beside her, "Nick. His name is Nick. Lives up past that big Ford dealership."

I looked to Diana. "Sorry," I murmured. "Didn't mean to add to the . . . you know."

She held up a hand, palm out. "I need a minute."

Carrie shrugged while Diana did the deep-breathing thing again, and I checked the room for anything more interesting than the back of Grace's head.

Everyone in Wenwood was not, in fact, present. For one, few of the town's retiree set had opted to attend. For another, not everyone would be accommodated in the small space. But the turnout was excellent, and the demographic predominately younger. It was the young professionals and families, after all, who seemed to have the greatest interest in moving Wenwood forward.

I scanned the groups of standees, hoping I might spot Drew. If we happened to be in the same place, I could present the whole needing someone to help out in his office as a "hey, by the way," and then hit him with questions about law offices and the benefits of fire. I spotted the girl who helped out at the bakery laughing with the gentleman who was the new manager of the grocery, and a couple of young mothers in earnest conversation.

Near the entrance, Melanie, Russ Stanford's admin, stood talking with Curtis the humorless, her face a study in sympathy. As though aware of my gaze, she turned toward me and waggled her fingers. I waved back as a man of vast proportions tipped his head sideways so he could enter the room: Gabe Stanford.

Something sour rolled across my tongue. Might have

been a little cheddar cheese aftertaste, but there was an equal chance it was a reaction to Gabe. I let out an involuntary "ugh."

"What?" Diana asked.

I glanced to the door. "Gabe."

"Figures," Carrie said on a sigh.

"Who's Gabe?" Diana asked.

"My ex-brother-in-law," she replied. "Because I haven't had enough crap this week."

Keeping my eyes on the man, I said, "Ignore him. There are a million other people here for him to aggravate besides you."

Diana glanced from me to where Gabe stood just inside the doorway, scanning the crowd. "Wait. That guy? Bruce Banner mid-shift?" She looked to Carrie. "That's your brother-in-law?"

"Ex," Carrie and I said together.

"Wow. A guy that big, I'd need a forty-four Magnum to stop him."

"Don't be silly," I said. "Regular weapons don't stop the Hulk."

I should have looked away sooner; there was no need for me to keep my eyes on Gabe for as long as I did. But his scan of the room eventually brought me into his line of sight and he focused his gaze in my direction, icy blue eyes piercing through the heat of the room and slicing through me.

I looked away, not wanting him to think I'd been staring at him because I found him interesting, appealing, or the least bit above pond scum.

The shift in perspective allowed me, at last, to catch sight of Drew Able, Esquire. Sandy hair, pale skin, and dressed plain as ever in blue shirt and khaki slacks, he crossed the front of the room and took up position behind the podium.

So much for catching him before the meeting.

He tapped the microphone a few times and invited everyone to find a seat if they could, while a line of folks whom I assumed to be the town council filed through a doorway and filled the chairs behind the conference tables stretched beside the podium.

At the podium, Drew invited those seated to stand and led the crowd in the Pledge of Allegiance. It seemed every man and woman in attendance recited the pledge with intent and enthusiasm. My spine tingled with pride at the sound of all those voices joined in support of our country.

The pride I felt was quickly doused as the previously empty seat beside me attracted an occupant, an occupant whose elbow pressed against my upper arm, while my shoulder pressed into his bicep. A sharp scent of disinfecting soap occupied the air around him, and he himself occupied every other square inch of space. I looked up, and up, and up at him, and Gabe smiled down at me, a little cheerful, a little superior.

I gave no smile in return, but looked to the front of the room where Drew called the roll of the town council members. Having ascertained all were present, he handed the floor to the council.

As the head of the council shuffled to the podium, the mood in the auditorium made a subtle downshift from convivial to cautious. I glanced left to see if Carrie or Diana seemed affected or could possibly explain the change, but they kept their eyes front, with the same sort of focus I'd witnessed in Friday when she was trying to work out what made ants move.

In a droning voice, the councilman began to read the minutes of the last meeting. Mention of an incentive to repave Grand Avenue between Paris and Rome passed without reaction—except from me, since my imagination flashed a kindergarten map of Europe, where a paving truck chugged along between the Eiffel Tower and the Roman Colosseum. I covered my mouth to hold in the giggles.

While I fought down my mirth and the smell of Gabe's soap faded, the minutes were passed with the bang of a gavel and the council moved on to new business. First order, the vote on who would be occupying 120 Center.

"Proposal 1312E, third reading. Occupation of the property at 120 Center Street by Stella Mason and Regina Henry, retail proprietors of Sweets and Stones, combination mid-range jewelry, gourmet chocolates, and traditional penny candies."

A smattering of applause erupted, quickly countered by general noises of dissent.

"Proposal 1312F, third reading. Occupation of the property at 120 Center Street by American Distributors, retail owners of National Wine and Liquors, full-spectrum liquor store."

The same combination of applause and disapproval rumbled through the room.

"I don't understand," I whispered. "There's more than one shop vacant on Center. Why the battle over this one?"

"Apparently this one has second-floor storage," Diana whispered back. She shrugged.

At the mention of the second-floor storage, I quickly recalled being inside 120 Center when it had been a hardware store and coming across the staircase in back that led to loft space. The amount of storage space upstairs meant more square feet for retail at street level. Part of me was surprised Carrie wasn't interested in relocating her antiques shop there, what with the current overcrowding in her back room. But I understood that the added space may not have been worth the effort. I knew all too well what a pain moving was. Sure, I'd moved personal stuff and not an entire retail store but I figured the aggravation was at least equal.

"All those in favor of granting tenancy to Stella Mason and Regina Henry? Show of hands, please."

Hands went up around the room. I was secretly pleased to see Grace's hand shoot up in the air, since so many others of her generation appeared to be sitting with their arms tightly folded, but kept my own hands tucked beneath my knees.

The vote was repeated for the liquor store. From where I sat there appeared to be fewer hands in the air. As I turned to check behind me to see what the vote looked like over my shoulder, I caught Diana glaring at me.

"What?" I said.

"You didn't vote."

"I'm not a resident."

"You've lived here half your life," she said.

"Not sequentially," I said. "More . . . intermittently."

Diana narrowed one eye at me. "But you're staying this time, right?"

I opened my mouth, already preparing a breezy assertion that of course I was staying, because it was so much quicker and easier than explaining my internal dilemma. But beyond a friend's insight, I knew the cop in Diana would see right through me. All I could do was shrug.

The gavel came down with a *crack* and the room quieted. Diana treated me to one last glare before facing forward.

"Popular vote goes to Stella Mason and Regina Henry. In the absence of overwhelming dissent that might require the Council to reopen discussion and by provisions of Wenwood articles of procedure, tenancy is granted to Sweets and Stones."

Cheerful whoops and applause erupted throughout the auditorium. A cluster of women at the front of the room jumped from their seats and hugged one another. At the center of the joy, Regina's and Stella's smiles sparkled. Even the councilman cracked a grin. "Congratulations, ladies."

Beside me, Gabe let out a huff that threatened to blow loose the bun on the back of Grace's head. He smacked his hands upon his thighs, stood, and stomped off.

Diana raised a brow. "I guess he wanted to buy whiskey by the barrel, huh?"

"If there's any justice in the world, he has no one to buy jewelry for," I said.

Much as I didn't want to give Gabe Stanford another moment's attention, I watched as he made his way around the back of the room and out the door. Maybe I wanted to assure myself he was really leaving. And while I watched a bit longer, presumably to make sure he didn't return and rob me of shoulder room again, a steady stream of people trickled toward the exit.

But even with the shrinking of the crowd, the change in atmosphere as the next order of business was read was palpable. While the councilmen reviewed the proposal by development company Spring and Hamilton to build a shopping promenade along the riverfront, the room erupted in murmurs and what sounded, remarkably, like hissing.

"Settle down, please. Settle down," the councilman requested.

"What's this all about?" I asked, leaning close to Diana and keeping my voice low.

Eyes on the councilman, Diana said, "Spring and Hamilton still doesn't have the approval of the town council to build their shopping center down where the new marina will be. The senior set is opposed, the younger set is in favor. What else is new?"

Carrie peeked her head around. "They'll get their approval. This is the second reading. Before next month's meeting the council will make their decision and take town sentiment into consideration. As you can see"—she waved a hand to indicate our surroundings—"there are more in favor than opposed. It'll go through."

"They just need to complete the land purchases and

tear down all those old houses standing in their way," Diana said.

"Your town council will hold one more roundtable meeting to discuss the pros and cons with the residents on September sixth," said the councilman. "Due to space limitations we request interested parties advise the council's office of their intent to attend."

Once again, murmurs rippled through the crowd, gaining volume row by row. The councilman cleared his throat, the sound crackling through the speakers like a Hollywood explosion. It took several long moments, but the room at last quieted enough for the councilman to proceed.

"At this time I would like to turn the podium over to Councilwoman Denise Cannon."

"A new speaker? You mean it's not over?" I asked.

Craning her head over her shoulder, Grace answered, "They still have to read out the new business. You have to stay for that."

"Or you could wait until Friday and read about it in the *Town Crier*," Diana muttered.

"So by staying we've got an inside scoop?" I said.

"Something like that." Diana folded her arms and sat back in her chair, eyes narrowed appraisingly at the short, rounded woman who ambled to the podium.

"As you are no doubt aware," the speaker began, her voice shrill and certainly not in need of a microphone, "the state has awarded licenses for four casinos to be built in the areas surrounding Pace County. Your town council has been meeting with representatives from neighboring towns to discuss the implication and repercussions these resorts may have on our local economies."

The woman continued to speak, providing highlights from meetings that seemed to have resolved nothing, and reinforcing the importance of the success of the proposed Spring and Hamilton promenade.

"That's what they're banking on?" I whispered to Diana. "They're hoping with successful retail they can get a cut of the tourist money headed for the casinos?"

Diana shook her head. "They're hoping to get retail in place, so when the next round of licenses are issued there aren't casino resort developers eyeing our waterfront."

I nearly asked why they wouldn't want a casino nearby but then recalled the crowded streets of Atlantic City, the neon lights of tower hotels, the weed-like increase of fast-food establishments. A town like Wenwood, with its quiet riverside charm and air of a simpler time, would lose its identity entirely were the sleek lines and hotel towers of a casino resort to cast their shadow.

I listened intently to the rest of the speaker's presentation and cheered and stomped my feet with the remaining attendees when she concluded.

If I were to make a home in Wenwood, my vote would fall cleanly in favor of kitschy gift shops and waterfront restaurants over roulette wheels and all-you-can-eat buffets.

All I needed to decide was if this was home.

8

Carrie had threatened to pick me up at nine forty-five so together we could open Aggie's Antiques at ten. Carrie was never on time. Nonetheless, I set my alarm as if she would be early, and by eight I was dressed and downstairs in the space I used as my glass workshop, making use of both the early light and the time I would normally spend waiting for Carrie to arrive.

When my grandmother was still alive and she used the room as an art studio, she set up her still lifes in the light from the windows. Now my stained glass worktable sat where those vases of flowers and bowls of fruit had once sat.

At the end of the table opposite the stack of outdated newspapers, pieces of my latest personal project—the sailboat on the blue-green sea—lay safe beneath an old floral sheet I had unearthed in the basement. Reclaimed Wenwood bricks weighed down the cloth, preventing curious paws from lifting corners—or worse.

I left the covering in place and opened my sketchbook in the center of the table. The covers had barely hit the surface before Friday attempted to leap onto the table by jumping for a corner of the sheet. The same sunlight that made this the perfect place to work lit her bright white fur with an angelic glow while her devil claws dug in and made me doubly grateful for the bricks.

I pried her narrow, fur-too-soft-for-words body off the sheet and placed her atop the table. She was only four months old, and I was new to owning a cat, but it seemed to me the fuzz I had taken for kitten fur truly was an indicator of long hair to come. A long-haired white cat. I could hear Grandy grumbling about it already.

Wide blue-green eyes fixed on the notebook, and she took a tentative step forward. I knew I had limited time before she plunked herself in the center of the paper, and for once, that was best.

Keeping one eye on Friday, I reached beneath the table and withdrew the old crafters' storage box—another basement find—from the shelf below and brought it up to the tabletop.

With the latch undone, the cover lifted to expose rows of square cubbies within. Bits of broken glass gleamed from inside each cubby, some larger than the others but none too terribly small. They were remainder bits from older projects, and I had taken to storing them so I had my own mini-library of colors and textures.

I had done my best to sort the pieces by color—moss with sage, sunflower with buttercup—though some were such a gorgeous conflagration of color variety that they had no single color place. But for this piece, for Trudy Villiers's window, I suspected she would prefer the simpler blends.

"Magnolias," I murmured.

Friday mewed back.

"Magnolias," I said, louder, smiling at her little white face. "They come in different colors."

The trick was to find a white with enough pink or a pink with enough white that the subtle color variation of the magnolia blossom would shine.

Again reaching below the tabletop, I blindly sought the box of latex gloves I kept below and pulled one free. I tugged the glove onto my hand as my eyes scanned the box of color. An assortment of pale pinks nestled in the upper left corner of the box. I stuck a gloved finger into the cubby and flicked past pieces one by one.

"Hmmm."

Mew.

I reached absently for her and scratched under her chin.

"Magnolia Bed and Breakfast," I mused. "She's got all those roses in the back. Maybe she'd rather have roses?"

I lifted a broken corner of milk-white glass streaked with pink and held it up to the light. "But she wants magnolias." I looked to Friday as though we were having a true conversation. "And I have a feeling Trudy gets what Trudy wants, always."

She had brand new sidewalks in a town that clung to its old brick walks with the tenacity of a cat on a mouse and she had someone keeping the lawn trim and the bushes shaped. I peered past the glass in my fingers, out the window onto Grandy's yard. There was some trimming and shaping to be done there as well. If only I had the money to hire someone to snip the boxwoods into shape.

"Some day," I said to Friday, giving her a final pat on the head.

She rubbed her soft cheek against my palm, emitted an uncertain purr.

"Yeah," I said on a sigh. "I don't know how long either."

There was a storm in the forecast for the afternoon, which was nice in its promise for a cool evening to follow, but bad news for people like me, who planned on walking home from the village shops with a fresh supply of bananas. Figuring with my luck I'd be walking when the storm was due to begin, I grabbed a compact umbrella on my way out the door and ran through ominously humid air to jump into Carrie's car.

"Sorry I'm late," Carrie said as I pulled closed the door behind me.

"Oh, don't worry about it. Worked out fine. I was all caught up picking colors for Trudy Villiers's window."

"Speaking of Trudy . . ." She smiled a little. "I got an e-mail from her last night. She wants to know if you can stop by tomorrow with sketches for the window."

The urge to squirm in my seat was so strong I nearly

twitched from the fight. "Just me? What about you? Wouldn't she rather work with you?"

Carrie let out a light bark of a laugh. "Georgia, you're the one designing the window. That makes you the one Trudy has to work with."

"No. No. You could just bring her the designs and let me know what she thinks. I'm fine with that."

"Don't be ridiculous." She glanced at me from the corner of her eyes. "Wait, are you . . . You're not afraid of Trudy are you?"

"Absolutely not," I said. "I'm not afraid of her. I just . . . don't think she likes me very much."

"Why would you say that?" Carrie asked over a barely contained giggle.

"Oh, I don't know. Maybe the way she kept squinting at me and saying 'Georgia Kelly' for starters."

Carrie chuckled as she turned onto Center Street. "You're sounding a little paranoid."

"Paranoid? She said flat out there's something wrong with me, which is exactly the sort of thing someone who doesn't like a person says."

"I wouldn't say she doesn't like you. More like she doesn't trust you."

While I wrestled with the quick-rising indignation—I was perfectly trustworthy, thank you very much—Carrie steered the car past the grocer's and turned into the access alleyway leading to the parking area. A turn to the right at the end of the alley would put us in the lot behind the market, but a turn to the left took us to the limited strip of spaces behind the smaller shops, Aggie's Antiques among them.

"All the more reason, then," I said. "You'll have to come with me or Trudy may not let me in."

Sighing, she parked the car and cut the ignition. "You're still acting like this is a personal affront. To people like Trudy who have lived here their whole lives, you're still an outsider—no matter how many years of your childhood you lived with Pete."

Those years weren't even consecutive. On and off my mother would move us back to her hometown, typically when she was between husbands. I'm hard-pressed to remember spending winters anywhere other than Wenwood.

"It's the adult Georgia they don't know," Carrie continued as we made our way across the thin strip of tarmac.

I huffed. "You didn't know the adult Georgia and yet we're friends."

She slid her key into the lock set in the steel door. "Yes, but I—" Before she had turned the key, the door creaked open.

It was only a fraction, but no locked door should pop open unless its lock had been released. Which could only mean one thing.

Carrie and I gaped at one another, jaws slackening.

"Did you forget to lock that?"

She shook her head. "I never forget. Not ever." Tentatively, she curled her fingers around the handle and tugged.

"Carrie, I don't think you should—"

"Oh, Georgia, I'm sure it's fine."

The door swung open and Carrie ducked inside. Maybe I did have a bit of paranoia going on. All those years living in the city might have made me somewhat overcautious. This was Wenwood for Pete's sake. It was more realistic for me to expect her to shut off the store alarm and shout to me it was safe to enter.

I did not expect a scream.

9

A half a second's hesitation was enough time for Carrie to come back out of the shop before I had a chance to go in. I grabbed her arm just above the elbow. "Are you okay? What happened?"

Carrie backed away from the door, pulling me along with her. "Someone was in the shop."

I sucked in a breath. "What? How—"

"Or maybe someone's still in there."

The sun blazed down on us, baked the tarmac beneath our feet. I managed to break into a sweat at the same time my blood ran cold. "Okay," I said, quietly. "Okay."

Carrie struggled to get her free hand into the purse hung from her shoulder but the strap was a few inches too short to make the movement possible. She knocked the bag behind her repeatedly in her attempts. "Nine-one-one," she muttered. "Need to call nine-one-one."

I nodded frantically and turned her away from the door to her shop. "Pharmacy," I said. "We'll call from there."

"Right," she said. "Safe there."

"Right." I agreed.

The idea that someone had gotten into her store was disturbing enough. The possibility that someone hadn't left the store made us move with an unstoppable urgency.

Little more than twenty feet separated the back door of Aggie's Antiques from the back door of Bing's Pharmacy, but the distance felt three-times farther. Maybe it was to do with the heat or the humid weight of the air. More likely it had to do with a sudden surge of adrenaline that made time seem to slow and brought the world into crisp focus.

At the pharmacy door—the same steel style as the antiques shop, with a buzzer placed to the left below a sign directing visitors to ring for deliveries—I finally let go of Carrie. With a murmured prayer of "please be open please be open" she tugged on the door, and we tumbled over the threshold and into a narrow passageway. We passed a series of colorful posters advertising diapers, vitamins, and support hose before the passage opened up onto the sales floor.

"Not open yet," a man called. A glass display case sat center store, while the walls were lined with over-the-counter remedies.

"Fred, it's me," Carrie called in return, her voice none too steady. "Carrie? From—from next door?"

"Carrie, is everything all right?" Fred's voice drew closer with each word. "You sound shook."

He appeared from a recessed doorway behind the register and hurried along the length of the sales counter, a small man with gray hair as thin as his frame. His bushy brows crinkled with concern.

"Someone broke into my shop," Carrie said.

"We're afraid they may still be in there," I added.

"I have to call the police."

Fred's chin fell. He looked from Carrie to me and back again. "Of course. Of course. Use my phone."

"I have my cell," I offered. I shoved a hand into my purse and surprised myself by locating the phone immediately. I passed it to Carrie, my own distress manifesting in the belief that only Carrie was capable of dialing the emergency operator.

"Good. Good." Fred dashed past us, down the passage to the back door. As Carrie dialed, a thunk reverberated through the quiet store. Fred was locking his barn after the neighbor's horses had got out.

Standing close beside Carrie as she made the call, it was easy to hear the emergency operator come on the line. Together we listened to the operator announce that nine-one-one was for emergencies only and a break-in is not an emergency. Carrie would have to call the precinct.

She told the operator, "I don't know the number for the precinct."

The operator rattled off the number. Before Carrie could go into a panic looking for pen and paper, I said, "It's in my contacts. Don't worry."

Carrie thanked the operator and disconnected the call. She handed me back the phone. "You call," she said. "They know you there."

I really wish that wasn't true.

Fred joined us as I scrolled through the contacts. "How did someone get into your shop? Didn't you lock up?"

"Well, yes, of course I locked up." Her voice broke on "yes" and deteriorated as she went along.

I placed my phone on the counter and put an arm around her shoulder. A continuing tremor ran through her. She wrapped her arms around her belly and curled into herself.

"What about your alarm?" Fred asked. "Did you remember to set it?"

Carrie let out the smallest possible peep of affront, and I glowered at Fred. "Maybe leave the questions for the police and instead tell me where she can sit down until they get here."

"Oh, well, I . . ." He rubbed his hands together like he was applying lotion and glanced back toward the doorway from which he had appeared. "I can't let just anyone in the dispensary. There are controlled substances back there. Why don't you go have a seat at Grace's?"

I clenched my jaw for a slow count of three. The luncheonette Grace owned and managed was a fine place to grab a cup of coffee and a bite to eat. It was also the ideal location for catching up on every morsel of gossip Wenwood had to offer, or, you know, becoming gossip. "Maybe you could bring a chair out here?" I suggested.

Fred raised two fingers to his chin and gazed at the ceiling in classic thinker's pose.

"Maybe now?" I snapped.

"Georgia, it's okay," Carrie said on a sigh.

"No, it's not okay." There was no reason for Pharmacy Fred to think twice about helping Carrie. I was pretty sure his hesitation violated some chiseled-in-stone law of small-town compassion.

Still, it was a small town. I had to remind myself that things were done differently in Wenwood than they were in New York City.

I took a breath, smiled softly, and said in a much calmer voice, "Fred, it would really be a kindness if Carrie could sit while we wait for the police. She's had quite an upset."

Whether it was my approach or whether Fred had reached his own generous conclusion, he scampered off to fetch a stool, then held Carrie's elbow as she lowered herself onto the seat.

Grabbing my phone from the countertop, I scrolled through the contacts until I reached the entry for Pace County Police Department. Hoping Diana was on the desk, I put the phone to my ear and listened to the ringing.

The grumbling voice on the other end of the line sounded unfamiliar to me and most definitely wasn't Diana's. I gave my name and provided the details of the break-in as I knew them—open door, disrupted interior, nonfunctioning alarm—while beside me Carrie muttered about the disruption in her back room. Smashed picture frames, toppled vases, shattered cheval mirror. I informed the desk sergeant we had no knowledge of whether the thief remained in the store, that we had not entered and were holed up in Bing's Pharmacy.

"They said you did the right thing by not going into the store," I said, dropping the phone into my bag. "And we should wait here until an officer arrives."

"Oh, dear. Oh." Fred set to wringing his hands again. "I have orders to fill before I open and . . ." He glanced behind him to the dispensary.

"And we can't be here?" I guessed.

He lifted his shoulders, offered an apologetic smile. "I don't mind Carrie waiting. I've known her since she needed all her medicine in bubble gum flavor."

It took me fully half a second to understand. Carrie was a local. I was still an outsider. At the beginning of the summer that treatment made sense. Now, after all that had gone on, my response to being viewed as an outsider was shifting from annoyance to hurt. A tiny little poison bubble floating dangerously close to my heart.

And yet, I rumpled my forehead and nodded as though his differing treatment made perfect sense and I should have thought of it myself. "That's . . . that's fine. No problem. I'll just . . ." What? Wait in the car? Wander around the grocery store?

Carrie rescued me, looking at me with clear eyes from her tragic pose on the stool. "Do you think you could get me a cup of tea?" she asked, stressing the second *you*.

I wasn't sure what she was getting at, if she was trying to convey some hidden instruction to me. But I was happy enough to have an excuse to escape Fred's lack of trust for a bit.

For his part, Fred was happy to escort me out the front door, locking it behind me. I knew the locking was nothing personal. Didn't stop me feeling that it was.

I stood on the sidewalk for a moment and weighed my options. Across the street to the left was Rozelle's Bakery. Because of her—ahem—affection for Grandy, I reasoned she wouldn't ask many questions about what I was doing in the village so early in the morning. And in her hope of moving on quickly to news of Grandy she would only half listen to the answers I gave about myself, so a simple fib about helping Carrie with inventory would suffice. The drawback was having to wait for water to boil and potentially miss the arrival of the police.

Across the street to the right was the luncheonette, where there was always hot water. There was also Grace and Tom and Dave and a potential host of regulars who had plenty of time to chat and weren't likely to let my story of something as dead boring as inventory stop them from asking a good dozen follow-up questions.

I could eeny-meeny but the wind gusted—a hot breeze with a metallic finish. Rain would come sooner than later. And my umbrella was in Carrie's car.

With a resigned breath, I checked for traffic then dashed across the road. Over and over in my mind I told myself the inventory lie, so that when I pulled open the door to the luncheonette and spotted Tom in his usual place at the counter I nearly blurted out the story instead of hello.

"Jeannine," Tom called. "Good morning, good morning, good morning." He raised his plain stoneware coffee mug in salute and gave me a giggly grin.

I approached cautiously, switching my gaze from Tom to Grace. She stood in her usual position behind the counter, one hand on her hip, the other tapping the eraser end of a pencil against the morning paper. "That's Georgia," she said.

Tom shrugged, boney shoulders shaping an inverted V beneath his New England Patriots golf shirt. "I got the name wrong, but the face is right," he said.

Well, that was good to know. I'd hate to have been running around with someone else's face. "Hi, Tom," I said, sliding onto the vacant stool beside him. "How are you?"

He flashed a grin. "Feel great."

"He saw some new doctor out in East Waring," Grace said. "Got poor Tom here taking hundred-dollar supplements to help improve his memory."

"It's working," Tom said. "Didn't I tell ya it's working?"

"You know, sometimes the right balance of nutrients really can work wonders," I said, not that I really thought any supplement, no matter how costly, could fully bring Tom back from his perennial forgetfulness, but I was happy to have his perhaps previously unreliable memory forestall the usual question of what brings me to town.

"See?" Tom jerked a thumb in my direction. "Jeannine knows."

"Georgia," I said.

But Tom laughed, slapping his palm lightly against his thigh. "I'm kidding. I know you're Georgia. My mind is clear as a bell. I remember everything."

Grace scowled. "Sure you do. Ask him about Terry," she suggested.

"Why?" I had never even met Terry, but knew from time spent at the luncheonette that he and Tom had been constant companions until Terry moved south to be with his daughter. At Grace's encouraging nod I swiveled the stool so I was facing Tom. "What about Terry?" I asked.

"Heard from him last night." Tom thunked his coffee mug onto the counter, smacked his lips. "How about a refill, Gracie?"

"You spoke to Terry?" I asked.

Tom nodded. "He's coming back up for a few weeks. Staying through September, he says. Too hot down Carolina in the summertime."

I checked with Grace, who raised her brows as the corners of her mouth turned down.

"He says Terry's going to take the train," she said, in a tone of shrewd disbelief.

I glanced at Tom then back to Grace. "And why is this doubtful?"

The bell over the door jingled in the same moment Grace said, "Tom says he's going to pick him up at the station. As if he's still got a driver's license. If Terry is really planning—"

"Ned!" Tom called.

Grace dismissed talk of Terry with a wave of her hand and a heavy sigh.

"It's Herb, Tom," the gentleman said, joining us at the counter. "You know that. Morning, Grace." He slid a careworn fishing hat from his head, revealing a wealth of freckles and age spots hunkered beneath a very few strands of hair. "And who is this young lady?" he asked.

"That's Georgia Kelly," Grace replied for me. "Her granddad runs the Downtown Dine-In."

"Oh, come now, Grace. I'm sure Miss Kelly has something to recommend herself apart from her relationship to someone else." He gave me a crooked smile bright with kindness and genuine interest. "How about it?"

"Okay, um . . ." If I wasn't Pete Keene's granddaughter, and I could no longer legitimately consider myself an accountant, then what was I? "I, um, first of all it's just Georgia," I said. "And I guess I might be a stained glass artist?"

Herb's smile widened. "That's wonderful. My wife, God rest her, was a big collector of blown glass. Picked some up everywhere we went. They're still attracting all the dust in my house, those pieces. I just haven't had the heart to pack them away."

"Well there's . . . no reason you have to," I said, hoping it was the right thing to say. "You're allowed to enjoy them, too."

"Now that is true. That is true," he said. "But where are my manners? Name's Herb Gallo."

I grasped the hand he held out to me but rethought a firm shake. His grip was cautious, and made me think at once of Grandy—still a strong bear of a man despite his age, whose handshake could still be intimidating. Herb Gallo, who looked to be of a similar age, shook hands with the force of a lazy breeze.

"We haven't seen you around here in some time, Herb. Been working hard, have you?" Grace asked.

"Oh, you betcha. On vacation this week though. Couldn't resist stopping by for some coffee and one of your cinnamon donuts."

Grace grinned. "Coming right up. How about you, Georgia honey? What would you like?"

"Just a cup of tea for Carrie and a coffee for me, please."

"To go?"

"Please," I said. Herb settled onto the stool to my left. He pulled close a copy of the latest *Town Crier* and scanned the cover page.

"Hey, how about my refill?" Tom shouted.

"Aw, it's coming. Quit your griping."

While Grace busied herself pouring hot beverages, Tom leaned forward to look past me at Herb.

"Say, Herb, what's your take on all this property Spring and Hamilton are grabbing up?" Tom had a habit of shouting, both when he thought he needed to speak over the noise in the room and when he had forgotten his hearing aid and couldn't even hear his own voice. Whatever the case may have been, I pretended to smooth down my hair, keeping my hand strategically over my ear to muffle what I could of Tom's voice.

"Well, I can't say as I'm opposed," Herb said without looking up from the paper. "I don't want to see Wenwood turn into some of those other rundown ghost towns. If this new shopping promenade can stop that from happening, then I don't want to be the man who stands in its way."

"But all those houses, Herb. All those people selling out to that company," Tom said. "For more shopping?"

"Oh, here we go again." Grace set two covered paper cups down on the counter, then tugged an empty paper bag free of the stack beside the register. "Not everyone got to retire wealthy like you, Tom." She winked at me to show her teasing as she nestled the cups inside the bag and pushed the package my way. "Some people still gotta make a living, and a little string of shops on the waterfront could be a blessing."

"It won't be a blessing. It will be a blight," Tom said at his default volume. "We can only hope someone doesn't sell. That'll stop the whole project in its tracks. I bet Pete sees it my way. Doesn't he, Georgia?"

I tugged a handful of singles out of the zipper pocket inside my purse and handed them over to Grace. "Why don't you ask me what I think, Tom?" I teased. "I live here, too. Don't I get an opinion?"

He gave me the same dismissive hand wave he had given Grace. "You're new," he said. "You haven't spent enough sweat here yet."

"Now Tom," Herb put in, looking up from the paper. "Miss Kelly has just as much right to an opinion as you."

"Herb's right." Grace passed me my change. "Don't listen to this old grump," she said. "He's still sore about—"

"Police are here," Tom announced.

"*Police*?" Grace spun to peer through the window, following the direction of Tom's gaze.

I grabbed the bag of caffeinated beverages. "Gotta go," I said.

"Georgia, do you know something about this?" Grace asked.

I shot her a little smile and hustled out of the store. Rude to leave without answering her question, I guess. But she and Tom would watch out the window anyway and have an excellent view of me approaching—

Detective Nolan.

Dang it.

10

"**Y**ou got here fast," I said when I caught up to him in the doorway of the pharmacy. His presence was no doubt a result of my call to the station or he wouldn't have parked in front of Bing's. The marked squad car had rolled to a stop in front of Aggie's Antiques.

He lowered his sunglasses so he could look at me from above the rim. Brown eyes serious and yet amused at the same time. "I've got a flashing red light that lets me exceed the speed limit."

"Oh. Right." I peered through the glass door, looking for signs of life within the store. I saw neither Fred nor Carrie, and opened my mouth to ask about their absence when Detective Nolan said, "Carrie went to find the proprietor. I presume he's the one with the keys."

"Oh. Right."

Well done, Georgia. Way to be repetitive with the handsome cop.

I bit the inside of my lip as personal punishment for thinking such thoughts.

"You ladies all right?" he asked.

I tried to meet his gaze but he had pushed his sunglasses back in place. All I could do was meet the reflection of my own eyes. "We're fine. That is, Carrie's a little shook up but that's all."

"And you're made of tougher stuff." He crooked a smile.

"I didn't go in," I blurted.

His half smile went to full and the brightness of it hit me like a cool breeze. Oh, this was bad. This was really bad.

For once luck was with me, because Fred was slipping the key into the door lock. The activity distracted Detective Nolan's attention from the blush climbing up my neck and onto my cheeks.

I stalled a few seconds at the doorway, allowing the detective to move well into the store before I followed.

Carrie waited beside the jewelry showcase, arms folded, shoulders inching toward her ears.

"You okay, Ms. Stanford?" Detective Nolan sounded sincerely interested rather than merely polite. At Carrie's nod he continued, "You wanna tell me what happened?"

As she recounted the story of our arrival at the antiques store, I pulled her tea from the bag and passed it over. I took my coffee out and bent back the tab on the lid. Maybe I should have been paying attention to what Carrie was saying and what Nolan was asking, but I knew the answers and could anticipate the questions. Instead, my mind hiccupped back to the luncheonette and Tom's talk of Spring and Hamilton and its bid for a shopping promenade.

When I teased Tom for not asking my opinion, there was perhaps more truth than jest in my words. I had refrained from raising my hand during the town hall meeting out of that same old fear of being an outsider, of thinking it wasn't my place and those around me might call foul. Deep inside, though, I heard an annoying little voice suggesting I was the one responsible for perpetuating that outsider feeling. And having and expressing an opinion on matters affecting the town might help me believe myself more of an insider.

"When the second squad car arrives," Detective Nolan was saying, "we'll take a look through the store, make sure no one's there—though I doubt anyone is."

"Why do you doubt it?" I asked.

"It's daylight," he said. "Anyone looking through the window would see an intruder."

"There could still be someone in back," I said. Carrie made a little whimpering noise.

"Could be, but not likely. Still. Can't be too cautious in a situation like this."

Fred Bing bustled out from the dispensary, tugging the door shut behind him. He held a flat plastic bin filled with small wrapped packages. He scuttled behind the customer service counter and slid the bin out of view. "I'll be opening soon," he announced in a tone that suggested we should think about other accommodations.

Detective Nolan squared his shoulders. "I want the

ladies to remain here until we've completed a search of Ms. Stanford's store," he said. "I'm sure they won't be in the way."

Pharmacist Fred scowled but thought better of arguing with the police.

Once the squad car arrived and Nolan went out to meet the officers, Carrie and I huddled shoulder to shoulder in the passageway to the back door, waiting for an all-clear.

"Don't you think it's weird," I asked. "First Russ's building and now your shop?"

As soon as the words were out I wished I could have them back. They seemed the sort of idea that shouldn't be uttered in a brightly lit space but whispered in darkness, as one might whisper about conspiracy.

"I don't know what to think." Carrie sipped at her tea. "I don't know if I want to think."

I wasn't sure I wanted to think either. But once the idea was out, it seemed to somehow solidify into a concept worth investigating.

We didn't wait long before one of the uniformed Pace County PD officers swung open the back door looking for us, letting us know Aggie's Antiques was free of intruders and we could return. After thanking Fred for his hospitality and managing to keep a straight face as I did, Carrie and I hurried back to the antiques shop.

Anxiety pinched the corners of Carrie's eyes and kept her shoulders tight. I didn't know how she hadn't given herself a headache. But then, maybe she had purchased some aspirin while hiding out in the pharmacy.

The officer tugged open the back door and held it while we passed through.

Every light in the back room was lit. In that brightness, what in my imagination was a tumbled mess was in reality a heartbreaking tableau. The poured concrete floor was coated with little shards of glass that we ground into both the floor and the soles of our shoes as we wandered into the center of the space. Crumpled papers, mangled picture frames, and empty jewel boxes littered the old table Carrie used to pack treasures for shipping. The only part of the room that appeared untouched was the spools of brightly colored curling ribbon affixed to the bottom edge of the table. I fingered a length of brilliant emerald as Detective Nolan stepped over a toppled floor lamp to meet us.

"I'm sorry to have to ask you this," he said, leaning down a little to catch Carrie's eye, "but I'm going to need you to take a look around and tell me if there's anything of value missing."

She lifted her chin. "Anything of value? Detective, all my merchandise is valuable."

Glass ground beneath his feet as he adjusted his stance. "Not valuable enough to have motion sensors installed though?"

In the same moment that her eyes glossed over with tears, she lowered her gaze. "Motion sensors are expensive."

"Everything in the shop is valuable to someone," I put in. "But these are antiques, grandma's attic type stuff, not highly prized collectibles. And if there was something worth stealing, why do all this?" I raised a palm to the ceiling and spread my arm, the gesture encompassing the surrounding destruction.

Nolan folded his arms, a movement that managed to pull his slate-colored tie a little farther askew. "This could be a diversion," he explained, "calculated to deflect attention away from what was stolen."

"No." Carrie shook her head. "Nothing that valuable."

The detective nodded. "In that case, what we're going to do is I'm going to write up a statement from you, and you're going to have to put together a list of what's missing."

"Or destroyed," Carrie whispered.

We stood in a silent triangle, letting the word *destroyed* fade away.

"I'm very sorry, Ms. Stanford." He paused. "I'm going to go out to the car and grab the paperwork. I'll only be a minute."

His departure didn't raise the same noise of grinding glass my and Carrie's footsteps had. I glanced over my shoulder at the oddity. Detective Nolan was tiptoeing through the mess, zigzagging his progress in an effort not to do any further damage.

"Oh, Georgia," Carrie said sadly.

I took a deep breath. "It's okay. We'll get this cleaned up."

"It's not that." She lifted a chin to indicate the shelving that ran along the southern wall of the back room. "Your glass," she said.

Turning, I scanned the shelves against which two of my stained glass pieces had rested. One had been a rectangular window, a simple fleur-de-lis design. But the other had been far more involved—a sixteen-by-twenty picture frame of white roses from buds to full blooms, with foil flourishes and the occasional soft green leaf. We'd been trying to find an old-timey photo of a bride to use to show off the intention of the frame. I supposed that search was over.

That familiar scratchy ache seized my throat. My nose twitched and my eyes burned. My heart seemed to fall into my stomach at the same moment the first tear fell. I had worked hard on that piece, had been particularly proud of it. And though I had long since come to accept that my own bridal portrait would never be framed by those white roses, still, to see the petals reduced to shards awoke an ache for losses more than material.

I sniffled in a most unladylike way. I wiped away the tear and turned to face Carrie again. "All right. Let's get started."

11

Unsurprisingly, Grandy felt I should go see Drew in person rather than chat with him over the phone. The job hunt game had changed a great deal since Grandy's day, but there was no telling him things were done differently now. That he had a computer in his office at all was borderline miraculous. Just don't expect him to research job applicants online or open an e-mailed résumé.

Still, I had to admit that doing things Grandy's way had one unexpected bonus: I was forced out of my summer wardrobe of flip-flops, shorts, and T-shirts and into a tailored dress and linen pumps. I took the time to flat-iron my hair and tie it back in a neat braid. I even went so far as to apply foundation beneath a soft swipe of blush. When I finished with some mascara and took one final look at myself in the mirror—a look at me as a whole and not the little pieces I'd been primping and polishing—my breath stuck in my chest.

The image in the mirror might well have had a caption beneath it reading "before." In the glass was the Georgia Kelly I had left behind all those months before. There was something sharp and sleek and downright smart about that Georgia. Gone were the frizzy red curls that made me look slightly ditzy and unkempt. Gone were the faint freckles and pale eyelashes. Gone were the shoulders rounded in defeat. I let my breath out slowly and wondered if I could still see myself in that image, if I felt more or less like myself in those shoes.

"You're going to be late," Grandy called up the stairs, derailing my train of thought.

I smoothed down the front of the aqua dress, took one last look in the mirror, and left my room. "I don't have an appointment, Grandy," I called back. "It's not possible for me to be late."

"I'm not worried about you being late arriving. I'm worried about you being late getting back with—"

"With the Jeep." I sighed as I reached the top of the stairs. "I know. I'm going."

As I clumped down the steps in my heels, Grandy made no secret of looking me over head to toe. "Don't you have a suit?"

"You look nice, too," I said.

He smiled and looked down at his feet, abashed as a schoolboy. "Quite right," he said. "You look lovely."

"Thank you," I said. "Directions?"

He handed me an index card on which he'd written

directions to Drew's office, complete with hand-drawn images of streets and intersections and a great big X over my final destination.

"Any messages for your lawyer?"

Grandy lifted his chin. "Give him my regards."

On my way through the living room, I paused by the couch where Friday was stretched out, belly exposed to the sunbeams streaming through the windows. "Be good, kitty," I said, scratching beneath her chin. She wrapped her front legs around my wrist and curled herself around my forearm. For her, it was probably just a bit of play. For me, it felt like she didn't want me to leave, and that made me feel a little bit special, a little bit loved. "I'll be back soon," I told her. She didn't let go, and I was forced to pry my arm away, fearful she'd give me a sad-eye look. Instead, she rolled over, sprang to her feet, and flew off the couch on her way to her favorite hiding place under the china cabinet.

So much for missing me when I'm gone.

I grabbed my purse and keys and headed out. The early morning cool had burned off and left the air outside well on its way to steaming. Across the street, leaves on the neighbor's maple tree hung motionless, sun glowing off the green. My luck. A perfect flip-flop day and I was in pumps.

At least the Jeep had air-conditioning. It kept me nice and cool while I struggled with the adjustments necessary to smoothly depress a gas pedal while wearing heels.

The ride to downtown Wenwood passed with the speed of familiarity. One minute I was backing out of the driveway, the next I was cruising past the grocer's where a large UNDER NEW OWNERSHIP banner stretched across two windows. Opposite the grocery was Rozelle's Bakery and, I suspected, the cause of Grandy's new strudel habit, Rozelle herself, sitting on a lawn chair in front of the shop chatting with a passerby. There was Grace's luncheonette, catty-corner to Carrie's shop, Aggie's Antiques, where Carrie had placed a pair of my stained glass panes in her window, and finally the vacant hardware store that Regina and Stella would soon take over with their candy and jewelry shop. From there the strip shifted from retail to private businesses—real estate (by appointment only), medical (same), and barber (both appointment and walk-in).

At the end of the strip, for the first time in memory, I turned left. Grandy's written instructions began at that turn, and I followed the left-right-straight indicators on his map until I reached the little white Cape Cod house with the shingle that read DREW ABLE, ESQ., ATTORNEY AT LAW hanging from a signpost. A smaller version of the same sign was propped in the picture window beside the front door.

I parked the Jeep at the curb, switched off the air conditioner in the last possible second before turning off the engine. With a deep breath and a self-deprecating shake of my head, I walked up the cracked concrete path to the front door and let myself in—per Grandy's further instruction.

The door opened into a small waiting room as nondescript as Drew himself. White blinds, beige walls, brown faux-leather couch. A coffee table held a selection of magazines guaranteed to never become dog-eared—*Scientific American*, *American Law Journal*, and *The Real Deal*.

Opposite the window was another door, this one open and showing a continuation of the riveting decor of the waiting room. A pair of button-tuck leather chairs faced the broad cherrywood desk behind which sat Drew Able—brown hair, white polo, pale skin.

"Georgia." He grinned and stood, revealing his customary khakis, these with a stain along the thigh that looked suspiciously like coffee. "Come in. Come in. What brings you by?"

I crossed the threshold into his office, then grasped the hand he extended in my best all-business shake. The little knot of nerves twisting in my belly gave an insistent tug. How best to approach him about hiring me for a job that didn't exist?

"To be perfectly honest, Gran—er, Pete Keene suggested I talk to you, but, uh . . ." Other than needing a brightly colored print or, ideally, a stained glass lamp or two, Drew's office didn't appear as disorganized as Grandy led me to believe.

"How is Pete?" Drew gestured to the visitors' chairs as he circled around me to close the door.

"He's well," I said, eyes on the door. "Am I interrupting anything? Are you expecting a client?" *In other words, can I change my mind and escape*?

"Oh, no, no. Not for another"—he checked his wristwatch—"twenty minutes or so."

It had not occurred to me that a small-town lawyer would have clients in on a Thursday morning. I somehow pictured Drew as having more time on his hands than work to do. Foolish, but not knowing much about how a lawyer keeps busy I'd come to my own conclusion. And yet . . .

A memory gnawed at the back of my mind, a passing comment Grandy made when he told me why Drew was his lawyer. He'd described Drew as the only decent lawyer left in Wenwood. I wondered if Russ Stanford had ever maintained an office in Wenwood. And if he did, was it important? Did it have a link to the fire at his office? Were Russ and Drew competing for the same client pool? Where did the break-in at the antiques shop fit in?

"What's on your mind?" Drew prompted.

I mentally shook myself back into the moment, gave a delicate little cough to buy time to recall why Grandy had suggested I seek out Drew. "I, um, Pete was concerned about not getting billed for your time from . . ."

"Ah." He nodded. He leaned back in his chair, its springs making a soft creak. "From the . . . yeah. Well. I didn't really do much, did I? You did more to get him exonerated than I did."

"You did plenty and Pete would like to pay you what you're owed." Even as the words came out of my mouth, they disintegrated. Then I really did shake my head. "I don't believe it. How stupid can I be?"

Drew leaned a little away from me. "Sorry?"

"Grandy—Pete—sent me here because he's convinced you haven't sent out a bill because you're completely disorganized and in need of my help. But in reality, you're being kind, aren't you? You know he's been low on funds, but really, business at the dine-in is picking up and—"

"Georgia." The tips of Drew's ears flushed red. "I wish I could agree to being the kind person you think I am but . . ." The red swooped down his neck. "Truth is, Pete's right. Sort of. Look, I know Pete doesn't have a lot of ready cash but he really needed my help. You, of all people, know how he is. He won't take anything for free."

"No," I agreed. "Free is the same as charity to him."

"Exactly. So we came up with a structured billing plan where he pays me—"

"A little each month," I put in.

"Exactly. But, I haven't sent out any bills because Pete's right. I really am disorganized."

With an effort at appearing overly obvious, I cast my gaze around the room. Sure, the furnishings were sparse, but that only enhanced the everything-in-its-place decor. The one aspect that hinted at disorganization was the closed file on Drew's desk, and that only because paper edges were sticking out at random points. "Yes, I can see you have a real problem."

Sighing, he stood, and crooked a finger at me. He led me to a narrow door in the corner of the office that I had presumed opened onto a water closet. But as I bravely followed Drew (because who wants to walk into a tiny bathroom with a lawyer?) I realized we were moving into another full-sized room. Filing cabinets big and small lined the walls. A table with four chairs gathered around it sat at the room's center. And atop the table, stacked on cabinets, in piles on the floor, were papers and files and files and papers. Every surface was covered.

I might have gasped.

"Current cases are on the table," Drew admitted in a small voice. "The rest . . ."

I nodded my understanding of the implication. "Grandy's file is in there somewhere." I took a moment to let the extent of the mess sink in. Then I turned to face Drew. "Have you ever billed anyone?"

"Of course!" He tucked his head back, affronted. "I've just been really busy lately."

"How long is lately?" I asked, eyeballing a collection of papers that had yellowed under accumulated dust.

"I keep meaning to get this cleaned up." He pushed a hand through his hair, sighed. "There's just no time."

I shouldn't have been surprised that Grandy had been right in his theory on why he hadn't received a bill. Grandy was sharp that way—and very likely had stumbled into this room at some point in a search for the bathroom.

"Isn't it, I don't know, dangerous to leave these papers lying around like this?" I asked, tracing my finger along the edge of a file.

He lifted one shoulder in a noncommittal shrug. "Doubtful. Rules of disclosure make these files practically public record."

I raised my brows.

"All right, not public record. But nothing is lying around that needs to be kept under lock and key. For those I have a fireproof safe."

"Fireproof?" I repeated.

Drew gestured to the far corner, where a boxy black safe huddled beneath a stack of phone books. Real, tangible phone books. I wondered if Carrie could use them for atmosphere at the antiques store. "I may be sloppy," Drew said, "but I'm not careless. Wills, prenups, powers of attorney, my computer passwords . . . all the important stuff goes in the safe."

My mind spooled out the memory of Russ's fire-damaged office. If the truly important papers needed to be kept in a fireproof safe, what good would it do to burn down the office? Nothing within the safe would be destroyed. Whatever the firebug had been looking for would have to have been tucked into a desk or a filing cabinet or something similarly minimally secured for the fire to do its job. Which meant whatever the arsonist was trying to destroy wasn't sensitive enough to warrant being stored in the safe. But then, what was easier to burn than steal?

Drew's voice shattered my musings. "Pete thought you could help with this?"

I nodded, distracted, thoughts shifting back to "the only decent lawyer" comment. What kind of lawyer was Russ? What if, despite being the nice guy Carrie claimed him to be, as a lawyer he was unscrupulous?

"Do you know Russ Stanford?" I asked.

Drew blinked rapidly, whiplashed by the question. "Wh-what?"

"Russ Stanford. Also an esquire. Do you know him?" I faced him, arms crossed against my chest, as he adjusted to the change in topic and considered the question.

His answer came slowly. "I knew him. Not well. Why do you ask?"

Why indeed? "Is he a good lawyer, reputable?"

Drew straightened a little, his shoulders squared. "I make it a point not to comment on the work of my fellow attorneys."

"Is that a no?"

"It's a no comment."

His face was inscrutable. And I was really looking. But his calm brown eyes and softly squared jaw revealed no emotion. I surmised his expression to be his "lawyer face." I bet it worked really well in front of judges. "Why did you come here, Georgia? To ask me about Russ Stanford, to settle Pete's account, or to offer to help me organize my office?"

Sadly, my bank balance was in no shape to settle Grandy's account. But he was right on the other two. Since I'd asked about Russ and got a politician's response, there was only one thing left. The nerves in my gut gave another twist. I ignored them. "All of the above, actually."

"You do filing?" he asked.

"I do books, Drew. I'm an accountant. And if you want to actually earn money as a lawyer you need someone to handle your books." I glanced around the room. "It doesn't look like you're much of a do-it-yourselfer in that area."

He pressed his lips tight, considered the idea. "That's how Pete thought you could help? By me hiring you?"

"You clearly need some help here, Drew." I waved a hand at the mess. "Before this gets worse. And I could use the work."

"I don't know . . ." His lips twitched as if he was biting the inside of his cheek.

"Yeah, I don't know how you waited this long to hire someone either," I said, grinning, teasing. "How about we call it a temp job? I'll get this place in order and give you a listing of who owes you what, and then you decide whether or not you want to keep me on to make sure you get paid."

"A temp job, huh?" he asked.

The pop and scrape of a heat-swollen door being opened carried through waiting room and office to reach us by the filing cabinet. Chattering voices followed.

"My next clients are here," he said. He dashed to the table. Pushing aside one file after another he muttered, "I know I left the file right . . ."

A rap at the open door made us both turn and look over our shoulders.

A man and woman stood in the doorway, looking as though they were both cut from the same brown-haired, fair-eyed cloth. "Sorry, Drew." The man flashed a quick grin. "The door was open. I was afraid we were late."

The woman beside him smirked. "You were afraid we'd be billed."

It was Drew who flushed with embarrassment, but his tone was confident. "Go ahead and have a seat. I'll be right with you."

The pair retreated, presumably to claim the chairs on the visitors' side of Drew's desk.

"Steve and Marcy Carney," he said, so quietly I struggled to hear. "Property sale. They're in for a nice windfall if I can find the file." He spun back to the cluttered table. "Where is it? Where is it?"

"Property?" My forehead furrowed as I added that

131

information to what little I knew of Drew. "I didn't realize you practiced real estate law."

"I practice a little bit of everything. That is, if I can find the—thank goodness!" Drew's fingers closed around a thick manila folder. Abashed, he turned around to face me. "You're right. I need help. Can you start tomorrow?"

12

The trip back to Newbridge, back to Broad Street and the scene of the crime, required just one U-turn after I went west instead of east. Considering I had only made the trip once before and as a passenger at that, I considered my otherwise direct drive a victory.

I parked the SUV on the same side street we had parked on earlier in the week, but this time found a nice shade tree to keep the vehicle cool. After locking the door behind me, I made a futile attempt at smoothing down the wrinkles in my dress and strode across the street.

Foot traffic and road traffic had increased since last I was in town. I presumed the bustle illustrated its ordinary pace. I passed by people running errands and kids gathered on the sidewalk asking one another the classic summer question, "Now what do you want to do?" My gaze strayed across the street, where the blackened hulk of stone that was once Russ Stanford's office slouched behind the chain-link fencing Carrie had paid to have erected to keep out the curious and the daredevils. My belly went hollow at the sight of the gutted building. The charred walls and boarded windows spoke loudly of loss and violence.

Why, then? Why had the antiques store been spared?

Standing and staring at the building wouldn't make the answer come. I needed more information.

Turning my back on the damaged building, I pulled open the narrow door to the coffee shop and stepped inside. The refreshing blast of air-conditioning made me aware of the sweat and vague nausea the destroyed law office had stirred. Hand on my stomach, I took a slow, steadying breath.

At fast glance all but four of the little tables appeared occupied, with a few people seated at the counter. The door opened behind me, and I shuffled out of the way of two late-middle-aged women, chuckling, heads bent over their smartphones.

A waitress buzzed by, pot of coffee in one hand, menus tucked under her arm. "Grab a seat anywhere, ladies."

I looked over my shoulder, realizing the waitress thought we were all one group. Worse, the waitress was not Susie, the dark-haired server I was seeking.

But the café was busy. I reasoned there had to be more than one waitress. Plus the aroma of coffee and grilled burgers scented the air. I strode to the counter and settled onto a stool, with the access to the kitchen farther down on my left and the closed end of the counter farther down to the right. Someone had left the day's paper within reach, beside a covered cake plate containing no more than half a dozen donuts. Tempting though the donuts were, I helped myself to the paper only and prepared to wait.

I was only three pages in and wondering how much longer printed newspapers would be viable when an earthenware mug was plunked onto the counter in front of me. Seconds later, the coffee was poured.

I looked up from the paper at the same moment Susie lifted the carafe of coffee away from my mug. Relief and anxiety moved simultaneously through me. Susie was the only chance I had at locating Russ's administrative assistant, Melanie. If Susie hadn't been working, I would have been sunk. Even though she was, there was still a chance she wouldn't help me at all.

But it was because of Carrie I had made the trip. Carrie who had fast become the friend I sorely needed after arriving in Wenwood. She was worth taking the chance.

"Coffee, right?" Susie asked after the fact.

"You remembered." I smiled, reaching for the cup.

"Menu?"

"Umm." I eyed the donuts. I knew I should opt for real food, opt for something with more protein and less sugar. Something whose ingredients were all sourced from a produce aisle. "Donut. Thanks."

The reduction in Susie's interest in me was almost a tangible thing. With coffee and a donut there wouldn't be much of a tip for her, making me a customer who required a little less attention. I needed to act fast.

"And I was hoping you could help me with something," I said.

"Jelly?" Susie asked.

"Jelly's good," I said. "You know Melanie who works—worked—across the street?"

She used a paper square to remove a jelly donut from the cake plate. Nodding, she withdrew a saucer from beneath the counter and set the donut atop it.

"I need to get in touch with her." I left the statement there, hoping Susie might offer her assistance. But her gaze flicked over my head and swept the room. She had other customers to see to, customers whose forks were tapping against plates and glasses were thunking onto tables. She shifted her weight, almost leaning, and I knew she was preparing to leave. "I don't suppose you could give me her number?"

Susie smirked, rolled her eyes, and took off to the closed end of the counter.

Drat.

I rested my elbows on the counter. Leaning forward, I kept my eyes on Susie, knowing she would have to come back past me.

When at last she spun around to head back to the kitchen, I held up a finger to flag her down. "Menu?" she asked again.

"If I give you my number, would you call Melanie and ask her to call me? Or maybe she could meet me here?"

"I'm working," she said, and kept going.

It took two more attempts, one solemn oath that all I wanted to talk to Melanie about was her job, and one plea that her boss's ex-wife might be in danger before Susie agreed to call Melanie on my behalf.

Rather than give Melanie my number and tell her to call me, Susie went right to the point and asked her to come down to the coffee shop. I suspected this was a ploy to get me to order something more substantial than a donut. But when Susie clicked off the call and slid her phone back into her apron, she said, "She can't come."

Stunned, I let my mouth hang open a moment before I found words. "Why didn't you give her my number? Or even just put me on the phone with her?"

"Because I'm not your secretary. Relax." Susie pointedly took away my coffee. "She's having a mani-pedi at Mindy's. You can go meet her there."

From the coffee shop it was a five-minute fight with my GPS and a fifteen-minute ride to Mindy's Nails. The cup of decaf I'd purchased for the ride tasted like the coffee was brewed with twice-used grounds and made me regret leaving an exorbitant tip for Susie. Still, she didn't make the coffee, and though she hadn't been quick to help, she had called Melanie in the end and that's all that mattered.

Unable to find a parking spot in front of the strip mall in which the nail salon was located, I left Grandy's SUV two blocks away and hoofed it. As I walked, seriously regretting my choice of footwear, sweat collected in my palms and across my lower back. I swore I could feel the sun burning my skin, transforming my Irish pale into freckled lobster faster than Friday chasing a firefly.

I waited to enter Mindy's while another patron waddled out, bright red toes held off the ground, car keys in hand. In that brief moment at the entrance to the shop, noise from inside assailed me. The television was blasting the midday news and the shop staff was busy shouting over it to converse with one another. The air smelled of nail glue and floral air freshener and my nose twitched with the threat of a sneeze. But the air, just that brief tease of it, was cooler, and I ducked inside gratefully.

Just over the threshold I moved out of the path of the doorway and paused, taking in the bright yellow walls, string of white manicure tables, and trio of beige pedicure chairs. In the chair farthest from the door, Melanie sat flipping through a magazine while a wiry gentleman with a thick head of black hair applied polish to her toes. I risked a deep breath, trying to still the sudden rush of anxiety cramping my gut. What made me nervous? It was just a few questions . . . that I had to ask of a virtual stranger.

As I blew out the breath and stepped forward, one of the blue-aproned manicurists rushed over and asked if I wanted a manicure. I pointed to the back of the salon. "Just here to see someone," I said, adding some volume to my voice to beat out the blare of the television.

Melanie glanced up, her gaze a mixture of curiosity and wariness. She flipped one more page of her magazine before setting the publication on the wide armrest and leaning forward. Her short denim skirt and pale pink camisole showed off newly sunned skin. Getting out of the office seemed to have done her good.

"Okay," the man at her feet said. "Now manicure?"

"Yes," she said, then turned to me. "Come have a manicure."

I did a quick mental calculation of my cash situation and a surreptitious check of the price list affixed to the wall. Knowing I would need to make a large cash outlay soon in order to buy sheets of stained glass I really should have avoided the little luxury. But I reasoned having my nails done would seem more congenial than straight out questioning Melanie. Plus, I was better at being pampered than I was at being an interrogator.

The staff picked up on Melanie's plan and a manicurist positioned herself behind the empty table next to Melanie's, smiling while I dashed to the wall lined with row upon row of polishes and grabbed the first soft copper shade I could find.

I passed the polish to the technician and settled into the chair to Melanie's left.

"So Susie says Russ's ex-wife had her shop broken into . . ." Melanie began in a fill-in-the-blank tone.

"Night before last." I rested the heels of my hands on the paper-wrapped block. "Did a lot of damage." The nail technician sprayed my fingertips with the scented sanitizer, and I realized this was the source of the floral fragrance, not air freshener.

"A lot of damage." Melanie scoffed. "Damage isn't as bad as burnt to the ground."

"No, it's not," I murmured. She was right, of course. The fire had done far more destruction to property. But at Carrie's antiques shop, more than just glass had been shattered.

When the technician inquired, I asked her to shape my nails nicely rounded. She set to work filing with an abandon

I wouldn't dare at home and I returned to questioning Melanie. "Have you heard from Russ at all?" I asked.

"Should I have?" She peered sidelong at me, big brown eyes shrewd.

"Doesn't he check in when he's away?"

Melanie lifted her shoulders in shrug. "Not with me. You know, Herb Gallo is the other attorney. If Russ checks in, that's who he calls."

"Wait. Herb Gallo? Older gentleman, widower, very polite?"

"Sounds like Herb," Melanie said.

Of all the dumb luck. I'd had him. He had been right there in the luncheonette and I never even knew. Of course, there was a slim—super slim—chance there was more than one Herb Gallo in the area. But I wouldn't bet on super slim.

"He might have spoken to Russ. Herb handles clients and covers cases and all that, so if there was anything need-ing to be done, he's the one Russ would call." She huffed a little and shifted the hair off her shoulder with a toss of her head. "All I can do is make photocopies and phone calls."

"I'm sure you do more than that," I said.

"No. That's about it."

If that was true, I may have spent my time better by hunting down Herb. But how to know for sure?

I waited while the nail technician guided my right hand into the soak then took the file to my left.

"You know, it's funny, really, that I came up to see you today because I just got a temporary job working for a lawyer myself."

"Yeah? Good for you." It was the look she gave me that conveyed the sarcasm more than her tone.

I chose to pretend I didn't understand her subtlety. "I'm a little nervous about it, honestly. It's my first job in a law office and I have no idea what kind of boss this guy's going to be."

Letting the statement lie, I focused for a bit on the technician sawing away at my nails with gusto. By the time she moved my hand into the soft soak and gestured for me to take my other hand out, curiosity prevailed.

"What's the lawyer's name?" Melanie asked.

"Drew Able? Down in Wenwood?" I waited for a nod of recognition, could practically see her mentally scrolling a contacts list.

"I don't think I know him," she said. "What kind of law?"

I bit back the "umm" I wanted to mutter. "A variety, I'd say. Criminal law and some real estate."

She sniffed a breath. "Russ and Herb don't do that stuff. That's probably why I don't know the name."

"No? What kind of law does Russ practice?" I sucked air through my teeth as the technician got a little over-zealous with the orange stick, pushing my cuticle back farther than nature intended.

"Didn't his ex-wife tell you?" Melanie's look was wary, suspicious almost.

I tried a smile. "She doesn't like to talk about him much. You know." I told the technician, "Careful, please."

She merely titched at me like I was being a baby.

"Funny. Russ likes to talk about her," Melanie said around a grimace.

"Really?"

"Russ does divorces, you know? So he's always telling his clients about his own divorce to kind of win their confidence." She looked away from me, then looked back quickly. "You're not divorced, are you?"

"Never married," I said, choosing to leave it at that. She didn't need my whole story. I doubted sharing details on my broken engagement would significantly endear me to her anyway. "So, is Russ working on any divorce cases now?"

"Oh, probably. Things are a little slow now, though. You know, summer."

I sighed. "But divorce. That doesn't fit," I muttered. The nail technician put down the orange stick and picked up the cuticle trimmer. I nearly whimpered in fear.

"What doesn't fit? Are you thinking there's some connection between the fire and the break-in?" Melanie asked.

I didn't know whether I was thinking or hoping. "How can there not be? But I can't figure out what that connection is. I can't imagine it being a divorce case. Sure, a bitter spouse on the losing end of a settlement might go after Russ for spite, but Carrie?"

A series of chimes sounded, growing steadily louder. Melanie sat up straight, peered at the purse hanging off the back of her chair. "Does anyone call when I'm getting a pedicure and my hands are free? No." She huffed out a breath and returned her attention to her manicure.

"Is that the only kind of law Russ does? Divorce law?" I asked. "Or Herb? Does he do anything else?"

"They do boring stuff. Contracts and wills and taxes."

"Contracts? What kind of contracts?"

She shrugged. "Like, rental agreements and property sales. Things like that."

I winced as the nail technician got a bit too eager with the trimmer, proving my fear was well-founded. I tried another "be careful" and got another "suck it up, buttercup" glare for my trouble. I opted to distract myself from the discomfort by taking another run at the questions swirling through my mind.

Carrie and Russ co-owned the property the law office sat on. What kind of agreement did they have with one another for payment of the mortgage, the taxes, and everything else that went with being a property owner? Were any of them more favorable for Carrie?

But that mental trail led me right back to suspecting Russ of burning down his own business and questioning what benefit he would gain from trashing Carrie's shop. It still didn't add up.

"How long is Russ usually gone for when he's off on these fishing trips?" I asked.

Again, she looked at me suspiciously from the corner of her eyes. "I really can't say."

As best I could manage with my hands outstretched toward the technician, I turned in my chair to face Melanie. "Look, you're protecting your boss, I understand that. I want to protect my friend. Even if Russ wasn't off chasing trout, I doubt we'd be able to get him and Carrie into a room together to try and sort out why they're both being targeted. So anything you can tell me about Russ's current caseload . . . I don't know if it will help, but it's a start, and I'll at least feel like I was doing something."

"Well." She blew out a breathy sigh. "Herb would know best what kind of work was in the office. You should try talking to him."

I almost said a silent prayer. "What's the best way to get in touch with him?"

"He has a house down in Wenwood. The address is in my phone. As soon as my nails are dry I'll copy it down for you."

Her nail technician set down the little bottle of primer and handed Melanie a pencil. "I will get your phone," he said. He scurried around the table and peered into the purse hanging off the back of Melanie's chair.

"Side pocket," Melanie said, watching over her shoulder.

The technician tugged the phone out of the purse and set it on the table face up.

"Oh," Melanie said, in a tone generally reserved for the moment you learn you're overdrawn at the bank.

"What is it?" I asked. "Something wrong?"

"That missed call." Melanie's gaze sought mine. "It was the police."

13

I waited at the salon long enough for my nails to dry and to learn the police had called because they had more questions. Trusting they were pursuing the likelihood of the connection between the fire and the break-in, and already imagining Detective Nolan's displeasure should Melanie tell him I'd been by asking questions, I gave myself a moment to admire my first manicure in over a year while I tapped Herb Gallo's address into the map app on my phone.

The Wenwood address Melanie gave me led to a road I was unfamiliar with in words, but I had my suspicions as I approached, and knew it by sight when I made the final turn onto Herb's street, Berlin Road.

Berlin Road curved gracefully along the waterfront, sometimes parallel to, sometimes turning away from

Riverside Drive—the road that functioned as a barrier between Wenwood and the river and led directly to the front gates of what was the old brickworks and what was becoming the new marina. The homes on Berlin were tiny compared to the near-palatial houses populating the lower Hudson Valley. These were homes built for brick-workers and their families nearly a century earlier, not for millionaires entertaining clients. And they possessed a charm that called to mind words like *cozy*, *quaint*, and *homey*, words that would never be applied to the show-place houses of other towns.

I flipped down the visor on the Jeep, blocking the worst of the early afternoon rays from blinding me as I searched for Herb's house. Having approached from the north end of the road, I watched the numbers on the houses de-crease, beginning at 102 and dropping by twos. When it became clear I was within three houses of Herb's, my heart sank at the same time my breath stilled.

Two police cruisers were parked in front of Herb's, number 44. Behind them, blocking the driveway, was an unremarkable silver sedan.

If the police were making the rounds of Russ Stanford's staff and stopping by just to ask Herb some questions, why would there be so many? The large presence couldn't mean anything good. And certainly meant I wasn't getting any information on caseload from Herb Gallo anytime soon.

I should have kept a steady speed and cruised on by the little saltbox house. But reflexes are funny things, and as I gawked at the scene, trying to catch some clue as to what had drawn the police, my foot lifted off the accelerator. Just enough so that the moment Detective Nolan stepped out of the silver sedan, there was no way to stop our gazes from locking.

The muscles in his jaw bulged and rolled and I could only imagine he was grinding his teeth. When he lifted a hand from his side I half expected him to wave me past. When instead he continued to raise his hand until he'd achieved the "stop" position, I brought the Jeep to a slow halt.

Sliding down the window, I opted against a fake cheerful smile, opted against playing innocent, and asked straight out, "Everything okay, Detective?"

One hand on his hip, one hand on the Jeep's door, he leaned close. "What are you doing here, Georgia?"

"I was hoping to talk to Herb Gallo," I admitted. What good would it do to lie? Detective Nolan would either see right through me immediately or find out the truth later on.

He let out a heavy sigh, as though I'd just confirmed a fear he didn't want to admit. "And what business would you have with Herb? You're not going to tell me he's your lawyer, are you?"

"That would be untruthful," I said. "Why are you here?"

Leveling his immutable brown-eyed gaze at me, he said, "I'm on police business, Georgia. Now tell me why you wanted to talk to Mr. Gallo."

I reached for the air-conditioning controls and increased the fan speed. What with the window open and Detective Nolan blocking the breeze, it was getting hot in the driver's seat. "He's Russ Stanford's law partner. He might have some idea what Russ was working on that warranted someone burning down the office."

His nostrils flared as he sucked in breath.

"And if I knew that, I might be able to figure out why that same someone would break into Carrie's shop and shatter everything they could get their hands on."

"You have no way of knowing if those two incidents are related," he said.

I let my head drop back against the headrest. "Oh, come on, Detective. There's no way they're random. Just like there's no way your presence here at Herb's house is a coincidence."

"Georgia." He shook his head, gaze on the ground. "What am I going to do with you?"

So much for relaxing against the headrest. His words, the tone of his voice, brought me upright in my seat. "That sounded almost friendly, Detective. Like you care," I teased.

He shot me the briefest half smile I had ever witnessed, then he slid back into stoic cop mode. "Listen, I'm not going to say anything stupid about only running into you when there's trouble. It's the nature of my job that I see people when the worst happens. But what I am going to do is ask you to head on home and stay there and not go poking around in Russ Stanford's law business."

"What about Russ's law business impacting my friend's business, and my business for that matter?" I asked. Visions of shattered stained glass danced through my head like serial-killer sugar plum fairies.

Detective Nolan huffed. "How about I do the police work

on this one and you get busy re-creating stock for Carrie's store?" He tapped the door of the Jeep with the flat of his palm. "Go home."

"Detective, I drove all the way out here—"

"You're not getting in that house, Georgia." His voice, his glare, his stance—all were unshakeable. "Go. Home."

With a hitch of his belt—very cowboy—he strode away, crossing the street and walking across the lawn of the little house.

I was dismissed. If I wanted to talk to Herb, I was going to have to wait until the police completed their questioning.

Unless they were questioning Herb because he was the number one arson suspect. But . . . Herb? With his classic fishing hat and fragile handshake? I supposed it was true that you never really know a person, but . . . hmm.

I powered up the window and stepped on the gas. Detective Nolan might have prevented me from pursuing one source of information that might help my friend, but lucky for me I had other sources.

"Oh, God, that's so Nolan." Diana rolled her eyes with such force she nearly toppled off the barstool.

The crowd at the Pour House, Wenwood's single watering hole, wasn't much of a crowd at all. A few long-term residents clustered at one end of the bar, elbows on its age-stained wood, eyes on the television above, showing a baseball game. At one of the four booths lining the wall opposite the bar, two couples shared a pitcher of beer and some manner of intense conversation.

Carrie, Diana, and I had taken our customary places at roughly the center of the bar and ordered our customary single glass of wine each.

I took a sip of my white, then said, "It's not like I wanted to barge in on his interrogation or whatever. I just—"

"Oh, it wasn't an interrogation," Diana said.

"Okay, questioning," I amended.

Carrie swirled the wine in her glass as though she were about to sip a more exclusive vintage than the House's seven-dollar-per-liter red. "Yeah, questioning sounds more like something that could happen at home. Or in a coffee shop."

But Diana leaned closer, pitched her voice low enough not to be overheard. "What I mean is, it wasn't any kind of question and answer. It was a crime scene."

"No no no no no." Carrie held up a hand. "Don't tell us anything that's going to get you in trouble. If it's official police business—"

"Don't listen to her. This is exactly what I wanted to ask you about," I said. "Tell us everything. What do you mean a crime scene? What happened?"

"It's okay. It's on the blotter. Public record, you know?" Diana paused to take a sip of wine, glance over her shoulder at the other patrons of the bar. "It will be in the news tomorrow. I just don't want to be answering questions from all the benchwarmers here."

"Fair enough." I leaned in, Carrie doing the same, so our three heads formed a human cone of silence.

Diana rested an elbow on the bar, gazed at us both from beneath lowered brows. "So. Nolan's been trying to get hold of Herb Gallo about the fire, right? But there was no answer at his house—at the door or over the phone. We've had a couple of uniforms checking during their shifts but there's been nothing until this morning when they noticed"—she dropped her voice to a whisper—"a kind of a, you know, odor."

"Oh my God," Carrie and I said in unison.

I had met Herb Gallo only once, and in the brief exchange we had at the luncheonette I took him to be a kind man, a gentleman of the old guard. Guilt at thinking for even a second that he might have burned down the law office made me momentarily queasy. And an irritating lump lodged in my throat as I thought of that lovely man dying alone, his remains undiscovered for days. My heart squeezed with sorrow. For a moment I couldn't meet Diana's eyes and instead focused my attention on my hands, on the abundance of tiny cuts and scratches that a kitten and a stained glass hobby made unavoidable. Those cuts were as bad as it got for me, but poor Herb Gallo.

"You said crime though," Carrie said, her voice small and shaky.

Diana nodded slowly, almost dramatically. "When the uniforms went in, they found the house had been tossed and old man Gallo murdered. He had his throat cut with a piece of broken glass."

Carrie's breath hitched and she put a hand to her throat. I grabbed at the bar, because the room seemed to tilt and threaten to knock me to the ground. Herb . . . murdered.

A piece of glass. He'd told me his departed wife had collected glass, told me he never had the heart to pack her collection away. And now . . . Dear heaven.

"Glass?" Carrie echoed.

Both sets of eyes turned to me.

"What?" I asked, lifting my head, trying to focus as I glanced back and forth between my friends. "Just because there was glass you think I have some insight?"

Diana lifted a shoulder. "Glass is kinda your thing."

"Yes, but I create things with glass. I don't—" I paused, brought my voice down to a conspiratorial level. "I wouldn't kill anyone with it. I wouldn't kill anyone at all."

"Oh, no, that wasn't even a thought," Carrie assured me.

"Point is," Diana said, "Herb Gallo is dead. It can't be a coincidence that Gallo and your ex were partners and the building they both worked in was—"

"I know," Carrie said. "I know."

She lifted her wineglass as the mood among us sank. I wracked my brain, looking for the right thing to say, looking for anything to say. But what was left that didn't either sound like a platitude or come off like I wanted to revel in her hardship?

"So you, uh, you talked Drew into giving you a job, huh?" Diana nodded, her eyes wide with encouragement telling me to follow along.

"Uh. Yeah. He didn't really take too much convincing. The man has paperwork everywhere." I lifted my wineglass. "It's not like his file room looked like something from *Hoarders*, but he really didn't stand a chance of pretending he didn't need help. Seriously, wildflowers are more organized."

"You'll still be able to help me clean up the shop, though, right?" Carrie asked.

My jaw fell slack. "Of course. You come first. How could you even doubt that?"

She turned the wineglass slowly in her hand. "You'd make actual money if you went to Drew's, though, right?"

"Carrie, you sell my stained glass pieces for me. I make actual money through you, too. Pick me up in the morning and we'll get the store put back together. I'll start at Drew's next week."

"What about your glass work? Like the window you're designing for Trudy Villiers? And pieces to replace what was . . . lost?" Carrie asked. "Will you still have time?"

"I won't be at Drew's every day," I assured her. "And it's not as if my nights are packed with romance and excitement."

Carrie reached out and patted my hand while Diana asked, "How can you say this isn't exciting?" She waved a hand to indicate the nearly empty bar and the old men intent on the baseball game.

"This isn't romantic," I clarified, and finally became aware of what I'd been saying. Was I really troubled by a lack of romance? Was I ready to start *dating* again? Or was it the wine talking?

I lifted my glass and held its rim against my lips. The pain of my breakup with my fiancée had seemed so acute only weeks earlier. But little by little, when I wasn't looking, it seemed, the wounds had begun to heal. I spent less time lost in sorrow and regret and more time laughing and looking ahead to tomorrow. Maybe the time had come when I could be open to possibility again. Not to say that I was ready to risk reopening some of the deeper cuts, risk—gulp—falling in love, but I might have been ready to share my time again. I might even have been ready to fall in like.

"Romance is only in movies," Diana grumbled. "In real life, someone has to do the dishes."

"Here here." Carrie raised her glass.

Diana obliged by tapping Carrie's glass with her own, the thick, cheap glass making more of a *clack* than a *ching*. "How are you holding up?" Diana said. "You know, what with being caught up in your ex-husband's mess and all."

Even in the half dark of the bar—or maybe because of it—the flush of color in Carrie's cheeks was obvious. She took a quick sip of her wine then half turned away. "Would you keep your voice down?" she asked. "Bad enough the whole town is talking about the break-in. I don't need them talking about me and my ex-husband, too."

"Are you kidding me? Have you forgotten you live in a small town?" Her tone was a bit too far into the realm of mocking, and I gave her a nudge. "What?" she asked me.

"Be nice," I said. "You're supposed to be being nice."

She raised her brows at me. "I am being nice. This is me being nice. Me being angry is why I don't carry a gun off duty."

I huffed and did half an eye roll.

"Fine." She turned back to Carrie. "Just so you know, I was on the desk the morning the call came in from the fire department about your ex's place. That's where I heard the news. It wasn't gossip I picked up at the lunch-eonette, okay? I don't know of anyone talking about it."

"So being on the desk, um, have you heard anything else?" Carrie asked, her hesitant speech and soft voice in danger of being drowned out by sudden cheering from the baseball fans.

"What do you mean?" Diana asked.

"Any leads yet on who might have set the fire?" I clari-fied. It hadn't taken the fire marshal long to officially declare the blaze the result of arson. But beyond that, Car-rie had no further news. At least, none that she'd shared.

"Nolan has his theories. So he says." She downed the remains of her wine and called a club soda order to the bartender. "But he wouldn't tell me what they are since he knew I was meeting you two tonight and didn't want me to divulge anything you couldn't learn from the six o'clock news."

I met Carrie's gaze. The pinching around her eyes told me she was thinking the same thing I was thinking: If Detective Nolan didn't want any information shared with us, he still considered Carrie a suspect.

Maybe it was the wine working—all four sips of it—but another thread of guilt passed through me. The guilt suggested I was somehow at fault for Carrie's predica-ment. I was pretty sure none of my friends or family had been suspected of a crime prior to my relocating to Wen-wood. And now, in three short months, my grandfather and my new best friend had become murder suspects, and a man I'd met only once had been killed. If I had just stayed put in the city, would any of this have happened? Mercy. How did Jessica Fletcher live with herself?

With a shake of her head, Carrie tossed her big brown curls back over her shoulder. "I'm sure Detective Nolan has reasons for managing the flow of information," she said.

Diana pulled a face. "I don't think he has any reasons. I think he just likes to act mysterious. But we can ask him if he shows up."

I managed to swallow my wine rather than spit it out. "Shows up?"

Swirling the ice cubes in her club soda, she nodded. "After I told him we come here every Thursday he said he might stop by and check this place out."

My stomach lurched. I didn't want to see Detective Nolan. No, I certainly did not. If I saw him again, with my mind so recently on my lack of romance, would I experience once more whatever heat-induced madness I had fallen victim to outside the torched law office and decide he has soulful eyes and strong hands? No. It was definitely best to avoid the detective. No good would come of me being involved with a cop.

"Drink up," I said, raising my glass. "If we can escape before he gets here we can still safely call this girls' night."

Of course, the problem with wine is that chugging it down is tactless. The problem with cheap wine is that chugging it down is nearly impossible; it was too sharp and bitter to be consumed at speed.

Despite a valiant effort from me, if I do say so myself, we were still bellied up to the bar when Detective Nolan arrived.

He stopped inside the door and took in the room in a sweeping glance. His gaze shifted quickly from patron to patron but I had no doubt that, if asked, he could recite a string of details about each one. When he returned his detective's attention to where we stood, I feared not only would he see the green top and jeans shorts I wore, he would also see evidence of every single cat hair I had painstakingly removed.

"Well. There goes the fun," Diana muttered.

The detective still wore suit pants, but he had discarded his jacket and tie and opened the top few buttons on his dress shirt and rolled his sleeves to his elbows. His clothes and his posture belonged to someone who was relaxed. His gaze remained intense.

He made no effort to pretend he had merely happened into the same bar where we were gathered. Instead, he greeted us with, "Good. You're still here."

This was enough to have Carrie and I check in silently with one another, trying to determine who it was the detective was addressing. By mutual, though still silent, agreement, we concluded he must be talking to Diana. Or maybe the conclusion would have been better termed as "hope."

"Oh, sorry to say, we were just leaving." Diana slipped her arm into the shoulder strap of her purse and pulled the strap up as she prepared to step off the barstool.

But Detective Nolan must have seen the move coming. He stopped behind her, blocking her escape, before her feet hit the floor. "Stay," he said, smiling. "Next round's on me."

"Oh, but we only have one drink each." Carrie lifted her glass, proof she had already reached the maximum.

Diana shrugged. "They're lightweights. And you're in my way. Sir."

Nolan signaled the bartender, making a circling motion to encompass our little group—the kind of motion that said another round for everyone.

"Just a soda," I called. Carrie echoed. Nolan grinned, and ordered a tap beer.

"Excuse me." Diana folded her arms and faced the detective. There was nothing friendly, nothing relaxed in the way she stood. I wondered if Nolan had somehow forgotten about her trouble with temper. Part of what was making it possible for Diana and me to build a friendship was my awareness of her anger management and aggression issues. I learned early on when not to push, when not to tease, and when to keep my mouth shut entirely. Nolan, it seemed, hadn't bothered with any of those lessons, and wasn't afraid of her willingness to throw punches.

He sighed, though, and dropped his arms. "I'd prefer you stay," he said, then shifted his gaze to include Carrie. "I only want to talk, see if you can think of anyone at all who might be holding a grudge. Someone's going to some pretty drastic measures to put you and your ex-husband out of business. The sooner we can determine who, the happier I'll be."

"Are you sure a bar is the right place for that?" I asked.

"It's informal." He dropped his voice low enough to not be overheard, locked his gaze on Carrie. "I could come back to your shop in the morning. I could send a squad car to bring you up to the station. Those are both good options if you want the whole town talking and speculating. Or we can talk here."

My chest froze, stilling my breath. I remembered too well the sense of being watched, the cold chill of knowing the folks of Wenwood were gossiping about me. I wouldn't wish that feeling on an enemy, much less a friend.

"Maybe a booth?" I forced a smile, hoping to encourage Carrie.

"Maybe not," she said. She turned in her seat, draping an arm over the backrest, and facing Nolan full on. "Look, Detective. I can't help you. Russ never shared his business with me when we were married and he certainly didn't start once we separated. And once we were separated, that was the end of me sharing my business with him. I don't have any more information than what I've already told you. And if I have to go up to the station and tell you the same thing just to make you understand, then I will."

Diana glared. "Nice going, Nolan." She huffed. "You gonna get out of my way now?"

Blowing out a breath, the detective stepped back and to the side, allowing Diana to pass. "Georgia, you need a ride?" she asked.

I pointed to Carrie. "She's driving me."

"All right then." Diana nodded. "I'll call you."

As the bartender set one beer then two colas on the bar, the detective moved into the space Diana vacated. He rested his arms along the backrest of the empty barstool and leaned in. "I don't want to make you angry," he said, face turned to Carrie. "And I don't want to upset you. I don't want to do that to a friend of Georgia's."

Before I could ask the meaning behind that newsflash, he continued.

"But Ms. Stanford, a building was burnt to cinders, your ex-husband is missing, your shop has been broken into, and—" He cut himself off, giving me the sense he was censoring his words. Maybe Carrie didn't fill in the blank, but I filled it in with *and Herb Gallo is dead* as easily as if the words had been spoken.

"I'm a cop," he said at last. "I need answers. And I'm going to get them." He reached forward and claimed his beer. Straightening, he pressed his lips tight together and nodded at Carrie. "I'll see you in the morning."

As he turned, he gave me a short nod, then walked to the end of the bar. He slapped one of the old coots on the back and asked about the score. All-business to all-casual in the time it takes a fastball to cross home plate.

"Carrie," I began, as gently as I could. "Maybe you should just humor him and answer his questions? Maybe something will come up that will help."

Her eyes went from wide to watery. "But don't you see? Of all people, you should understand. I don't want to remember. I want to put everything about Russ behind me and leave it in the past. Nothing I can say will help Detective Nolan. It will only hurt me."

A finger of sympathy poked at my heart. I reached out to rest my hand on her forearm. "You're right. I'm sorry."

She laid her hand over mine. "He's going to show up at

the shop in the morning, Georgia. He's going to ask more questions about Russ." Eyes downcast, she sniffled. "Will you stay there with me until he comes, even if all the cleaning is done? I don't want to face him alone."

"Of course," I promised. "Of course." Because as Carrie herself had told me at the start of our friendship, no one should have to face the police alone.

14

As I had done earlier in the week, I set my alarm extra early and spent those peaceful morning hours in the workshop humming show tunes and cutting glass for the sea and sailboat panel. Friday exhausted herself trying to take down a fly from midair, so that by the time Carrie arrived to pick me up for the drive to her shop, the kitten had fallen asleep at the foot of the staircase, so utterly and so deeply she didn't stir when I rubbed her belly and promised to see her later.

"Hey," I said, climbing into the car. "Do you know if it's supposed to rain today?"

Carrie made miniscule adjustments to the mirrors while I wrestled with the seat belt. "I didn't hear the weather."

I froze with my hand over the seat belt latch. Carrie always heard the weather. She sought it out on television and radio. In summertime a good portion of her business was foot traffic; the weather forecast was the same as a business forecast. "Are you okay?" I asked softly.

She nodded. "Yeah, I'm okay. I mean, I'm better today." She flicked on the indicator light and pulled away from the curb.

"As opposed to . . . ?"

"Last night. I took some time this morning to just try and get my head together, and . . . I'm calmer, you know?"

I let her statement sit for a while before admitting, "I'm not sure what that means."

She wrapped her fingertips around the steering wheel, eyes scanning the road. "Like, I thought about it really hard and I think I can do it. I think I can talk to Detective Nolan about Russ. I mean, I'm not promising the claws won't come out if we start talking about his inability to remain faithful to a woman for more than six minutes, but I think I can get through whatever questions Detective Nolan throws at me."

I shook my head, puzzled by this new attitude. "What changed? Last night you didn't want to have to dredge up any of your history with Russ. And now . . . ?"

"I still don't want to do any dredging, and I think I won't have to. Detective Nolan can ask all the questions he wants. I doubt I'll know the answers to any of them."

Her fingers rolled tighter around the wheel and her knuckles began to brighten. A peek at her face revealed eyes a little too wide, lips a little too tight.

"You might," I said. Still, I wasn't ready to let my

question go. "But what *happened*? What made you change your mind? You were so adamant last night."

She shook her head. I couldn't tell whether she meant the motion to indicate she didn't know or she wouldn't tell me. Either way, I let silence overtake the cab of the car while Carrie drove us toward the highway.

"Did you ever meet him?" she asked, her voice barely above a whisper.

"Who?"

"Herb Gallo."

I nodded. "Once. Just the other day." In the time it took for Carrie to turn onto the highway, the penny dropped for me. "Oh, gosh. Herb was Russ's partner. You must have known him really well. Oh, Carrie, I'm so sorry."

She waved away my sympathy even as her eyes welled with tears. "He's a sweet man." Several hundred feet of highway blurred by before she spoke again. "It's only that . . ."

After giving her the space to continue, I finally resorted to prompting. "Only what?"

"First the fire, then my shop, now Herb. Who's doing this? What do they want? And how far . . ."

Her voice trailed away, and I did my best not to let the question complete in my mind, but it was no use. "How far are they willing to go?" I asked.

Silent, hands gripping the steering wheel like a lifeline, Carrie nodded.

We both knew the answer, neither wanted to speak the words. Whoever was behind all this was willing to go all the way to murder.

* * *

I spent the morning with Carrie, answering more of Detective Nolan's questions and listening to his advice to be careful, but not give in to panic. The police department was confident that some of the avenues Herb Gallo's death pointed to would prove invaluable in the investigation. He never said right out whether they were narrowing the suspect pool, whether the new source of clues would lead to an arrest. He only reassured us the case was a top priority and he was doing everything in his power to find the person or persons responsible.

When he left, Carrie was once again facing two options: She could give in and hide from the world, locking herself away in her apartment until the investigation concluded. Or, she could give her fear the respect it deserved, be careful and cautious, and keep on living her life.

She opted against cowering in her apartment. I opted against trying to convince her that getting a cat to keep her company would make becoming a recluse much more palatable. Then I gave her a hug, and vowed to watch her back.

We passed the afternoon in the slow process of reorganizing the backroom stock. We sorted and counted and shelved until Grandy swung by the store to pick me up on his way to the dine-in. I didn't like to leave Carrie, but she was wearing her brave face and I knew she wouldn't be alone for long. As soon as word had gotten out about the break-in different merchants from downtown Wenwood had begun taking turns stopping by the shop, helping Carrie clean up the mess and put her sales floor back in order, offering lunch, or just offering company. She was in excellent care. And besides, no way could I blow off going to the dine-in, not on payroll day.

Grandy drove through the late-afternoon thunderstorm while I sat in the passenger seat, visor down, mirror open, and fought with my hair. On an average day the kinky, curly mop was tough to manage. On a humid day it reached cartoon monster proportions.

"Who had this hair, Grandy?" I asked, shoving a bobby pin so tight against my scalp I feared blood. "Does this come from the Keene side, or the Kelly side?"

He kept his hands at ten and two and merely flicked a glance my way. "Your grandmother had hair like yours."

"Yeah?" I asked.

"Darker, though. More bronze than brass."

"Why don't I remember that?" Grandma Keene had passed away when I was eleven. I had been old enough that I should remember her, but young enough that I forget much of her.

A smile played along Grandy's lips. "She liked her kerchiefs. Said they kept the dust out of her hair and her hair out of trouble."

I smiled myself, to hear the tone of fondness in Grandy's voice. It was so unlike his typical rumble. It was audible evidence of the loving man residing deep inside in his tough old soldier persona.

Twisting a hank of hair with one hand, I fished another bobby pin from my lap with the other. "I don't think I'd look especially fashionable wearing a kerchief."

He smiled wider. "No, I suppose not. In those days . . .

Well, it was a different time. We were different. The town was different. Brickworks was still running. I hadn't even conceived of buying a movie theater."

Not that I didn't like hearing Grandy talk about "the old days"—he could tell a good story when the mood was on him—but often as not he'd end up morose. From there it was a very short trip to cantankerous, and we had a long afternoon and night ahead of us. "Speaking of," I began, though I had no intention of staying on the same topic. "I ran into Tom Harris the other day at the luncheonette."

Grandy made a noise between a huff and a laugh. "Tom Harris. What's he done this time? Mistaken you for your grandmother?"

"Um. No." I made a mental note to dig out some old pictures to see if that was even possible. "He asked what you thought about the plan to open that shopping promenade on the riverfront."

"And what did you tell him?"

"I didn't tell him anything. Well, I did tell him he could ask my opinion, but he's only interested in yours. You haven't said anything about the plan though. I figured I'd get your take on it." I shoved the last bobby pin in place and sat back in my seat, content to have wrestled my hair into a vaguely elegant twist back bun that had the added bonus of reducing my odds of getting hair in the customers' food.

Grandy scowled at the road ahead. "Must we talk about this now?"

"Ah. That means you're not in favor. Why not?"

"It means no such thing. All it means is this is bad weather and I need to concentrate."

For nearly a mile I let the car fill with the sound of wipers sluicing water off the windshield. Then I couldn't take the quiet anymore.

"So that means you are in favor?" I asked.

This time it was a full-on huff. "As it happens my feelings are mixed on the subject."

I waited, knowing if I gave him the time he would explain.

"I like to think there's something that can be done to bring this town back from the brink. The marina is a good start, but it's not enough to turn the town back into a place where people want to stay and build a family. It's not easy watching all you young people run off and leave the rest of us here to wither away."

His voice sounded like he meant to continue. Instead he fiddled with the wiper speed until I prompted him to continue. "But?" I said.

Grandy filled his chest with a deep breath. "But I also worry that catering to seasonal tourists will change the town for the worse. Summer is a short season. What happens when winter comes? What keeps us from becoming the kind of place no one would even dream of raising children?"

I thought of some of the seaside towns I had been dragged through by my wandering mother. When I was young those towns looked bright and exciting and filled with fun. As I grew older, I began to see the other side of the fun. I saw the cheap plastic that the shiny keepsakes were made from. I saw people barely scraping by in the shadow of a luxury resort. I saw the broken and desperate side that Grandy didn't want to see in Wenwood. My heart ached a little.

"That makes sense," I said. "I can see why you'd be conflicted."

"Conflicted." He harrumphed. "Fancy psychiatrist talk."

"I know, I know. You're not fancy," I teased, perhaps more to cheer myself than him. "What I mean to say is that I understand your concerns. They're good concerns. I don't know if there's any answer, though. Things can't go on as they are."

"Hmph. Regulation, might be an answer. Proper zoning laws."

"Resulting in more fireworks at town meetings."

"I told you not to go."

"I know. But what else do I have to do on a Wednesday night?"

Grandy wisely didn't answer. Not that I truly thought he would, but now and again he'd suggest I do something more than "fiddle with glass"—like pull weeds or clean out the back shed. Oddly, he never suggested I find another job and get out on my own.

I think he enjoyed having me around, but knew he would never admit it.

We reached the Downtown Dine-In without managing to overtake the storm. Grandy parked the Jeep in his usual spot opposite the front door and we slogged through the rain to the shelter of the marquee overhanging the lobby doors.

Through the lobby, past the ticket booth, and inside to the gray and navy interior, we shook off the rain that clung to our shoes and umbrellas and went our separate ways. Grandy went off to check with the kitchen staff on the night's dinner preparations and specials and to make certain there were sufficient supplies. I went to Grandy's little office at the back of theater, on the opposite side of the house from the kitchen, and settled in to do payroll the old-fashioned way, with bound charts and a ten-key adding machine. Tools from a different time. I had tried more than once to get Grandy to update to an easy computer program or outsource the task to one of the dozens of companies that prepared payroll, but he preferred retaining the ability to backtrack to find every penny if the need arose.

In under two hours I had the payroll complete and I wandered out of the office in search of Grandy. In the lobby, the high school kid who worked concessions was opening the stand and I waved the pay vouchers at her in greeting. She gave me a silent, double-fisted cheer and I laughed as I kept on my way.

I pushed through the doors into the theater auditorium, where the seating area no longer held rows of auditorium seating but strings of tables and club chairs, where moviegoers could order a light meal brought to their seats and enjoy it while they watched the evening's film. A door in the back of the house led into a short corridor that terminated in another door, the duplication intended to keep the noise from the kitchen out of the auditorium. Once past that second door, the heavenly aromas of cheese and bacon swirled through the air and made my mouth water. I followed my nose through the swinging door into the kitchen and directly to where Grandy's head cook, Matthew, stood, hands on hips, glaring at Grandy.

"Don't you think I thought of that?" Matthew demanded. Even at eighty years old, Grandy was a good foot taller than Matthew, but Matthew didn't appear inclined to let Grandy's size intimidate him. "I'm removing the top and stripping the seeds out, that reduces the heat by, like, a million."

"Is that a unit of measure you learned in culinary school?" Grandy practically sneered. "*Like a million?*"

For a long time Matthew made me seriously nervous. For a short time I thought he killed Andy Edgers. One of those reasons was why I still approached cautiously. But neither Grandy nor Matthew had any fear of each other. For reasons I could only blame on testosterone, snarling at one another was how they got along.

"So . . . what's tonight's menu fight?" I asked, purposely keeping my tone light.

"No specials tonight," Grandy said at the very same time Matthew said, "Jalapeño poppers."

"Poppers?" I inched closer to the metal worktable across which the men had drawn their line in the sand. "Would you be wrapping those in bacon by chance?"

"Georgia, I'll thank you not to interfere," Grandy said.

Unlike Matthew, Grandy didn't scare me. I plopped the pay vouchers on the table and gave him a hard look.

"Bacon-wrapped poppers taste crazy good, and they're just spicy enough to keep the patrons ordering sodas and beers but not spicy enough to make them . . ." I stumbled in my search for a polite descriptor of the less desirable effects of spicy foods. "Uncomfortable."

Matthew snorted. Grandy glared. I backed away. "Okay then. I'll just go get changed and let you two work it out."

That was the other half of my Fridays at the dine-in. After I finished payroll I had roughly forty-five minutes to change out of my day clothes and into the black pants and white blouse of a dine-in waitress. There was a critical lack of glamour to the job, and waitressing wasn't my forte, but the tips were enough to keep me in sunscreen and pay for my weekly tipple of chardonnay at the Pour House. Things could be worse.

Back in Grandy's office I locked the door and did my quick change routine. I swung by the ladies' room to tuck away any stray strands of hair, then stopped back into the kitchen to shovel down the salad with grilled chicken that Matthew always had one of his cooks prepare for me.

Wendy, the other waitress, a recent high school graduate with green hair and a stud earring below her lip, joined me in the kitchen as the lobby filled with the early-show crowd. Always smaller than the eight-thirty "late" show, the early crowd tended more toward families with children, thus more toward hot dogs and soda pop. Two waitresses were enough, and I would be able to cover any tables ordering alcohol.

Between shows and against my usual dietary cautions, I stood with Wendy in the second passageway and indulged in half a dozen (or more. Who's counting?) poppers. We were joined there by Liz, a late-twenties pistol of a girl who had been at the dine-in since Grandy opened the business, moving from concession to ticket sales to waitress.

"I have a new plan," she announced, shaking out her wet umbrella. She tossed it carelessly into the corner beyond the pass-through to the kitchen. "I'm going to open up a shop once that new promenade down in Wenwood is done."

"Cool," Wendy said. "Cool" was her stock response to each of Liz's plans for financial solvency and independence. "What are you going to sell?"

"I've given this a lot of thought." Liz picked a popper from the plate. "I figure, easiest thing to sell to tourists, you know, other than key chains and T-shirts will be—wait for it—antiques."

With a bite of popper in my mouth, I sucked in a breath. A piece of jalapeño adhered itself to the back of my throat and ignited.

Tears filled my eyes and quickly overflowed. I coughed and smacked my chest and bent double. Wendy shouted back to the kitchen for some milk while Liz asked, repeatedly and unhelpfully, if I was okay.

I coughed and cried and wheezed. And all the while, and despite the pain of jalapeño throat, all I could think was *another antiques store*. Why had that never occurred to me before? Why had I never thought that of all those nice new stores that might one day line the waterfront, one of them might be an antiques store? Or a bakery or a luncheonette? What would become of the merchants in the village of Wenwood? Would they survive the competition? Fold? Relocate?

Someone—I presumed Wendy—pressed a glass of milk into my hand. I braced against the urge to cough, holding my chest tense, and tried to drink. I failed to suppress the cough and spluttered into the cup. My breath against the milk forced the liquid to rise and splash me in the face, dribble down my chin.

I fared better on the second attempt and at last the fire receded. Liz slipped a paper napkin into my field of vision. With a nod of thanks, I took the napkin and wiped down my face.

"Are you all right?" she asked again.

"Duh," Wendy said. "She just choked on a jalapeño and she has more mascara under her eyes than on her lashes. Of course she's not all right."

Oh, mercy. I swiped under my eyes, knowing by the smudge of brown-black that came off on my forefinger that the effort was useless.

"Go get cleaned up," Liz said, tugging the napkin out of my fingers. "I'll start your tables."

I thanked her and handed over my order pad.

I sneaked back through the movie house, past the lobby beginning to fill with patrons, and on to Grandy's office and the meager stash of makeup I kept in my purse.

Thoughts of the riverside promenade troubled my mind as I did my best to repair the damage the jalapeño popper had wrought.

The new marina was under construction on the faith that the restoration of the old brickworks would bring new visitors to Wenwood. If shops along the promenade could meet all of a visitor's needs, what reason would they have to venture into town? Grandy's visions of the future of Wenwood took on a new and troubling possibility. Would staying in Wenwood permanently be the smartest choice? Or would it soon be time for me to plan my return to the city?

For certain, it was past time for me to get back to work. Satisfied I no longer looked like a raccoon in mourning, I scrambled back to the theater to reclaim my order book from Liz.

"You only have one table with kids," she said. "Trade?"

"How many do you have?"

"Three."

Tables with kids were never as profitable as tables with beer- or wine-drinking adults. It was simple percentages. Still, Liz had done me a favor. "Fine," I said. "I'll take the kids' tables." Drat *Star Trek* and its cross-generation appeal.

"Here." She held out her own order pad. "Let's just swap the house."

For waitress stations, the theater proper was divided into three sections in much the same way theaters with stadium seating were set up: lower tier, upper left, and upper right. Wendy worked the lower tier, and Liz upper right, leaving me upper left. Left, right, kids, beer . . . I had more important things on my mind.

I traded pads and flipped through pages to see if any early drink orders had been taken. Spotting a pair of alcohol orders, I went back to the kitchen to draw two beers and pour two glasses of red wine.

The house was packed, as was typical for the second show on a Friday night. I took no special notice of the patrons filling the seats until I left off the beers with a couple of middle-aged men in Starfleet T-shirts and moved to the fair-haired couple who had ordered the wine.

I might have continued to only half-register them until I had settled both glasses atop a cocktail napkin, but the gentleman greeted me by name.

My gaze flicked up from the table, and locked onto blue eyes the color of morning glories. Tony Himmel. Handsome enough to slow my breathing—humiliating though that might be—and charming enough to make my knees a little weak—even more humiliating.

"Georgia," he said again. "It's good to see you."

I nodded, thoroughly unable to close my gaping jaw. To me Tony was completely out of place. He ran a construction business, he drove a Jaguar, he wore ties to dinner. He did not belong here, in my grandfather's movie house, waiting to watch *Star Trek*.

"This is my sister, Karin. Karin, Georgia Kelly."

Mouth already open, I managed to squeak out a "hi."

Karin, a female version of Tony—same blue eyes, pale hair, elegant jaw—smiled. "It's nice to meet you," she said. She glanced sidelong at Tony. "Since you know my brother, should I expect preferred service, or deplorable service?"

I returned her smile, but faced Tony. "I, er, I suppose that remains to be seen." I tucked my tray under my arm. "I'll be back to take your order."

Putting my back to the Himmels, I headed up the steps

to the top of the auditorium, ready to begin collecting dinner orders . . . as soon as my pulse slowed.

For the love of all that's holy. Tony Himmel. The man behind the marina, the face of Stone Mountain Construction. We'd had dinner together once, after Andy Edgers had died and while I was trying to determine why anyone would kill the man. At the time I made an effort to keep the dinner impersonal—as in, all business, nothing romance-y. At the time, with residual aches from my breakup with my fiancé, all-business was my best choice. And for weeks after, I told myself I was grateful he never phoned again.

Now . . . now I watched the back of his head as he leaned toward his sister. His hair was longer, lighter, and he wore a long-sleeved T-shirt that fit snugly in the right places. Now maybe keeping that dinner on a platonic level looked like an error.

At least I had the good fortune to have incinerated my throat on a jalapeño, thus necessitating fresh makeup. I reached a hand to my hair and ran the tips of my fingers against the ends of bobby pins, assuring myself all the strands remained in place. I didn't look tragic, I reasoned. I had that going for me.

With an inward sigh and a steadying breath, I marched to my first table and managed to keep from stammering while my heart rate slowed and I recommended the jalapeño poppers. Table by table I announced the evening's special menu item, reminded guests to order all items at once—there would be refills on beverages but no additional food items—and promised kids our chocolate milk was extra chocolaty. All the while, anxiety simmered in my belly. I would have to face Tony again, and though I promised myself I would treat him and his sister with the same courtesy I provided to guests at my other tables still I wondered whether, given the option, I would rather treat him with preference or indifference.

At Tony's table, I did my best to remain professional as I delivered my spiel. Of course, professionally I was an out-of-work accountant, not a movie theater waitress. I spent a lot of time trying not to meet his gaze and shuffling from foot to foot.

When I finished the speech and requested their order, Karin narrowed her eyes speculatively. "Hm. Interesting," she said. She flicked a glance at her brother. "This is a new response. Are you sure you two have met?"

Tony sighed and lowered his head. He rubbed—one-handed—at his temples. "Karin . . ."

I tried a small smile and searched for the right thing to say to keep her from speculating. "Your brother was a big help when I needed some information on the agreements between the town and his construction project."

Then I made myself look directly at Tony without flinching, without breaking eye contact. "How are things progressing down at the brickworks—I mean—the marina?"

"We're back on schedule," he said, pride broadening his chest. "You should really come down and see it. A lot has changed since you were last there."

"Ah, well." The one and only time I had stopped at the site I had been politely sent on my way. I wasn't eager to repeat the experience. I lifted a shoulder. "I'd hate to trouble you while you were working."

A measure of brightness left his eyes.

"And here we are holding you up while you work," Karin said. She lifted her menu, held it like a script while she ordered a grilled chicken sandwich, hold the bun.

"Same," Tony said.

I collected their menus and opted not to press them about ordering the jalapeño poppers.

The poppers. Liz's plan to sell antiques. The promenade.

Two steps away from their table I paused, turned back. No sense passing up an opportunity.

"Tony," I said, leaning nearer than I would if I were asking if he wanted ketchup. "Can I ask you something?"

His face softened as he smiled. "Of course."

Balancing with my fingers against the edge of the table, I knelt down beside his chair. "What do you know about the Spring and Hamilton plans for the riverside? Do you know anything?"

He sighed and gave a short, sharp nod. "Some," he said. His smile, and whatever emotion it represented, vanished.

I had the vague sensation my question disappointed him somehow, but didn't have the time to reason out what the cause might be. I let the feeling go and pressed on. "The town council," I began, and Tony grimaced, having had his own issues with the controlling board of Wenwood in the past. "They set a deadline for—"

"Miss? Excuse me, miss?"

Letting my eyes fall closed for a moment, I smiled at Tony, then turned to the summoning voice. "Yes?"

"We have a question about the menu." At a table behind and to the left, a woman with twin boys perhaps eight years old held out the menu. With her attention on me instead of them, the boys took speedy advantage of her distraction and shot spitballs at one another. The woman might have been spared that knowledge, but I wasn't, and I would have to clean up before heading home.

"Excuse me," I said to Tony. "Sorry." I stood and hustled to the troublemakers, doing my best to replicate Grandy's displeased scowl.

I must have nailed it. The boys' eyes went wide as they put their straws and ammunition on the tabletop. "And clean it up," I said, before turning to their aunt or mother or whomever was brave enough to take them to the movies. "What can I help you with?" I asked.

And before I could finish my testimonial on the charm of the jalapeño poppers, the house lights dimmed and advertisements began playing on-screen.

Duty called. I had to get my dinner orders into the kitchen and get the drinks service under way. Once again any questions I might have for Tony Himmel would have to wait.

13

Friday lay half on my shoulder, half on my neck, her head tucked under my chin. I peered at my alarm clock and was surprised to see I'd woken before the alarm sounded. Must have been the weight of my living scarf.

I reached to run a hand down her kitten-soft fur. Or maybe it wasn't kitten-soft. Maybe she would be that soft forever. I had no past experience with kittens to guide me. Nor cats, for that matter. When I asked the vet, she hesitated to commit to an answer in the long versus short hair, soft versus sleek hair questions. I suspected she really did know, but only told me she didn't so that I would continue to love the feline no matter what.

As if there were any doubt.

With a turn of my head I pressed a trio of noisy kisses between her shoulders, then gently slid her off me so I could rise. She relaxed on my pillow while I showered and dressed, then she followed me down to the kitchen where she banged her little head against my ankle and mewed pathetically until I set a dish of moist food by her paws. Then and only then, once the kitten was appeased, was I able to put up a pot of coffee.

Coffee brewing, I dashed downstairs to my workroom. I grabbed the big leather portfolio I'd found among my grandmother's things and slipped my window designs inside. The bits of glass I had identified as potential colors I had wrapped in newspaper and nestled into a small paper bag. I paused, debating whether or not to bring the samples along. The last thing I needed was for Trudy Villiers to slice open a finger handling the glass.

In the end, I decided having her approve the glass might be best, and I fished a pair of cotton gloves out of my glass-cleaning supplies. As long as Trudy would agree to wear one, all should be well.

Carrie texted me that she was out front as I was finishing up my note to Grandy. I'd told him several times that I was heading over early to Trudy's, but for him, a thing wasn't happening unless it was in writing.

I ruffled the gray patch between Friday's ears and told her to be good, then I was out the door and on my way down the still-damp sidewalk to Carrie's car.

Before I'd even closed the door behind me, I asked, "What happened after I left?"

She gave me a wry half smile and pulled away from the curb. "Rozelle brought chocolate éclairs."

In my effort not to laugh, I nearly choked myself. For

sure, I had flashbacks of stuck jalapeño. I coughed once, hoping not to irritate my throat. "Because fresh pastries are always the answer."

"When hot tea just isn't enough," Carrie added. She steered the car off of Grandy's block and toward the boulevard that would take us out to Trudy's.

"Did you hear anything more from the police? Do they have any leads?" I asked. And though I said "the police" what I meant was Detective Nolan. I didn't want to risk sounding like I was more interested in the detective than the crime. Mainly because I was beginning to wonder about my interests myself. I thought it was an easy question but running into Tony Himmel had set me back on the answer. Nolan was handsome, dedicated to his work, and made me feel safe. Tony was handsome, dedicated to his work, and made me feel appreciated.

Where were the chocolate éclairs when you needed them?

"If Detective Nolan has any leads, he's not sharing them with me. The only thing he said was that he suspects it's someone from my and Russ's past—you know, as Mr. and Mrs."

"Were you and Russ married long enough to make enemies as a couple?" I asked.

Carrie widened her eyes and shrugged, never taking her hands off the steering wheel. "I wouldn't have thought so. But I guess you never know who you're going to really tick off."

"Did you forget to send one of your wedding guests a thank-you note?"

She shot me a sidelong glance but otherwise pretended I'd never said a word. "So now I have to make a list of anyone Russ and I had a disagreement with while we were married. Which means I have to spend my time *thinking* about when Russ and I were married."

"What about after you split up? There's no one you were both still in contact with? I realize if we're talking about the same person being responsible for everything that's happened, we're not talking about someone you were friendly with, but . . ."

"But someone we were enemies with?"

"Someone you didn't get along with," I said. Somehow "enemies" seemed extra harsh. "You know, like Gabe. He seems pretty ticked at Russ for the whole prenup thing. That could easily be the falling out Melanie referred to."

Carrie made a noise generally regarded as doubtful. "I don't know, Georgia. I can't see Gabe as an arsonist or a burglar."

"It's always the quiet ones that end up as news headlines," I murmured.

She peered at me from the corner of her eyes. "You've met Gabe. How could he possibly sneak around unseen?"

We turned onto the broad street that would lead to Trudy's. Maple trees in full leaf lined the roadside, their branches spreading wide above us so that it seemed we drove beneath a sparkling green canopy.

"I don't know," I said. "Maybe he's extra light on his feet. Have you ever seen him tiptoe? Or, you know, do ballet? Do they make tights that big?"

I could almost see Carrie's imagination spinning as she

mentally painted the picture of Gabe creeping around like a cartoon cat burglar, complete with the special toes-only walk at which cartoon crooks excelled or bounding across a stage with a tiny girl dressed as a swan. When at last she laughed, I laughed along with her.

Trudy's door swung open the moment my foot hit the curb. For a moment I feared she planned to shout out at me to go away, and I stayed put until the slam of Carrie's door told me she was out of the car and visible. Only then did I extricate myself from the car, clutching my portfolio like a shield.

"Thanks for doing this," I said, when I joined Carrie on the sidewalk. "I appreciate the company."

"She doesn't hate you, you know," Carrie said. "She's always like that. I think she's decided *Downton Abbey* is a tutorial on how to manage 'the help.'"

From the open doorway, a low-flying blur of white and tan catapulted itself in our direction. Both Carrie and I skittered backward in an attempt to soften the impact. Whether the move worked or not was hard to judge. Fifi pushed her snout into my shin with enough force to move me back one more step. Her stubby tail wagged enthusiastically, pulling her hindquarters side to side along with it.

"See? Fifi loves you," Carrie said, as I bent to ruffle the soft fur atop the bulldog's head.

I giggled as Fifi changed tactics and snuffled my toes. "She smells Friday, that's all."

"In which case she should be mauling you."

The murmuring of voices reached us, and Fifi lifted her head. Nostrils twitching, eyes on the open door at the top of the porch steps, she emitted a rumble like a precursor to a growl.

Two figures emerged from the doorway. One was Trudy Villiers, thin and regal and dressed in a high-necked chiffon blouse with matching ivory slacks. The other was a man with dark hair and a thick mustache in need of a trim. I was sure I didn't know him, yet he looked familiar.

"Who is that?" I asked Carrie, keeping my voice low.

"I don't know. I've seen him somewhere before, though."

"That's what I was think—oh! That's Curtis," I said. "He was at the town hall meeting the other night."

Trudy stepped onto the porch, her good-bye carrying clearly while Curtis strode down the path toward us.

I weighed the wisdom of greeting him by name. Diana hadn't introduced any of us, after all. Using his name might make even small talk awkward. I settled on a simple, "Good morning," and Carrie did the same.

"Morning," he said. His eyes narrowed a little, and I reasoned he might be thinking we looked familiar as well.

Fifi shuffled sideways so that she stood in front of and roughly between Carrie and me. The rumble intensified as the man drew nearer, until he was close enough to elicit a throaty growl followed by a single bark.

Curtis lifted both hands, palms out. "Relax dog," he said. "I won't come any closer, I promise."

"Fifi, come," Trudy called from the porch.

But Fifi only persisted in growling, until Curtis lunged

at her, then feinted left. The poor dog barked with such vigor her front paws came up off the ground.

Curtis laughed, a mirthless sound with a hollow echo, and headed down the sidewalk to his car.

Fifi's head swiveled as she tracked him. She stopped barking, but the low-throated growl continued.

"What a jackass," I said, none too quietly, not caring if my voice carried.

He pointed a key fob at a late-model Toyota that had a volunteer fireman's emblem on the back window and the faded outlines of a stick figure family. The car chirped its response.

Carrie shook her head in disbelief, gaze on Curtis as he climbed into the driver's seat. "I don't know," she said. "*Jackass* might not be a strong enough term."

"Girls come inside, come inside." Trudy beckoned us closer with her fingertips. "And bring Fifi if you will."

With my toe I nudged Fifi's back paw, hoping she would precede me into the house. I kind of liked having a defender, even though that defender was less than two feet tall and had failed to take a chunk out of Curtis when she had the chance.

The dog ambled forward, rolling a bit from side to side. Carrie and I trailed behind her, climbing the top step of the porch well after Fifi had disappeared indoors.

"Sorry about all that," Trudy said, her voice every bit as proper as I recalled. Stepping back to allow us to enter the house, she continued, "Fifi just gets so riled up when she sees him. And I haven't got the heart to lock her away in the bathroom. I don't know what I'll do if she's still here once I have paying guests."

We waited inside the foyer while Trudy closed and locked the door. I couldn't help noticing, though, that her hand was trembling as she turned the lock. When she faced us once again, I took a second to really look at her, study her face without worrying what she thought of my behavior. And what I saw surprised me.

Trudy Villiers was shook. Distressed. Her cheeks were in high color, her brow and lips pinched. Her fingers fluttered at the fashionable gold chain draped low on her chest, and her gaze remained resolutely on the floor.

"Ms. Villiers, are you all right?" I asked. In the same moment Carrie said, "Trudy, is everything okay?"

She clutched at the gold chain. "Oh, he rattles me so. And then all of Fifi's barking." She tsk-tsked, presumably to herself, and gestured for us to continue on through to the living room where once again we took seats on the ivory couch. Within moments, Fifi jumped up and wedged herself into the space between us.

Trudy huffed as she settled into the wingback chair opposite. "And now she's on my couch again."

"I'm sorry," Carrie said, sliding a hand beneath the dog's belly. "Do you want me to move her?"

"No, no, don't bother. I believe it's already too late for that couch."

"Would you like me to keep an eye out—" Carrie began, but I interrupted her. I had to. I couldn't take it anymore.

"Who *was* that guy?" I blurted. "He got you all upset and Fifi ready to snack on human flesh. What was he doing here? Do you *know* him?" I simply couldn't believe Trudy would willingly associate with someone like Curtis.

Her rigid posture softened and her eyes momentarily slipped closed. "I suppose you might call him the rightful heir to that dog." She tipped her head toward Fifi. "But you've seen how well they get on. I really thought I'd seen the last of him when I agreed to watch over her until I could find her a home. Some people, though . . ." Her voice and her gaze trailed away, and she shuddered.

I looked to Carrie. She was so much better at the little social graces than I.

"Well, um, let's talk about some pleasant things," she said brightly. "Georgia brought some design concepts for you."

Taking a deep breath for courage, I laid my portfolio on the coffee table. I unzipped the portfolio and withdrew the sheaf of papers showing sketches and color concepts for her window. On the first, the text read MAGNOLIA. I had surrounded the stylized lettering with an oval of blossoms. Keeping that sketch to the top, I fanned out the remaining pages.

"What's this?" Trudy shifted her weight to the forward edge of the wingback chair and leaned toward the table without relaxing her spine. She reached out and slid one of the sketches free of its place below a pair of others. "These look like roses."

"A-a-and magnolias," I muttered.

Carrie gave my side a quick jab with her elbow, disturbing Fifi who grumble-growled her displeasure.

I shot Carrie a look that asked what it was she expected me to do.

Her eyes went wide and she tipped her head in Trudy's direction.

Right. Sell the idea.

I forced a smile. "I thought since you have such a beautiful rose garden you might like the flowers included."

Trudy arched a brow. "Magnolias and roses?"

"As you see," I slipped another colored drawing out from beneath the image of plain magnolias, "including roses also allows more color."

Slowly, ever so painfully slowly, Trudy turned toward Carrie. "Did you know about this?"

My pride stirred. It straightened my spine and lifted my chin and reminded me I had faced far more intimidating people than Trudy Villiers and I had not bent before them.

I kicked my vocal volume up a notch. "Before we came I informed Carrie that I would be presenting several options. And that is all they are. Options. As you can see, I've prepared two with magnolias alone." With my fingertips I fanned the drawings separate.

"But you mistake me, my dear. I quite like this floral mix." She centered the drawing over the table and released her hold, allowing the paper to float down among the other renderings. "It's the colors." Her attention remained fixed on Carrie. "Would you be able to incorporate these colors in your search for decor? Nothing large. Perhaps a few accent pillows or lamps."

A better, more experienced businesswoman than I, Carrie confined her response to a sage nod.

Trudy blew a breath through her nose—the subtlest of huffs—and shuffled the other drawings around.

I raised a hand to my cheek, allowing me to cover my mouth with my palm and preventing me from speaking. Better to let her reach her own decision.

At last she lifted the first drawing, the one of MAG-NOLIA surrounded by an oval of blossoms. "Can you add roses to this design?" She raised her eyes to look at me and her face fell slack. "My word," she said on a whisper.

I dropped my hand and slouched a little.

Carrie half rose from her seat. "What is it? Trudy, are you all right?"

For a moment she sat as frozen as a statue of a queen, holding forth the drawing, chin dropped. "So familiar," she murmured.

I sneaked a peek at Carrie, but her attention was fixed on the older woman.

"*Kelly*, you say your name is?" Trudy asked.

Wheels spun in my mind and I offered the information I determined she was after. "My mother was Patricia Keene. She was Peter and—"

"Florence's daughter," Trudy finished for me. She bobbed her head slowly, a physical motion that seemed to say the pieces had come together for her. "Flo's grand-daughter. That's why your appearance is so familiar. I didn't see it until . . ." She laid a hand alongside her cheek.

That made twice in one week someone had remarked on my resemblance to my grandmother. I conjured a memory of her—standing in front of the range top, wooden spoon in hand and grinning over her shoulder. Over her dress she wore a pink apron with little images of poodles drawn in black and on her feet a pair of low-heeled black shoes. Her hair lay in tight curls against her head, and her lipstick was a vivid red. In this memory my grandmother was the image of at-home elegance, and I wondered if I would ever feel as self-assured as she always seemed to be.

"We played mah-jongg together, Flo and I," she said. "Oh, my. I haven't thought of that in years."

"Did you know my grandfather—Pete—also?" I asked.

She let out a short laugh. "It was another time," she said. "I never met Peter. I never met many of the husbands, only those whose wives I was very dear friends with. Dotty Crawford. Adele Chesterton. Madge Heaney." Her voice softened with each name until it faded away entirely. Her gaze drifted around the room. "It's Madge's generosity that's allowing me to make these changes. Yet all I have to remember her by is a dog I can't keep."

Then she took a breath that halted any melancholy and smiled. "At least Betty Weeks is still among the living. She's the last of that old crowd. Apart from myself, that is."

Once more, Trudy extended the drawing toward me. "Please make this." She pulled another sheet from the table and passed that to me as well. "With these roses added in."

The blooms in the drawing were yellow and coral and a delicate sienna. Their color would offset prettily the slight pink and lavender and bright white magnolia blossoms. A tremor of excitement danced through my veins at the prospect of finding those colors in glass. If I didn't linger after Carrie dropped me back home, I could easily drive to the stained glass shop and return in time for Grandy to leave for the dine-in.

I gathered up the sketches while Carrie asked a few additional questions about the antique pieces she would be on the lookout for. I was anxious to get to work, ready to put fires and break-ins and murders and devastatingly handsome construction foremen behind me.

Someday I would have to learn to adjust my priorities.

16

When I arrived home, Grandy was ensconced in the kitchen, daily paper spread before him on the table, coffee and toast with jam at his elbow.

"What's news?" I asked. I dropped my portfolio on the counter and grabbed an empty coffee mug from the cabinet.

"Our best pitcher tore a rotator cuff during last night's game. Might as well end the season right now." He took a man-sized bite of toast, more than half the slice disappearing into his mouth.

"Yankees?"

"Of course Yankees," he grumbled through a mouthful of bread and jam.

I lifted a shoulder. The Yankees may have been Grandy's favorite team, but so were the Dodgers, the Padres, and the Brewers. He could have been talking about any one of them but there was no need to point that out.

"Where were you this morning?" He pushed his plate of toast toward me and made a little noise meant to tell me to help myself. After spending months under the same roof we were beginning to operate in shorthand.

I helped myself to a triangle of toast. "Went out to Trudy Villiers about the glass project."

He looked up from his paper, looked at me with sincere concern and a hint of hopefulness. "Oh? How did she like the designs?"

"She liked them. Liked the roses." I couldn't stop the little smile pulling at my lips.

Grandy grinned and nodded. "Very good. She'd have been daft not to."

"You have to say things like that. You're my grandpa."

"I don't have to do or say anything. I'm an eighty-year-old man and I've earned the right to silence or honesty as I see fit." He gave one more short, firm nod then looked back to his paper.

As I took a bite of toast, there was a soft tap on my leg. I glanced down, unsurprised to see Friday balanced on her hind legs, one foreleg tucked close to her body, the other braced against my calf. "Meew," she said.

"Beggar." I scratched between her ears and she pushed back against my fingertips, eyes half closing.

"She's nearly out of cans," Grandy said.

He blustered about Friday being in his way, sitting on his favorite chair, or swatting at the ticker running across the bottom of the television screen. But he kept an eye on her food and water and now and then I would catch him with telltale white hairs clinging to the breast of his navy bathrobe. Let him claim he never cuddled with the kitten; those white hairs were strong evidence.

"There's some in the back of the Jeep. I'll bring it in." I took a careful sip of coffee—Grandy's brews tended toward hair-on-your-chest strength—and the heat nearly scorched its way down my throat.

"You've got a lot of junk floating around the back of the Jeep," he said, eyeing me over the top of his reading glasses.

"I know. Sorry. It's all this rain. I'll bring them in later." Apart from the case of kitten food and a gallon of all-purpose cleaner, better known as white vinegar, I had two twenty-pound tubs of cat sand and an industrial pack of paper towels in the back of the Jeep. It was practically extended storage.

"Hey, by the way, are you certain you never met Trudy Villiers?" I asked. Holding my hands over the now empty toast plate, I brushed the crumbs from my fingers.

"I said no such thing," Grandy murmured. "I said I don't remember her."

Half grinning, I rolled my eyes to heaven, making no effort to hide the gesture.

"You try remembering everyone you ever met, see how you do."

I sighed. "She said she knew Grandma. Said they played mah-jongg together."

He thought for a moment then smiled, the way he often did when a particular memory of Gram overtook him. "Oh. Oh yes, she did play mah-jongg for a time. Every Wednesday lunchtime. That was some years ago, though. The brickworks was still running back then. Your mother was still in school."

I braved another gulp of coffee. "I didn't know Gram played mah-jongg."

Grandy nodded. "That she did. And rummy and canasta. She and her lady friends used to sit at that table"—he pointed to the dining room, where a heavy mahogany table for six waited for a big family to gather around—"playing cards and laughing until all hours."

As Friday nimbly leaped into my lap and curled into a little ball, there was no keeping the smile from my face. The look of happy memory lighting Grandy's eyes, taking years from the wrinkles in his forehead and cheeks made shared happiness irresistible.

"She loved a good game, your gran did." He tipped his head and gave me a contented smile. "She would have enjoyed having you here. You would have lost every cent you have to her playing gin but she would have been happy."

"I would have liked that, too," I said.

Grandy turned his gaze back to the paper. "Maybe this Trudy person would like to teach you."

I thought of Trudy and her perfect posture and pristine home. "She doesn't strike me as the laughing-until-all-hours type," I said. I shifted in my chair, lifting one foot to tuck under my opposite leg. Made of liquid as she was, Friday simply sloshed from one side of my lap to the next without protest. "But she did say the same thing you did, that I look like Grandma."

"So you do."

"Why did you never tell me that before?"

"You never looked like her before," he stated, calmly turning the page.

A most unladylike bark of a laugh escaped me. "Are you serious?"

"Georgia, it may surprise you to know I didn't know your grandmother when she was a little girl. It's only now you're grown that the resemblance is clear."

"Yes, but you must have some idea what she looked like as a child. You must have pictures somewhere."

He nodded and turned the page on the news. "Somewhere."

A strong urge to see the pictures swept through me. Did I really look so much like my Grandma as a woman? Were we that dissimilar as children?

I would have to take some time to locate Grandy's old photo albums. But there were more pressing matters to see to first.

"Would you mind if I borrowed the Jeep for a while? I'd like to take a ride out to the glass shop."

"For this new project?" he asked, turning the page on the paper.

"And to make some new pieces for Carrie's shop."

Looking up from the news, he questioned me on whether there had been any police progress following the break-in, and when I informed him there was no news, he asked after Carrie's well-being and how she was bearing up under the strain. I informed him she appeared to be doing as well as could be expected.

"I just don't understand why someone would break into her shop and destroy . . ." Sighing, I scooped Friday up into my arms. "It doesn't make sense. Russ's office, Herb Gallo, Carrie's shop . . ." I tucked the kitten below my chin and against my chest and snuggled her close. "Russ and Carrie aren't together anymore," I said, stroking Friday's soft fur, thinking aloud. "So what's the connection?"

"Georgia." His voice was strong, stern, forcing me to meet his eyes. "You're not thinking of getting involved in this, are you?"

"I'm kind of already involved, Grandy. Carrie's my friend. I'm worried about her."

"Then be involved as a friend. Be supportive, keep her spirits up, give her a shoulder to cry on. Do not go poking into places only the police should."

"I wouldn't—"

"You would. And I'm telling you not to. You could have got yourself killed sticking your nose in over that whole Andy Edgers affair."

"You were in jail," I squeaked. "Did you honestly expect me to do nothing?"

"I expect you to use common sense and not put yourself at risk. Especially not for me. Promise me you'll keep your nose out of this one and let the police do their job."

Truly I hadn't had any urge to go poking my nose anywhere . . . not until Grandy said I shouldn't.

"I promise," I said. "I will let the police do their job."

* * *

A variety of roads led from Grandy's house to the inter-state. Some were back roads, one was a highway, and one was fairly out of the way but ran alongside the river for a good stretch.

I pretended to myself that I had elected to take the scenic route, and stubbornly ignored the voice that insisted I'd chosen a route that would take me past the old brickworks. Whichever was the truer of the two, the riverside route was the path I took.

This far north of the city, the Hudson River was a rich blue with sparks of sunshine glinting off the swells. Sail-boats slid through the water with the effortless motion of gliding birds while speedboats raced past, bows bouncing against the subtle waves.

With the press of a button, my window slid down, and the rich, crisp scent of the river's muddy banks filled the interior of the Jeep. I took a deep breath of the clear air, let my head fall against the headrest, and smiled. There was something simultaneously soothing and energizing about being so near the water, so close to nature. You know, despite the whole SUV-and-paved-road thing.

I guided the vehicle around one of the many wide curves that seemed to lead away from the river and tried to picture the land side of the road remade to include a shopping promenade where now there was only the occasional bun-galow. I thought in some respects the change in view would be a good thing, a move toward the twenty-first century.

But in other respects, the loss of the bungalows and their hint of the area's history seemed sad and shortsighted.

One more curve back toward the river and there, at last, rose the old brickworks. Except . . .

The building I had known, the building that featured so prominently in Wenwood's history . . . the only thing the structure retained from those long-gone days was its view of the river.

I lifted my foot from the accelerator, flipped on the turn signal in a move more reflex than choice. The Jeep bounced merrily along the broken-down road that led to the place that I needed to learn to think of as the marina. Eight-foot-tall chain-link fencing wrapped the site as it had the last time I ventured out that way. And just like the last time, inside the perimeter a Jaguar sat in front of a trailer.

Turning the SUV parallel to the fence, I drove a short distance off road and cut the engine. I took the time to swipe a little extra sunblock across my nose before I stepped out of the vehicle, hand to my forehead to deflect the strong rays of the sun.

With my back to the marina, my new vantage point afforded me an unbroken view of the riverside property Spring and Hamilton was busily acquiring. Whether they would be able to convince the town to allow them to build was another matter. But yes or no, the property they were accumulating was marginally scenic. Stunning? No. The slight rise away from the riverfront could only be called a hill in exaggerated terms, and the view of the other side of the river was less than idyllic. I began to suspect that a promenade of shopping and casual dining might not be the worst addition.

Behind me came the *clink-clank* of the latch on the chain-link fence being opened. I took in a breath, shoulders going rigid. Footsteps crunched across loose pebbles and then Tony Himmel's voice said, "Nice view."

I glanced over my shoulder to find his gaze fixed in the same direction mine had been. Willing myself to exhale, I asked, "What are you doing working on a Saturday?"

He grinned and looked down at me. "What are you doing checking up on me?"

Heat flooded my cheeks. "I'm not checking up on you. I just wanted to see the—the—" I waved a hand in front of my mouth as though that might draw out the words. Tony laughed.

Darn it, he had a nice laugh. And he looked as good in today's faded black T-shirt as he did in the suit he wore the first time I'd encountered him—and when Friday had tried to adhere herself to him. Smart kitty.

"I'm teasing you," Tony said, humor lacing his tone. "Relax. It makes sense you'd want to have a look."

"It does?"

"After your interrupted questions last night, of course."

"After my . . . ? Oh, no, that's not what . . . I wanted to see the progress you were making on the brickworks. I mean, on the marina."

Smiling, he tipped his head in the direction he'd come and spun away from me. He pushed his fists into the front pockets of his loose-fit cargo shorts, ambling toward the gate. "It just so happens I'm the one person who can grant you exclusive, behind-the-scenes access."

It took me a few scrambling steps to catch up to him. We passed side by side through the wide gate onto property that appeared transformed since my last visit. Where not six weeks ago the main building had been a mix of bare wood framing beneath a half-open roof, now the walls were closed, the roof cleanly halved with a full added story on the land side, and a flat, finished balcony space on the river side.

"Patio dining," I said, eyes on the roofline. "That's going to be nice."

A small measure of his cheer dimmed. "I hope so. I really hope so." He took long strides forward, forcing me into a half jog trying to keep up. "The marine shop beneath is nearly ready for occupation. Last I checked there were—"

"No, wait, wait." I hustled to get ahead of him. "What do you mean you hope so? You've seen the drawings or plans or whatever it is the construction crew works from. You've approved them. You've had this planned since . . ." I didn't remember how long he told me he had harbored dreams of rebuilding the marina, but it wasn't a recent idea.

He pushed a stray hank of hair back off his forehead, let it fall. "Once Spring and Hamilton secure all the property, they're likely to get approval for their retail plan. This restaurant needs to build a steady customer base before any competition arrives."

"I don't think you need to worry," I said, wrapping my

arms around my belly. "What's your competition now, the luncheonette?"

Tony huffed a mirthless laugh and walked forward again, leading me closer to the redesigned building. "Down here I figure we'll stay open past eight o'clock."

"You might cause a scandal." I hoped to joke him out of his sudden bad temper, but he said nothing in the few steps we took before we reached the front of the building.

He stopped in front of a large window set alongside a double-door entrance. "I can't show you the inside—it's still a construction zone—but you can take a peek."

Accepting his invitation, I stepped up to the window and peered inside.

What had been bare plank floors on my last visit was now covered wall to wall with drop cloths, presumably to protect the flooring as the interior dividing walls went up and were painted the same marine blue as the outer walls. I crouched a little to get a better look at the ceiling, where exposed beams crisscrossed the expanse, allowing—if I remembered the plan correctly—for mast storage.

Nothing at all remained of the brickworks.

A little knot of sorrow lodged itself in the back of my throat. Rationally I knew this was an important step for the future of Wenwood. But new beginnings seemed always to keep company with memories of things lost.

Standing straight, I turned my back on the window and gazed along the riverfront. That view, too, would change if Spring and Hamilton had its way.

I shifted to face Tony, his words echoing through my

mind. "Did you say Spring and Hamilton haven't secured all the land they need yet?"

He kicked at some loose dirt, nodded. "That's what I hear." Then his eyes flashed to mine. "Why do you ask?"

"No reason," I said, perhaps too quickly.

Tony looked down at me, a breeze ruffling his hair. His expression said he didn't believe me.

"Okay." I relented. "I was just thinking about change and when it's a good thing and when it's a hard thing. And I wondered if maybe that conundrum was holding up the property acquisition. You know, for whoever's selling."

The quirk of his smile and his stifled laugh made me immediately doubt my theory.

"Or maybe it's a money thing," I added, the heat of embarrassment undoing the good work of the cool breeze off the water. I waved away my words. "Forget it. I just—I don't know what I'm talking about."

"Ah, Georgia," he said on a heavy sigh. He rubbed a hand around the back of his neck, shook his head. "One of these days I *won't* owe you an apology. I'm sorry. I got a kick out of you using *conundrum* in a casual conversation, that's all."

"Oh." And yet somehow I didn't feel much better. I felt, instead, concerned about the next phrase that might fall out of my mouth. "But you don't owe me any apologies."

"Don't I?" Hands back in his pockets, he shifted away from me and began ambling back toward the gate. "Isn't that what last night was all about? All very cool and impersonal?"

"At the dine-in?" Had I been cool? In my effort not to

appear overly interested in him, had I gone too far in the wrong direction?

"My sister is trying to figure out where you and I stand with each other. She can be a bit nosy and overbearing." He grinned. "And I suppose her confusion makes sense. We didn't get off to such a friendly start you and I. And once construction here got past that . . ."

Still overconscious of choosing words poorly, I kept quiet, turned my attention away from him and back to the strip of riverfront property ahead and the rest of the world beyond the fence. Traffic moved briskly along the road in both directions, no one slowing, everyone intent on continuing past.

"Once we got past that supply delay the crew and I started making up for lost time around here, hoping we still had a shot at getting the project finished on schedule. I haven't had a lot of free time to make sure you and I didn't slide back into that unfriendly place."

Bad enough I doubted my speech. Now I doubted my hearing. Or, perhaps more accurately, my understanding. "I don't follow."

Tony's expression was apologetic. "We met for dinner. And kept things understandably . . . businesslike. I should have called you the very next day and invited you to dinner for reasons not so platonic."

I was instantly interested in the ground beneath my toes, hoping if I kept my gaze on something dull and innocuous I wouldn't blurt out something juvenile that might change his mind. But it was mere moments before I knew I had control of my words. "I doubt it was the right time."

He squinted against a sudden splash of sunshine. "How about now?"

Now?

A slew of thoughts assailed my mind. At their forefront, a burned-out building, shards of glass on the floor of an antiques store, and Chip Nolan's face when he sent me away from Herb Gallo's house.

Disappointment stabbed through me, leaving my limbs feeling heavy. I backstepped toward the Jeep. "How about you call me in a few days?" I said. Keeping my eyes on him, I reached behind me and opened the door on the vehicle. "And we'll talk."

That fast, Tony Himmel went from successful, grown man to despondent puppy.

"Maybe over coffee," I said with a grin, then ducked into the Jeep and slammed the door behind me.

I forced myself to keep my eyes ahead and not look back at Tony. I didn't want to know yet whether I had chosen my words wisely or poorly. For a little while at least, I wanted to hold on to a fun mystery.

17

In my three-plus months in Wenwood, I'd made only a few trips to the stained glass shop, primarily because it was more than an hour's drive in each direction. More than that, glass could get expensive.

I parked the Jeep around the corner from the store where an old maple tree provided shade. Breathing deep of the dry inland air, I steered my wayward mind back to the business at hand: Trudy Villiers's window. In my purse was a rough copy of the design and broken bits of glass closest to the colors and types the design required. I only hoped the design and glass would come together as I envisioned.

The electronic door chime sounded as I entered the shop, sharp and unsettling. I much preferred the delicate jingle of the store bells in Wenwood.

Unlike previous visits when I had been one of very few

customers in the store, today the shop floor was crowded with men and women, patterns in hand, strolling back and forth along the glass-filled cubbies. I spotted the proprietor—a tall, thin woman with dark hair caught in a heavy bun at the back of her neck—mingling among them.

"Be brave," she called out. "If you see something that intrigues you, pull it out. Take a good long look. You can't get a true impression of the glass without handling it and holding it up to the sun or resting it on one of the light tables."

She spotted me hovering just inside the doorway and smiled. "Hi there. Anything I can help you with today?"

A short, round woman paused near my left and gazed down at the pattern she held. A simple tulip. I guessed no more than twelve shapes in the design, and that's when the pieces clicked together. I had not stumbled into an unexpected rush at the glass shop, but rather I'd stumbled into a beginner's class.

"I need some glass," I said, as if stating the obvious were somehow illuminating.

The woman pointed to the start of the glass cubbies along the east-facing wall. "Right over there."

Of course, I knew that already but smiled my thanks all the same and ambled over to the wooden cubbies. Large, nearly two-foot-by-three-foot glass sheets resting on their short edges filled the lower cubbies. Sheets cut to half or a quarter of the size filled the upper cubbies, and it was from those upper cubbies that I pulled the first sheets of glass.

I wanted first to find the streaky pink and violets for the magnolia blossoms. Without the right mix of color—that ideal combination of soft and bright—the flowers would be lost in the overall design. Not to mention that the cost of the opalescent pinks would require a big chunk of my budget. I needed to be cautious with my selections to prevent having to skimp anywhere.

As I slid the square of violet glass out of its cubby, my cell phone erupted with Idina Menzel's voice declaring it was time to defy gravity. Heat suffused my cheeks. "Sorry," I muttered to several startled stained glass students. "Sorry."

Glass in hand, I hurried to the large light tables in the center of the space and carefully laid down the sheet. In so doing, I caught sight of the price written on the corner in grease pencil. Almost thirty dollars. I would need a large sheet. A little bit of financial fear gripped me. Between the outlay for this window and the cost of creating replacement pieces for the antiques shop . . . Let's just say it was a good thing Grandy was letting me stay with him rent free.

The phone stopped ringing before I could open my purse. And even though I knew that if it had been Tony Himmel who called, the ringtone would have been the innocuous factory-installed tune—as it was for all people not in my contacts list—still I felt a little flare of hope. And that said something.

But the missed call, when I checked the screen, had come from Carrie.

I looked from the phone, to the glass, to my fellow shoppers, weighing the wisdom of returning the call right away, after having attracted so much attention.

I had just decided to mute the phone and call Carrie back later when Idina rent the air again. Quick as a blink

I pressed the proper button to accept the call while at the same time hustling away from the crowd.

"What's up?" I asked. "Is everything okay?" Two calls in fast succession did not bode well.

"Russ called," she blurted.

"What? When?" I worked my way to the rear of the shop, in among shelves lined with bottles of soldering flux and finishing patina and varying size bottles of cutting oil. Finishing hooks and hanging chains were displayed in open cardboard boxes.

"Just now. He said as soon as he hit the state line, his phone went crazy with messages."

"Of course it did. Cell phones are very territorial like that."

"Yeah, well, whatever. He said he's going to go see the building and then he's coming here." Her voice squeaked, and I couldn't help but picture her pacing behind the register at her store, white-knuckling the phone and trying to straighten her wavy hair with sheer force. "What am I supposed to do? I don't want to see him."

"Under the circumstances, I don't think you're going to be able to avoid him," I said. No sooner did the words leave my mouth, though, than I wondered why Russ would be so intent on seeing Carrie. Surely whatever they needed to discuss could be done over the phone. Unless Russ had somehow gotten it in his head that Carrie was responsible. "You know what," I said. "Why don't you call Diana and ask her what she thinks, you know, from a professional law enforcement perspective?"

Carrie gasped. "Yes! Good idea. I'll call her. But can you come over to the store? Keep me company?"

I peered at the crowded shelves around me, at the stained glass panels hung from the ceiling, at the students pulling stunning sheets of glass from cubbies. "Of course," I said. "I'm up in Chalmers, though. How far out is Russ?"

We worked out how long we thought it would take Russ to get to the antiques store. Or rather, Carrie did, as she seemed to keep a map of the state in her head. Determining I had enough time to select at least the pink glass and a few other sheets from which to make pieces for the shop, I assured Carrie I'd be there and got to work. I had less than an hour to purchase glass and an hour to get back to Wenwood . . .

Just in time to stand between my best friend and her ex-husband.

I was going to be late returning the Jeep to Grandy. Well, late according to Grandy, for whom "late" meant not arriving early. But it was his vehicle and his rules and I was willing to follow. Usually. Now and again I lost track of time. The best way to appease Grandy in those instances was to bring a peace offering.

Behind the grocery store on Wenwood's main drag, I parked the SUV beneath the branches of my favorite walnut tree. Purse in hand, sunglasses in place, I pulled out my cell phone and made a quick call to Carrie.

"I'm going to Rozelle's and then home and I'll have

Grandy drop me off by your store on his way to work," I said when she picked up. "Anything more from Russ?"

"He asked me to meet him at the luncheonette after I close up here," Carrie said.

I locked the Jeep and headed down the entrance toward the street, the sun's heat reflecting up from the blacktop and making my knees sweat. "Did he say why he wants to talk to you?"

"I imagine it's about the building and about Herb and all but I couldn't ask. I had a customer. Thank goodness it's been busy today. It really kept my mind off of . . . everything."

"That's a good thing," I agreed. I waited at the sidewalk while traffic passed up and down the main road bisecting the village. "How about Diana, did you speak to her?"

"Left a message," she said. The tone and volume of her voice shifted. "Hi there," she said, clearly holding the phone well away from her mouth. "Welcome to Aggie's Antiques."

"All right. Go help your customer. I'll see you in a little while."

The single traffic light shined red, stopping cars long enough for me to dash across the street. I reached the door to Rozelle's Bakery at the same time as a balding gentleman in his late forties. He opened the door and rushed inside ahead of me, leaving me dumbfounded on the sidewalk.

"Tourist," I muttered. I shook my head and tugged open the door. One step across the threshold, the shock hit me. That man, with the sunburned bald patch and bad manners, was a tourist—to me. He was an outsider. Making me . . . a local?

Shuffling to the nearest showcase, I rested a hand against its chrome edging and gazed at the colorful frosted cookies within. My mind turned at high speed, trying to grasp the realization that I had come to consider myself a local. How had that happened? At what point had I stopped thinking of myself as a temporary resident and started thinking of myself as permanent?

"Georgia, honey! You need more bread already?" Behind the counter, Rozelle bustled toward me, pastry box in one hand, square of wax paper in the other. The tourist walked with her, display cases dividing them.

"I was curious what sugar-free special you have today," I said, aware that even the fact that Rozelle made different sugar-free concoctions was something she didn't advertise. She always had sugar-free cookies, but Wenwood residents knew there was always something more.

"I'll have to check," she said before turning her attention to her other customer.

I looked on as the balding gentleman pointed to different trays of cookies. Rozelle, whose sensible shoes might have put her one gray curl over five foot, expertly scooped the cookies with the wax square and dropped them in the pastry box. Her movements were economical and sure, and after each handful went into the box she gave the box a little shake. Having witnessed this behavior enough, I knew she was estimating the weight. Further, I knew her estimates were accurate to within an ounce.

"Eat," she said, handing me a jelly finger. "You have to learn to appreciate the sweet things."

"I do appreciate them," I said.

Rozelle gave me a look that called me a liar.

I took a bite of the cookie and made an extra-loud *mmmmm* noise so she would be sure to hear me. Of course, I could have told her about the donut I'd treated myself to at the coffee shop. She might have told Grandy, though, and the last thing I needed was Mr. Kettle crying foul against Ms. Pot.

As Rozelle walked back to the register, the sweet goodness of the cookie woke my taste buds and my belly. Sudden, intense hunger followed. I tried to calculate how long it had been since my last meal but apparently it had been so long the brain cells containing my math skills had starved to death. Leave it to me to be so distracted by a good-looking man and a store full of glass that eating lunch became a nonnecessity.

Of course, I was chomping on the sort of bakery cookie for which a tall glass of milk was not only a good idea, it was a requirement. Tasty? Yes. Dry as dirt? Ditto.

One of Rozelle's counter helpers came out of the back of the shop and took over ringing up the sale for the bald tourist. Rozelle ambled back to me, wiping her hands on her ever-present apron. "Now then," she said. "You need something special for Pete?"

I swear her eye twinkled. Rozelle had been sweet on Grandy since long before I arrived in Wenwood. I didn't know how long before; I was frankly afraid to ask. If I knew how long she'd carried her torch, I ran the risk of feeling sorry for her, and I'd much rather be encouraging than sorry.

"I've had his Jeep out all day," I said.

Rozelle nodded sagely. "That might put him in a mood."

"I just don't understand why." I huffed. "That is, I do. It's his, but—"

"Pete's lived on his own a long time now. Maybe too long?" she asked, almost hopefully. "I expect he's still adjusting to sharing his home and his things." I opened my mouth to protest, to remind Rozelle that I was Pete's granddaughter not some stranger, but she kept on speaking before I got a word out. "It's not about you, Georgia. He's happier to have you than he lets on. It's no fun being old and alone. But it's still an adjustment when things are no longer where you left them, from a coffee cup to a car."

I sighed. "Or all the hard candy I take away."

Her giggle would be best described as a titter. "That especially." She straightened her shoulders, smoothed down the creases in her baker's apron. "Let's see what I have to take his edge off today."

She wandered farther along the counter and I wandered with her, passing by the two tiny tables squeezed into the opposite side of the store, and eyeing, as always, the collection of teapots and cup-and-saucer sets filling the cubbies along the wall.

"How about a cheesecake?" Rozelle suggested.

"Sugar free?" I asked, as the entrance of another customer set off the bell over the door.

"Sugar free. I used a little artificial sweetener. Only a little, I promise."

"That's fine," I said.

Rozelle's eyes widened in surprise. I'd been in the bakery

enough looking for sugar-free deliciousness for Grandy that she knew my reservations about artificial sweeteners. But in Grandy's case, sugar was the greater evil.

"Really," I said. "It's fine. I'll take it."

Without further comment, she boxed the cake and rang up the sale, while her fresh-faced employee waited on the other customer. The clerk, one of the girls Rozelle hired to help out during the summer, had the clean-scrubbed, ponytailed appearance of a New England college student. When her school years were done, would she remain in Wenwood to begin her life? Would there be anything here to keep her?

Rozelle snapped me from my thoughts by handing my change over the counter. "Thanks, Rozelle." I accepted my change and the cake and smiled my gratitude.

"You'll be sure to give Pete my regards, won't you?"

I forced my smile wider, forced down the little flare of feeling badly for her. "Of course." I took a step back to leave but stopped at Rozelle's next question.

"Wait. Tell me. How is Carrie? So scary what happened."

"She's okay," I said.

"Do the police have any idea who broke in?"

I shook my head. "Not that I've heard."

"Such a terrible thing. And poor Herb Gallo, too. My. This used to be such a nice, safe place."

I reached across and gave her hand a squeeze. "It still is, Rozelle. The police will figure out who's responsible for all of this."

"I hope they figure it out soon," she said on a sigh. "A lot of people are trying to make this town something again. I hate to see all that work come to nothing because folks are too afraid to come here."

"It won't." I wasn't sure I believed myself, but it seemed like the words needed to be said.

Rozelle only nodded, waggled her fingers in good-bye, and turned to help the next customer who had wandered in.

Bakery box in hand, I left the shop, thoughts of Wenwood's future clouding my mind. Rozelle was right. Between the early summer murder of the hardware store owner, the break-in at Carrie's shop, and the death-by-misdeed of Herb Gallo, not to mention the willful abandonment of the kitten who now happily curled up on my worktable each day, Wenwood was in danger of losing more than a measure of its charm.

And that brought up a whole new line of questions. Was someone out to tarnish Wenwood? Was there something to be gained by keeping the town down? But then why set fire to the law office?

As the next thought hit, it hit hard enough to make me pause just outside the grocery store. The law office was in Newbridge, burned to an unsightly, blackened crisp. Carrie's shop had been broken into and its merchandise destroyed but the building itself was undamaged. We'd thought the thief had avoided breaking the front windows to gain access because of the risk of witnesses. What if the thief kept the window intact so as not to stain the face of Wenwood's village?

A flurry of excitement in my gut told me I was onto something, something important. If the police were looking for someone who . . . wanted the best for Wen-wood? Wanted . . . wanted what? Why?

In my purse, my cell phone burst to life, the voice of a movie trailer narrator ominously proclaiming, "In a world where grown children move home . . ." Grandy. "I'm on my way," I said by way of greeting.

"Just wanted to remind you," he responded, "to remember the cat food. The little devil is into everything looking for something to eat."

I grinned. "She's not looking for food, Grandy. She's looking for trouble."

"Hmph. That's worse." He sighed. "Why did I ever let you keep that thing?"

"Because you love me," I said.

"That must be it."

My grin faded, but the warmth expanded in my heart. "I love you, too, Grandy. I'll be home soon."

Grandy gleefully proclaimed the cheesecake a bribe to make him forget I was late returning the Jeep. Though he swore to not forget, he did forgive and downed a generous slice before getting dressed for his night at the dine-in.

I did my own quick change, switching my cotton T-shirt for a pale green blouse and trading my shorts for jeans. The days might still have been sultry, but the nights were blissfully cool. I tried tugging my hair back into a loose ponytail, but my wayward locks were having none of that. A couple of hairpins keeping the mop off my face would have to do.

Inside the SUV, Grandy made a show of readjusting the mirrors. He turned down the volume on the radio before switching to the all-news station, and finally, after he'd shifted his seat forward and back one last time, he turned to me. "Are you ready?" he asked.

"You're not going to check the tire pressure?"

"Put your seat belt on," he grumbled. He backed out of the driveway once I proved to him my seat belt was securely fastened, then waited until we reached the end of the block before springing the latest news on me. "Your mother phoned."

A mélange of dread, guilt, and curiosity churned through my stomach. I knew she felt I didn't call her as often as I should, so when I did catch her on the phone she proved what a star player she was at the Irish Guilt Game. She could make me feel thoughtless in under four breaths. And still I loved her a ton and eagerly asked, "How is she? How's Ben?"

"Claims she's happier than she's been since before your father passed away."

"That's nice," I said, hoping she meant it, hoping this time the feeling would last for both of them.

Grandy eased the SUV gently around the corner, heading for the boulevard that led to downtown Wenwood. "She said they're thinking of making a fall foliage tour."

I did the mental math in record time. "Which means they're coming here," I deduced.

"Ahh-huh. She's going to call with the details during the week."

"She's going to stay with you—with us?"

"Ahh-huh."

I allowed myself a moment to let the news sink in, to really see how I felt about the upcoming visit. "That will be nice," I said, nodding. "It will be good to have a visit with them."

"Good," Grandy said. "I'm glad you feel that way. We'll put them up in your room. You can sleep in the spare."

My brows crept up my forehead. "Great. Sure. Yeah." The spare room. The one with the narrow single bed and faint outlines of unicorns on the walls. The room I was relegated to during childhood stays. "I can hardly wait to be twelve again."

I told Carrie the news of my mother's impending visit while I helped her close up the shop. I exaggerated a little here and there, hoping to encourage laughter to break through her tension, but she remained as nervous as a first-time actress on opening night. The prospect of meeting her ex-husband had her distracted and clumsy.

"I've only seen him once since we signed the papers." She tugged a plastic cover over the cash register. "And that was only to close down the joint checking that funded the auto-pay for the Newbridge property."

I swirled a feather duster across the edges of an old armoire. "It will be fine," I said.

"Promise?"

"Promise."

When she could no longer put off leaving, she locked the front door, then shut off the lights. We exited through the back storeroom door, where I ducked out while Carrie set the newly repaired alarm.

Without another word, we walked the parking strip behind the shops and passed through the alley leading to Center Street. Across the road and to the right, the business sign above Grace's luncheonette was flickering to life. We followed it like a beacon—well, I did anyway. Carrie moved like someone was pushing her from behind.

But at the door, she took one deep breath, then another. She straightened her spine and lifted her chin. "I'm going to be Trudy Villiers," she said. "I'm going to be cool and elegant and unaffected by petty things."

I refrained from pointing out that what's-his-name had rattled Trudy last time we saw her. Better to have Carrie following the strong example in her mind.

As ever, the bell overhead jingled when I pulled open the door. Carrie entered first, walking past the counter to the left and the spinning rack of postcards to the right to stand at the center of the dining room and peruse the booths.

The air smelled faintly of French fries and disinfectant—neither of which struck me as appealing. When Carrie started moving for a booth and I caught sight of Russ Stanford, still more of my appetite fled.

Though Russ was clearly three-quarters the size of his brother, he was undoubtedly Gabe Stanford's sibling. Dark hair, sharp blue eyes, and the kind of expansive posture I often saw in dine-in customers who thought they belonged to some higher echelon. Couple that with the knowledge that he had cheated on my best friend and my instant dislike was sealed.

He held a cell phone to his ear and waved Carrie closer with big, sweeping gestures.

I trailed along behind her, waited until she'd slid all the way into the booth before I took the seat next to her. Russ raised his brows at me, looked to Carrie with the question, all the while continuing his telephone conversation.

"Sweetheart, I understand. I promise I'll be there as soon as I wrap this up. I promise." He was one of those people who didn't know how to conduct a cell phone conversation quietly. "Absolutely, I'll bring home Chinese food. You want those little fried wontons?" He held up a finger to indicate he'd be right with us, and I turned to Carrie.

"Was he always this rude?" I asked.

"Maybe," Carrie said, softly. "I wouldn't know. I used to be the one on the other end of the line."

I sucked in a breath, nudged her gently with my elbow. "Trudy Villiers," I reminded her.

She nodded and sort of wriggled her way to a more upright pose.

"Okay. All right. Love you, too. Bye, honey. See you soon." Russ disconnected the call and tossed the cell phone onto the table. "Who are you?" he asked, squinting at me.

Before I could open my mouth, Carrie said, "This is my friend Georgia. I invited her to join us."

"What'd you do that for?"

I swear she sounded just like Trudy when she said, "I didn't want the evening to be completely unpleasant."

"Why would you . . . ? It's not going to be unpleasant, Car. We're past that, aren't we?"

Carrie's right eye twitched, and I couldn't tell if she was dubious or trying not to cry.

"Okay, kids," Grace began before she'd even reached us, "what can I get you?" She set three glasses of water on the table, then stood, hand on her hip. "I got open roast beef with a side of fries on special tonight."

"Just coffee for me," Russ said before Carrie or I could speak.

It was a little thing, a minor thing. Maybe I was still a little raw over having to wait for him to conclude a cell call. Maybe I'd been living too long with Grandy and his values were rubbing off on me. Maybe I'd always had my own ideas about what constituted a gentleman and Russ was simply reminding me of them. Regardless the reason, I couldn't stop the little sting of insult I felt at Russ giving his order first instead of politely deferring to the ladies at the table.

"A bowl of today's soup, please," Carrie said in the tone of a minor royal.

I ordered the same, and Grace held herself to one disbelieving look before walking away.

Russ leaned back, rested his arm atop the back of the booth. The woman in the booth behind him turned to glare before shifting to her left, out of range of his elbow. "You look good, Car," he said.

The compliment hung in the air a few seconds before Carrie responded. "Thank you," she said carefully.

A busboy strolled by, slid the cup of coffee onto the table with practiced ease.

"I guess this whole fire-and-murder thing isn't really bothering you, huh?" Russ tugged the cup closer to him.

Carrie huffed and shook her head. "You still have no idea how to say something nice without saying something worse."

"Fine. You're right. I'm sorry." He poured what I considered an excessive amount of sugar into his coffee. "Okay? I'm sorry." He stirred his coffee, the spoon clanging against the porcelain cup. "Look, I gotta get home, so let's make this quick," Russ said.

"You have to get home? You're the one that asked me to meet you," Carrie said. "And now you're in a rush?"

"Gimme a break, Carrie, huh? I had a long day."

"You?" Carrie asked.

Russ ignored the question. "I come home from what was supposed to be a relaxing vacation to find out my office has burned to the ground, my partner's been murdered, and the police think I had something to do with it. Then I spend the whole afternoon at the police station answering questions for some uptight detective before—"

"And my shop was broken into and half my stock destroyed," she put in.

"Before . . ." Russ paused, tipped his head in concession. "And your shop was broken into. I was sorry to hear that," he said. He had the shred of decency necessary to wait a polite amount of time before returning to his own agenda. "But at least your business is still standing."

"Oh come on, Russ." Carrie huffed and slumped a little, totally breaking character. "Don't turn this into a competition."

He held up a hand. "I'm just saying—"

"What did you tell the police?" I asked, reaching for my glass of water.

"What?"

"What did you tell the police?" I repeated. "What did they want to know?"

Russ's forehead furrowed, his brows crinkled and dimmed the blue of his eyes. "What business is it of yours?"

"It's just a curiosity question," I lied. "We've—Carrie and I—we've spent no small amount of time answering questions for the police. I wondered if they asked you the same questions they asked Carrie."

He cut his gaze to Carrie. "And what questions would those be?"

I spoke up quickly, forcing him to return his attention to me and keep it there. "How much the building was insured for, whether you owe anyone any money, whether you had any kind of damning evidence in your office that would be better off not found, that sort of thing."

As soon as the extensive fibbing left my lips, Russ's jaw dropped. He swiveled his head toward me, the motion exaggerated, and he lowered his arm from the back of the bench. "Are you . . . are you insane? No, I don't owe anyone any money and no I'm not defending any kind of underworld criminal." Innocence seemed writ large in his wide eyes and easy breathing. If I was still harboring any suspicions about Russ Stanford burning down his own business, they would have faded to nonexistent. "What kind of a friend are you?" he asked.

"The best kind," Carrie said. "She's just looking out

for me, Russ. The police have been asking me those questions about you for days, questions about your work and why I didn't sell my half to you and who we knew in our past that might want to ruin us." She took hold of a glass of water and downed a few gulps. "It hasn't been easy."

He let out a long sigh. "Okay, okay, maybe you're right. I'm sorry, okay? It's . . . this is all still a . . . I'm still adjusting to all of this. It's not easy coming home and getting hit with all this either, you know."

"I know," Carrie said softly.

"And we still got the insurance thing to do and then figure out . . . how am I going to work? What . . . my whole business." He snapped his fingers. "Poof."

Beside me in my seat, my purse vibrated a split second before the factory-preset electronic ringtone of my cell phone blared from its depths. "I'm so sorry," I muttered, without any degree of conviction. I was mostly thankful for the interruption, for the brief respite from Russ's blather. "I'm sure it's no one."

It had to be no one. Factory preset meant I didn't have the incoming phone number stored in my contacts. No doubt another wrong number for "Shorty."

I lifted the phone free and read the display: Stone Mtn. Const.

Tony Himmel.

I glanced at Russ, glanced at Carrie.

I couldn't leave her; I was her moral support. But I didn't want to have to ignore the call. And it would be rude to take the call at the table.

I glanced at Russ again, and raised the phone to my ear,

pressing to connect the call as I did so. "Hi there," I said with a smile.

Tony's voice reached deep inside me, hot cocoa on a cold day. "Hi yourself. How are you?"

"Pretty good now that I'm hearing from you." I said it (a) because I meant it and (b) because I thought Russ deserved a little of the same treatment he'd given us. Except I suspect I couldn't keep from my voice the little thrill I felt at receiving Tony's call.

As proof, Carrie turned to me and mouthed, "Who is it?"

I shifted the speaker away from my mouth. "Tony Himmel."

Evidently I didn't move the speaker far enough. Even as Carrie shooed me out of the booth, with a "Go talk to him," Tony asked, "Am I interrupting something?"

I asked him to give me a minute, covered the phone. "Are you sure?" I mouthed to Carrie.

"Go," she said.

I gave Russ a fake smile and did my own Trudy Villiers impersonation. "Excuse me won't you? I'll just take this outside."

Sliding free of the booth, I ducked around Grace as she made her way past with a plate of spaghetti and meatballs and hustled out of the luncheonette.

"I'm back. Sorry about that," I said when I'd reached the outdoors.

"Is this a bad time?" he asked. "I know you said to call later in the week but—"

"It's fine. It's a fine time."

"I can call back."

"No, no, don't," I blurted. "What I mean is, now's fine. I'm at the luncheonette. I just came outside so I could hear better. What's up?"

He pulled in an audible breath. "Uh, here's the thing," he began.

That fast, such a simple phrase, and the thrill drained away. My shoulders sagged and I let my head drop forward. "What?"

"Thing is, truthfully . . ." He paused, I leaned against the building behind me for support. "I'm really not that big on coffee. It's crazy, I know. I'm in construction. I should have very strong feelings about coffee, positive feelings. But that's just not me."

"And so . . . ?" What did this mean? He'd decided he didn't want to see me again? And he was using coffee as an excuse?

"And so I was hoping you might reconsider dinner," he said.

My eyes slid closed and I shook my head. Stupid telephones. So much easier to stand face to face with someone, read their expression, evaluate their body language. Over the phone I had no way of knowing if Tony was being earnest about the coffee, or cute. I sighed. "I don't believe this," I said.

"Is that a no?"

"You couldn't have started with that? You had to do a whole bit about coffee?"

"I wanted to be honest," he said. "And if you could accept my honesty about that, you might accept my honesty when I tell you I didn't want to wait until some vague day in the future to call you and then wait for another vague day to see you. I feel like I've lost enough time with you. I don't want to wait."

I kept my eyes closed, let the smile spread across my face. He was good. He was very good. "So what is it that you're honestly saying?"

"I'm honestly saying let's have dinner. Me, you, Cappy's Seafood, tomorrow."

"Tomorrow?" My voice might have cracked a little.

"Yeah, I know, it's short notice. But tomorrow's Sunday and Sunday's pretty much all I have for now. I'm at the marina site every other day. So what do you say? Take a chance on a short-notice, honest guy?"

There was no stopping my humiliating giggle. "Can I order crab legs?"

"You can order whatever you want."

"Okay. Tomorrow. Cappy's. You're on."

I gave him the address at Grandy's house and we said our good-byes and the smile was still stuck on my face.

Yes, the timing was terrible. I was frightened for Carrie, worried about what was going to happen next, sad to be facing another wake and funeral for a Wenwood resident. But really, who was I kidding? No timing was ever ideal. And maybe, very likely, taking a chance on a little happiness was just what was needed.

Sucking in a deep, cleansing breath, I looked up and down Center Street, at the little village of Wenwood and nodded to myself. Happy was just what the doctor ordered. Not that Tony was any sort of guarantee, but it would be nice to find out.

I headed back into the luncheonette planning to rejoin Carrie and Russ. But before I'd even drawn level with the counter, Russ was moving fast toward me. Worry instantly gripped me. "What happened?" I asked.

"Nothing," he said. "I told you I had to leave."

He shook his head like he couldn't understand how I would forget such a thing, then pushed past me and out the door.

Dumbfounded, I walked to where Carrie stood, arms folded at the end of the table.

I tried the same question on Carrie. "What happened?"

"I asked Grace to bring to-go containers for the soups," she said. "This was . . . Russ left and I just . . . I just want to go home and get into bed and forget this week ever happened. Is that okay?"

I wrapped my arm around her shoulders. "Yeah, it's okay. You deserve the break. You've been through a lot."

With the hot soups stored in paper containers, one bagged for me and one for Carrie, we retraced our earlier steps, back through the alley and into the parking strip behind the shops. Not a word passed between us as we got into the car. Not a word passed as Carrie drove me back to Grandy's.

I broke the silence only when I stepped out of the car. Leaning back in I said, "I'll call you tomorrow, okay?"

She gave me a half smile. "You know where to find me."

I slammed the door closed and made my way up the brick walk and into the house. All the while, I tried to keep from my mind a sudden, troubling thought.

Who else knew where to find Carrie? And would they go looking?

18

The soup lost none of its blistering temperature in the short ride home from the luncheonette. I poured it into an oversized cappuccino mug, and the sound of the splashing drew Friday from whatever furniture she'd been napping under . . . or on top of. I dished some of her canned food into her little kitty bowl and set it down on the floor in front of the sink.

"Live it up, kitty. Celebrate. It's Saturday night." I made stupid six-shooter motions with my hands. Friday twitched one ear and nibbled daintily from the bowl. She was unimpressed. I didn't blame her. Saturday night and what was on my agenda? An evening of stained glass. Just me and the kitten.

After switching on the radio I kept in the corner, I opened the packaging on the glass I'd purchased that morning. The pinks I wanted for Trudy's window, once located, I stored on end in an old apple crate I kept for such purpose. Left with the glass I had selected for antiques store projects, I looked from a white, gold, and blue mottled glass I'd bought more for its possibilities than for a plan to the glass I had cut for the sailboat panel.

When I began the piece, I had done so because the pattern caught my eye. I thought working on the project would be a good way to stir my creativity so I could design a window for Trudy. In the back of my mind I saw the piece one day hanging from one of Grandy's windows—a just-for-fun piece turned into something decorative. Now I supposed it would do more good hanging in Carrie's shop.

The temptation to start work on a new pattern, to begin cutting the glass I'd bought on impulse, coursed through me with the same allure as "just one more cookie" or "just one more pair of shoes." The desire was both hard and easy to overcome. All it took was a deep breath, closed eyes, and the firm action of closing the paper wrapping over the exciting new glass and setting it aside. Best not to jump into anything, anyway.

I gathered up a small handful of already cut glass, aqua and vermillion and gold-flecked white strips that curved like waves on the water, and carried them into the garage.

Grandy had built a tool bench at the back of the garage, against the common wall between the garage and the workshop. With his permission, I'd cleared a space at the near end of the bench, closest to the doorway that led to the workshop, and there set up my glass grinder. Now, after making sure the water reservoir was full, I nudged the foot pedal out from under the bench with my toe and powered on the grinder.

At the center of the hard plastic grating, a diamond-head grinder bit spun at a respectable three thousand rpm as soon as I applied pressure to the foot pedal. I grabbed the first blue glass wave, set it flat on the horizontal grating, and pushed the edge of the glass against the whirring bit.

Water sluiced across the surface of the glass, gently washing away the miniscule shards being dislodged by the grinder, splashing them against the square of plexiglass I'd leaned against the wall to protect the pegboard.

Splashing.

I lifted my foot from the pedal and huffed. Safety goggles. Why did I never remember to put on the safety goggles first?

Taking a step to the right, I searched the tool-covered pegboard for the safety goggles I typically hung there. Not finding them, I sifted through the bits of miscellanea that had collected atop the workbench, but still had no luck. I really wouldn't leave the workshop or garage with—

I rolled my eyes at my own forgetfulness. I had worn the goggles outside when I was doing some yard work. Not because I thought using a manual hedge shear was particularly dangerous, but because not wearing the goggles would be a foolish move. Also because Grandy insisted.

The question was, where had I left them?

I turned a circle in the garage, scanning the neatly stored collections of seasonal implements—an assortment of rakes and cases of heavy-duty trash bags for autumn, ice melt and three kinds of shovels for winter, and hedge clippers, half a bag of mulch, a spade and hoe for spring and summer. My goggles weren't anywhere.

Thinking perhaps I had left them in the kitchen when a hot morning's yard work required a cold glass of water, I went back into the workshop and up the stairs to the main floor of the house. I might have left the goggles on the counter or hung them from the back of a chair. But when they were nowhere to be spotted, I ducked into the dining room to check the sideboard and groaned.

Despite my best efforts, the sideboard continued to be the place where Grandy piled all the things for which he didn't have a ready place. Months of AARP magazines, packages of opened batteries, and pages of half-finished crossword puzzles typically crowded the surface. And there, leaning atop an old scrapbook and against a ball of twine, were my goggles.

As I reached to grab them, I realized what I had thought was a scrapbook was instead an old photo album.

Moving the twine to the pile of magazines, I opened the cracked leather cover of the album and peeled back the heavy tissue paper page to admire the first set of photos.

Six people gathered around a picnic table, four men, two women. One of the women wore a floppy hat, obscuring her face. The other looked boldly into the camera, smile wide, head wrapped in a cloud of red hair. Grandma Keene.

I lifted the album and turned to the dining room table, intending to take a seat and peruse the album slowly. As I spun, the photos on the first page sailed off, some sliding to the floor, others dropping to the table. I retrieved the trio from the floor, photo corners still clinging to the snap-shots.

"Huh. Adhesive dried," I muttered, flipping over the first picture. Scrawled across the back in faded blue ink were the words *July 4 at Barbara's*. I looked at the front again. Barbara must be the woman under the hat. Or maybe she was the one who took the picture?

The phone rang, putting an end to my brief wonder-ings. Hugging the photo album to my chest, I cut through the kitchen and grabbed the handset from its dock. As I brought the cordless phone to my ear, I caught a glimpse of "Unavailable" on the caller ID display.

Dreading the possibility that someone on the other end of the phone was going to try to sell me an upgrade to Grandy's cable television plan, I phrased my "hello" as if I'd just been dragged from my deathbed.

"Damn. Did I dial the wrong number? Son of a—"

"Diana?" I asked, voice back to normal.

"Georgia, you sounded like you were dying," Diana said. "Don't scare me like that."

My forehead rumpled as new confusion overcame me. "Why are you calling my house phone? Are you looking for Grandy?"

"I'm looking for you. Carrie's apartment was tossed while she was at dinner."

I felt the blood drain from my face, rush to my heart, chilling me with fear. "Oh my God. Where's Carrie? Is she okay?"

"She's fine. She's home. I'm on my way there. You need a pickup?"

Carrie's apartment. What next?

I dropped the photo album on the table. "I'll be waiting out front."

This time I didn't feel a moment's surprise to find Detective Nolan on the scene. I would have been shocked if he wasn't there.

He prowled around Carrie's apartment, looking oddly too large for the antique furnishings, as if he alone could take up the entire span of the love seat. He'd never struck me as a big man before, though, and I registered the thought that perhaps it was his confidence that made him seem large, his self-possession.

"Evening, Detective," I said.

He gave me a tight smile, then crooked a finger at Diana. "Davis," he said. "Can I have a word with you?"

As she moved toward Detective Nolan, I turned to the little dining room, where Carrie sat at the cluttered table. Seated in one of the mismatched chairs, she leaned forward on her elbows and spoke softly to a uniformed officer seated at the head of the table. The officer was filling out a form affixed to a clipboard. Incident report, my late-night television brain informed me.

I shuffled in beside Carrie, careful to step over a heap of paperback novels scattered on the floor. I laid a hand on her shoulder and gave her a quick hug. "How are you doing?" I asked.

The words felt foolish on my lips. Just looking around the wreck of her home was enough to make an educated guess at how she was feeling. But to not ask seemed somehow insensitive.

She turned bright eyes on me. "Angry," she said. "I'm feeling angry. It wasn't enough he broke into my store, but to break into my house, too?" She shook her head as a bit of the fight seemed to leave her. "And then I think of Herb and . . . thank God, you know?"

"I know," I murmured. I didn't want to dwell too long on what might have happened had Carrie been home when the intruder arrived. It was enough I was aware; dwelling would cripple me.

The officer looked up from his clipboard. "You're saying *he*. Do you have some idea who might have done this?"

Carrie sighed, looked back to the cop. "He. She. They. I don't know."

Nodding, the officer asked, "Anything else missing?"

"I wrote it down," she said, pushing a piece of paper in his direction. "The rest is just . . ." Carrie lifted her head and gazed around the apartment.

I did the same, taking in the scattered books and emptied knitting basket, balls of yarn unraveled across the carpet as though they'd been used for peewee soccer practice.

Pinning Carrie's list behind the incident report, he clicked his pen closed and stood. "Call the precinct tomorrow. They'll be able to give you a report number for your insurance. You'll have to—"

"I know," Carrie said, making no move to rise. "I have to file a claim."

Slipping his cap back on his head, the officer tucked the clipboard under his arm and gave a nod of finality.

"I'm sorry for your trouble, ma'am." Then he eased away from the table and headed for the door.

As Carrie met my gaze, the rumble of men's voices reverberated along the entrance hall. Diana strode into the living room, came to a hard stop as she took in the obstacle course the apartment had become.

"Don't worry about it," Carrie said with a wave. "At this point it doesn't matter what you step on."

"No, I won't step on anything. It's not that bad." Diana picked her way across the debris on the floor to the opposite side of the table and leaned her hands against the back of a chair. "Officer Beaumont is going to do some canvassing, see if any of your neighbors heard or saw anything."

"Someone must have." I infused my voice with as much certainty as I could fake. "No one could make this much of a mess without making noise enough to draw attention. Right?"

My statement was met with silence.

"Fine," I said, standing. "Let's at least get this place cleaned up."

"Leave it," Carrie snapped.

Diana met my gaze across the table, wordlessly agreeing that this behavior was out of character for the usually chipper Carrie.

"Carrie, sweetie," I began, bending down to bring my head more level with hers. "How about I make you a cup of tea? Some chamomile or Soothe Me?"

"Or a hot toddy?" Diana put in.

"I don't need tea," Carrie said, biting off one word at

a time. "Or whiskey. I just need this nightmare to end. My property, my shop, my apartment. What's next?"

I didn't want to think about what was next, didn't want to recall the scene outside Herb Gallo's house. For all the hardship Carrie had suffered, she's also been lucky. So far. I had to hold on to that.

I put a hand on her shoulder. "Okay, this is what we're going to do." I locked gazes with Diana, silently asking her to back me up. "Diana and I are going to pick up a little bit—"

"I said don't—"

I kept talking, speaking louder to drown out her protests. "And while we're doing that, you're going to pack a bag with whatever you think you'll need for the next few days. You are not staying here. You're going to come stay with me and Grandy."

I expected a protest. I expected her to insist she wouldn't be frightened out of her home. But Carrie raised her head and looked at the wreckage surrounding her. As she stood from her chair, I stepped back out of her way.

"Okay," she said. "Okay."

Relief relaxed my shoulders, and I noted Diana's posture softening also. We both watched as Carrie walked over strewn papers, kicked a remote control out of her path as she made her way out of the dining room and through the short hallway to her bedroom.

"It's a good idea," Diana said, "having her stay with you."

Bending to lift a tumbled bookend from the floor, I shook my head. "I just couldn't imagine her staying here by herself. At least not tonight, not until we can get this cleaned up, get new locks installed, all that."

Diana crouched and scooped together a half-dozen matched coasters. "Smart," she said. "Whatever this guy is looking for, there's no way to tell if he found it, if he'll be back."

"That's what worries me."

We worked in silence for a little while longer, gathering papers into neat stacks, blotting moisture from the floor where a vase of flowers had fallen. Neither one of us was inclined to attempt to rewind all the yarn. Instead we lifted the strands as neatly as we could and laid the tangle of color in the basket from which they'd come.

A tap on the door made both of us jump. My heart pounded and fear clogged my throat in the split second before I recalled burglars didn't knock.

Detective Nolan ambled back into the living room, one hand tucked in the front pocket of his jeans.

"I thought you left," I said.

He shook his head, turned to Diana. "Where's Carrie?"

"Getting a bag together. She's going to stay with Georgia for a couple days."

Looking back to me, he tipped his head in the direction of the door. "Let's take a walk."

"Who? Me?" I squeaked.

"You. Georgia Kelly. Let's walk."

I glanced at Diana, who said, "I'm here. Go ahead."

I grabbed one more stray magazine off the floor and set it on an end table. Detective Nolan waited to be sure I was coming then turned and led the way out of the apartment. He stayed a couple of paces ahead of me down the hallway to the top of the stairway.

"You know," I began, finally catching up to him. "When someone suggests taking a walk, they usually intend to walk *with* the other person, not race ahead. What's the rush, Detective?"

He sighed. "Christopher."

"What?"

"My name is Christopher." He walked down the stairs, and this time it was my hesitation that made me have to rush to catch him.

"I thought your name was Chip," I said from a step behind him. "That's what Drew Able says."

Detective Nolan—Christopher—reached the landing and paused. "I was Chip in grade school. And middle school. And people that knew me then are having a tough time letting me grow out of it." He leaned toward me, bringing his face closer to mine. "But I promise you, I'm all grown up now. And you can call me Chris."

All the wayward thoughts I'd had about the man returned in one knee-rattling rush. Eyes shrewd and warm, enough salt in his hair to wipe away youthful foolishness, smile all the more delightful because of its rarity.

I had to close my eyes and take a deep breath as I shook those thoughts away . . . again. "Um. Okay. Chris. Where are we going?"

He jogged down the remaining half flight of stairs and this time I decided he could just wait until I caught up. No way was I going to run.

Plus, it gave me a few more moments to gather my wits

and remember Tony's call, remember his laugh, remember we had plans. A little shiver of happy anticipation danced across my skin. Tony. I was going to a non-platonic dinner with Tony. At last.

At the bottom of the stairs, the detective held open the glass and steel door leading onto the steps of the apartment building. I passed through with a muttered thanks, dimly aware that the air-conditioned indoor temperature was a few degrees warmer than the outdoor air.

"So what's on your mind, Chris?" I skipped down the trio of steps and kept walking once I hit the sidewalk. Two could play the chase-me game.

He fell into step beside me. Once again he slipped his hands into his pockets. "I wanted to get your take on all of this."

I opted against pretending cluelessness. "Mine? What good is my opinion? You're the professional here. And come to think of it, why are you here? Aren't there other detectives? Don't you ever have a night off?"

And there was one of his rare smiles. Wow, that was hard to resist. You know, for some people.

"Pace County currently has three detectives. We really could use one more, but no one's hitting exhaustion while we're short staffed."

"Yeah, but—"

"But yes, I do have the occasional nights off. Yes, tonight was one of them. But at this point, the desk gets a call from anyone connected to Russ or Carrie Stanford, I'm the one they contact."

"Okay. So it's your case is what you're saying? And

you really have connected the dots and admit these crimes aren't random?"

He let out a heavy sigh. "I connected those dots a long time ago, Georgia."

We walked without speaking for ten feet or so, long enough for the subtle sounds of the neighborhood—a loud radio somewhere out of sight, the splash and shrieks of kids in a pool—to make an impression on me, and for one and only one car to zip past on the street.

"So then what do you need from me?" I asked. "What's the point of this stroll?"

"You know Carrie better than I do," he said. "Naturally."

"Naturally," I echoed.

"And she'll tell you things she wouldn't necessarily tell me."

"You mean you, Chris? Or you, the Pace County detective?"

He gave me a tight smile. "Both. Either."

I stomped on a weed growing boldly in the crack of the sidewalk. "What makes you think I'd tell you anything she'd rather keep private?"

"I wouldn't ask you to do that," he said. "What I am asking is your impression. She's insistent that Russ Stanford is her ex, but she still co-owns property with him, she still uses his last name, and she had dinner with him tonight."

"So?"

"So are there any lingering feelings there?"

My forehead scrunched as I tried to sort through the logic. "What difference does that make?"

"Emotions are a difficult variable to pin down. If she still has feelings for him, she may be withholding information, suspicions . . ."

"You mean like if Russ was actually the guilty party here and Carrie was still in love with him, then she'd keep certain details to herself to protect him."

He nodded. "Exactly that."

"Or do you mean," I started, and almost couldn't believe I was going to ask, couldn't believe I was suddenly worried about the answer, "that if Carrie is still in love with Russ, there's no point in you asking her out?"

Detective Nolan came to an abrupt stop. He pulled his hands from his pockets and set them on his waist. "Honestly?"

"Yes, honestly," I said.

He shook his head. "No. I mean honestly, that's what you're getting out of this? I thought you had sharper skills of observation."

I stood still, managed to do nothing other than blink rapidly. I knew the ground beneath my feet was solid, flat, and steady, yet I somehow felt I had lost all balance. "I'm . . . really confused."

Huffing, he looked away from me, up the street where no traffic passed. "I have no interest in Carrie Stanford that isn't professional. And may I repeat, I thought you had sharper skills of observation."

Shuffling backward a little, putting enough space between us that I could see his face and his posture and potentially read both, I nonetheless remained confused. It was my turn to huff. "Look, you know what? It's been a long day. And the first person in this town that I could call a friend is packing her bags in a crime scene. So please, can you just ask direct questions and not play this police interrogation game where you try and trick me into giving up information I'd rather keep secret?"

His smile started slowly, but grew into a grin that seemed to dislodge the weight of law enforcement from his shoulders. "All right, then. Do you think Carrie is protecting Russ?"

"No. Next question."

"Do you believe Russ's brother Gabe may have set fire to his office to destroy the prenuptial agreement between Russ and his new fiancée?"

I drew a breath through my teeth. "Not sure. He has motive, he has access to accelerants, and he's a serious jerk. But he would have no reason to break into Carrie's shop or her home. So I have to go with no."

His brows rose and he nodded appreciatively. "What about the fiancée? Could she be trying to scare Carrie away, make sure she has no place in Russ's life going forward?"

I tipped my head. "Could be. Can I interrogate the fiancée?"

"No."

"Then no comment. Next question."

"Will you have dinner with me on Wednesday?"

Prepared to shoot back a quick yes or no to a question about Carrie or Russ, I opened and closed my mouth like a goldfish navigating sparkling water. The only word that threatened to fall from my tongue was *Tony*.

"Okay." He nodded. "That's a no. Fair enough. You were right about asking direct questions. Much faster."

"Oh, no, wait." I had to explain. I couldn't let him think I had no interest at all, right? Because there was interest. And because what if me and Tony didn't really click after all?

Detective Christopher Nolan held up a hand to stop me. "One more question. Do you have any theories on what our perpetrator is looking for among Carrie's things?"

"No," I said. "But can we get back to—"

Again, the hand came up. With his other hand, he reached to his belt and pulled a cell phone from its case. And in that one move, he put the cloak of law enforcement over his shoulders once more. "Thanks," he said. "That's all I have. You can go back upstairs now." He turned his back on me, phone to his ear, and started walking. "Nolan."

I took one step, ready to hurry after him.

"Yeah, Steve, what do you have?" His voice faded as he moved away, and I stood still, incapable of taking another step. Unbidden, Grandy's voice rumbled through the back of my mind. *Don't chase after boys, Georgia,* the voice advised. *If he's really interested, he'll be back.*

Frustrated and disappointed in myself, I scanned the sidewalk cracks for more weeds. Reaching down, I grabbed a handful of dandelion leaves and wrenched them out of the earth. With a grunt of aggravation, I threw the weeds at the street. But they were weeds, leaves heavy with moisture from humidity and rain. Rather than sail toward the street and land where a passing car would crush them beneath unforgiving wheels, the weeds dropped directly to the ground in a stunning display of the effects of gravity.

"Perfect," I muttered. "Just perfect." I sighed and headed back toward Carrie's apartment building.

"Well," I told myself. "At least I will always have my cat to keep me company on a Saturday night."

And then I swallowed down the lump of self-pity in my throat and went back inside.

19

Diana offered to stay behind at the apartment and wait for the twenty-four-hour locksmith to arrive. Of course, Carrie argued, feeling more herself and unwilling to impose on anyone. But Diana and her badge insisted. She promised to meet us there in the morning with the new key and help in the cleanup and inventory of Carrie's belongings.

Carrie clutched her weekend bag in two hands as we made our way down the stairs and out to the parking lot located adjacent to the building.

"Give me your car keys." I held out my hand, waited while Carrie gaped at my palm. "Please," I added.

With jerky motions, Carrie shifted the weekender to one hand and tugged her purse off her shoulder. "My keys," she said. "To my car."

I took the weekend bag from her, freeing her hands to dig through her purse. Circling around the back of the car, I said, "Pop the trunk when you find them." Then I waited while Carrie, who swore she was calm and capable of driving her own car, found the keys in her bag and dropped them three times before pushing the button to unlock the vehicle.

The trunk lid lifted on its hinges enough for me to get my hand under and pull up. Inside, Carrie had a set of jumper cables coiled at the bottom of a milk crate, a snow scraper, a half-full container of windshield wiper fluid, a cardboard carton, and a plastic grocery bag stuffed with papers.

Cardboard cartons and plastic bags should not look familiar. But the bag was yellow, and the carton had a U-Move-It diamond logo emblazoned on its side.

I relocated the grocery bag to the milk crate and dropped the weekender into the trunk. When I returned to the front of the car, Carrie had settled herself in the passenger seat, belt and all.

Climbing into the driver's seat, I learned that though Carrie and I were of similar height, our driving styles differed. I reached beneath the seat to find the lever to slide the chair back. "Why is that carton in your car?"

The frisson of renewed energy that passed through Carrie was nearly visible. When she turned to me, her eyes were clear and color had returned to her cheeks. "Ugh. I was going to give them to Russ but after all his pathetic begging it went right out of my head," she ground out.

"Ohhhh," I said. "Is this the part I missed while I was on the phone?" I threw the car into gear and guided the vehicle out of the parking lot and onto the quiet road. "Start at the beginning. What did he say after I went outside?"

"I thought we would be discussing the property and working out when we could go together to the insurance company and take care of whatever paperwork we needed to handle, maybe work out whether to rebuild or sell or whatever."

"And that's not what happened?"

"No, I started to ask him what day would be good for him but then our food came"—she glanced to me—"and then he apologizes for not being able to eat with us and decides to explain why, saying he has to get back because, 'oh, you probably heard me promising to bring Chinese food' and 'I should probably tell you I'm involved with this girl.' He starts in trying to *break it to me gently* that he's going to go ahead and propose to his girlfriend."

"Would that be Brittany who likes fried wontons?"

"That would be Brittany. But he's telling me about her, praising her to high heaven and watching me like he's waiting for me to fall to my knees crying." Carrie's laugh had bitter undertones. "As if I'm going to have some sort of breakdown because he's off the market *after* I've divorced him."

I sighed and shook my head, happy to commiserate on the oddities of men if it kept Carrie's mind off the break-ins. "Incredible," I offered.

"Oh, you haven't heard the best part," she said.

"Which is?"

"Do you know why he wanted to talk to me face-to-face?"

I obliged by shaking my head and asking why.

"It wasn't to talk about the fire or Herb or make plans to talk to the insurance company. No. He just figured with everything going on I was bound to hear that he planned on getting married again. He wanted to ask me not to contact Brittany and tell her any stories that make him look bad."

"What?" I nearly shrieked. "Are you serious? Why would he think you would do that? Why would he think you even know who Brittany is or how to contact her?"

"That's what I asked him," Carrie said. "I don't know where he got the idea that I would even want to know the girl's name much less seek her out and warn her against Russ. Although"—she shifted in her seat, moving the seat belt farther out against her shoulder—"now that he's brought it up, I am beginning to feel like it's the least I could do for her."

"Out of the goodness of your heart?" I grinned and turned onto the boulevard leading from Carrie's end of Wenwood to mine.

She turned to face me. "It's that old question. Would you want to know in advance if the guy you're thinking of marrying is a jackass? Would it matter? Or would you rather take that leap of faith?"

The tires *shoosh*ed against the pavement, the only sound that remained in the car after the internal echo of Carrie's question faded. Because I had to give that question hard thought. By some accounts—my own included— I'd been lucky to split with Eric before the walk down the aisle made it a legal issue. In that respect, I had known before the "I do" what I might have gotten into. But if someone had told me the hue of Eric's true colors before I saw them myself . . . well, I don't know if I'd have believed what I was being told. Worse, I might have thought things would be different with *me*.

A signal light switched from yellow to red, breaking me free of the cobwebs of my thoughts. Applying the brake, I brought the car to a nice, smooth stop.

"Well?" Carrie asked. "Which would you rather?"

"I'm probably not the right person to ask." I shook my head. "I'm afraid I might fall into the leap of faith category. Or I used to, anyway. Might be different now, I suppose."

She folded her arms brusquely. "I'd want to know," she said.

When the traffic light turned green, I started off again, watching for the turn I needed to take to get to Grandy's. "So are you saying you've decided to track down Brittany and tell her that Russ is a philandering donkey?"

"Jackass. And I wouldn't have to work hard to track her down. The police have already spoken to her. I could probably get Detective Nolan to give me her last name at least and after that she's just an internet search away."

"Speaking of Detective Nolan," I began. Once the words were out of my mouth, though, I wasn't sure what I wanted to say. I felt the swift sensation of wanting to keep my confusion to myself for a while, at least until I had time to sort out any deeper feelings lurking beneath that confusion.

"Speaking of Detective Nolan?" Carrie prompted.

I flicked on the turn indicator, thought fast. "Speaking

of the detective, did Russ tell you anything about what the police asked him? You know, while I was out?"

She held up a hand. "Please. All that man could talk about was—" She stopped herself and took a deep breath. "I'm not being fair," she said on a sigh. "Here I am about to say all he could talk about was Brittany and the work he's going to have to do to reopen the office—even in a temporary space. But I would probably do the same. I probably have done the same."

Making the final turn onto Grandy's street, I switched the headlights to high beams. The wide bright light illuminated not only a squirrel scampering across the road but the tree trunks and low-hanging branches on either side of the street, and managed to make the grass look as if the blades were glowing.

"Wait, so he went on about Brittany and about how much he has to do to set up shop again? What about what happened to Herb Gallo? Didn't he have anything to say about that?" I asked.

Carrie nodded. "He did mention that his workload would double since he has to take over Herb's clients, too."

"Seriously, I think I'll never understand men," I said, bringing the car to stop at the curb. I cut the lights and the engine and looked over at the house. Grandy had left a light on for me in the living room. Friday, backlit in the window, came to her feet and stretched like a miniature Halloween cat.

"Oh. I forgot about the creature," Carrie said in a small voice.

"Not a creature," I said. "Small cat."

She sighed and pushed open her door. Releasing the seat belt and stepping out of the car she said, "I'm much more of a dog person, but I can't have one in my apartment. If I had a dog, I bet no one would have broken in."

I walked to the back of the car to take Carrie's weekend bag from the trunk, but she beat me to it. "I think that would depend on what kind of dog you had. Not sure a Chihuahua would keep away a criminal."

Both hands on the handles of the bag, Carrie turned for the house. "I always thought a German shepherd would be nice."

"You wouldn't want a dog like Fifi? All slobber and noise?" I teased.

"Only if I could also have a German shepherd."

With the keys to Carrie's car tight in one hand, I dug in my purse with the other. Somewhere in its depths I had house keys.

Carrie let out a noisy yawn as I unlocked the house and waved her inside. "Sorry," she said. "Day's catching up to me."

I gave her what I hoped was a sympathetic smile. "Don't worry about it," I said.

She declined that soothing cup of tea after all, and I settled her in the spare bedroom with clean sheets, extra pillows, and a half a dozen cartons containing various remnants of my former life.

"Hey, I never asked you," she said, sinking to the bed. She tugged the pillow from under the spread and hugged it tight. "What did Tony Himmel want?"

Probably any other day I would have added happy energy

to my response. Things being what they were, I kept it low-key. "He asked me to dinner tomorrow. I accepted."

She waited a moment, I guessed for me to say something more, but I shrugged.

"That's it?" she asked.

"That's it. Just dinner."

"Where is he taking you?"

"Cappy's."

She nodded abstractly. "They have the best crab legs there."

Wishing her a good night, I headed back downstairs. I grabbed my purse from the old wingback chair on which I'd dropped it and continued on into the workspace.

Perhaps I should have been tired. Maybe physically I was. But my mind was racing at top speed. Crawling into bed at that point would result in more tossing and turning than sleeping and dreaming. Plus Friday tended to be intolerant of my tossing and turning.

I flipped on the overhead light and the gooseneck lamp clamped to the end of my worktable. Before I stuffed my purse into an empty spot on the little bookshelf, I pulled out my cell phone and called the dine-in.

After I told Grandy that Carrie's apartment had been broken into, I waited what I thought was a reasonable amount of time while he went off about how things like this had never happened back when the brickworks was still in business. I thought he would eventually wrap up his diatribe and I could let him know I'd put Carrie in the spare bedroom. But he knocked that plan askew when he said, "This is why I told you to let the police handle things,

Georgia," he said. "Nothing good would come of you sticking your nose where it doesn't belong."

I wanted to inform him that Detective Nolan—Christopher; no, best to think of him as Detective Nolan—said I had good observational skills, but instead I went with, "If it wasn't for me sticking my nose in, you might still be in jail."

"And you were damn lucky you didn't get hurt. Or worse," he grumbled. "And this situation will get worse before it gets better, mark my words. After what happened to poor Herb Gallo"—his sigh echoed hollow on the phone—"Carrie's lucky she wasn't home at the time."

But was she lucky she wasn't home? Or did the thief/burglar/perpetrator know she wouldn't be there? Whoever was behind the sudden crime wave clearly knew both Russ and Carrie. It wasn't out of the realm of possibility that either one of them had unknowingly told the criminal that they would be out to dinner.

"Well, she's here now," I said. "I didn't want her to be alone, jumping at every gust of wind. She's in the spare bedroom."

"With all those boxes? That may be braver than staying on her own."

"Ha-ha very funny." I pointed out that Carrie would have to be up and out in the morning to open the shop, that I'd be going with her, and apologized in advance if either of us woke him.

It wasn't until after we'd said good-bye and I plugged the phone in to be charged that it occurred to me: Grandy never said Carrie was safer with us than at her apartment.

He simply forgot, right? He really did believe she was safer where the arsonist/thief/murderer couldn't find her, didn't he?

Unless the criminal had set up his own personal stakeout and waited for Carrie to leave her apartment. In which case he knew what kind of car Carrie drove . . .

And he could have been watching while we all arrived after Carrie discovered the break-in. Watching while the police went in and out, while Detective Nolan and I strolled the sidewalk, when Carrie and I left. Had someone followed us? I never even thought to watch my rearview. There had been cars behind us at various points, of course. After all, it was Saturday night. People still went out. But had I not noticed anyone following us because I hadn't seen anyone? Or because I had no real experience in detecting a tail?

I hurried up the stairs to the front door. Usually on Grandy's nights at the dine-in I left the door unlocked for him. I flicked the locking lever. Tonight he'd have to use his key. I closed and locked the living room windows next. Anyone could walk up onto the porch and punch out a screen. Carrie was right: A dog was a good idea.

The dining room and kitchen windows sat too high off the ground for anyone to crawl through. Those I left open, happy to have at least their small breeze.

Back down in the workshop, I pulled closed the door that led to the garage and locked that, closed and locked the windows and the door to the yard. Clasping my hands tightly before me, I looked around the room, reviewing.

Doors locked. Windows closed. Nothing else I could do, really. I considered calling Diana, asking her if she could put in a request at the station to have a police cruiser ride by a few times.

Upstairs, something crashed to the floor. I froze. Held my breath. I'd locked everything. Who could have—

Friday came tearing down the stairs as if her tail were on fire. Every hair on her little cat body stood straight on end, effectively making her look twice her size.

"Jeez, Friday," I said on a relieved exhale. "You scared the pants off of me."

She leaped onto the lowest shelf of the bookshelf, where an absence of books gave her the right-size space to hide in.

"Got room in there for me?" I asked.

With the windows closed the air in the workroom was well on its way to stuffy, but it was too early to retreat to my air-conditioned bedroom for the night. I suspected, in fact, that sleep was a long way off. I gathered up my Homasote board, the spool of foil to wrap the glass edges, and the fid to flatten the foil. With those and the jig—the temporary wood framing that held the pattern and the cut and buffed pieces in place—I returned to the main floor of the house, intending to set up shop at the dining room table.

Arriving in the dining room, I located the evidence of Friday's destruction. On her way across the sideboard to—or from—the window, or in search of some fresh vegetation, she had knocked over the vase in which I'd placed some cuttings of black-eyed Susans. The vase itself had rolled to the floor while the flowers had been scattered over the sideboard and water spread across the surface and down the front of the doors.

I muttered curses as I dashed to the kitchen for some paper towels to sop up the mess. The spreading water crept around the base of an old pewter basket of my grandmother's and under the stack of photo albums I had left there days before. Snatching up the albums, Grandy wiped dry the back cover of the bottom album and plunked the pile onto the dining table. I repeated the lift-and-dry method for the pewter basket then finally scooped up the tumbled blossoms and empty vase and carried them into the kitchen sink.

I followed the wiping up of water with some soft rags and furniture polish while marveling at Friday's wisdom in hiding from me.

After pouring myself a cold glass of water, I settled down at the head of the table and picked up my first piece of glass—a trapezoid-shaped piece of white muffle that, combined with two other like pieces, would compose one of the boat's sails.

Holding the glass in my left hand, I pulled free the edge of three-eighth-inch copper foil from its roll with the same action used to pull free a piece of cellophane tape. I pressed the adhesive side of the foil against the edge of the glass and slowly, carefully wrapped the entirety of the glass's edge with foil. Keeping the foil straight and its edges even on either side of the glass was a challenge— hence the slow and careful. Once I had the foil in place, and had snipped the piece free of the roll, I pinched the foil-wrapped edge of the glass between thumb and fore-finger and, working my way around, pressed the edges down onto the glass. At completion, the glass appeared as though it had a decorative copper outline.

I picked up the flat fid—a strip of stiff plastic that I often thought would be excellent for frosting miniature cupcakes—and used it to smooth out any bubbles or wrinkles in the foil as best I could. The more accurate I had been when applying the foil in the first place, the fewer the wrinkles.

One down, dozens to go.

I repeated the process piece by piece, working through both sails and the hull of the boat. The repetition of the deceptively simple task allowed me to keep my hands occupied while my mind wandered free. It wasn't long—and wasn't a great leap—before I went from looking at the image of the sailboat taking shape in my jig to thoughts of Tony Himmel and his long-held dream of building that marina.

What must it be like to have a plan you held in your hopes for so long finally take shape? How must he have felt at each challenge, each setback? Before I knew him I had thought him capable of going to any lengths im-aginable to overcome the obstacles and see his dream realized. Once I learned to know him better, I understood there were lines he would not cross in his quest.

But that was Tony. Plenty of other people were willing to cross even the deepest line in the sand to get what they wanted. People like the guy who had burned down Russ's law office, killed Herb Gallo, and broken into Carrie's shop and home. There was a reason behind those actions, a plan someone had that was being threatened, a dream that faced death. But who was that guy? What was that plan? And was he yet lurking in shadows preparing to cross another line?

20

I was still asking myself those questions the following day, as Sunday brought residents and travelers alike into the village of Wenwood. The line of patrons waiting to choose their treats at Rozelle's Bakery seemed inexhaustible despite the occasional light rain shower. Umbrellas were employed as needed and carried dripping into Aggie's Antiques as folks wandered in searching for the something rare, something eccentric, or something that brought their memories back to earlier days—their own or someone else's.

Carrie threw herself into her work at the store, wrapping herself in her shopkeeper persona as though wearing armor. She chatted with every customer who came through the door. She laughed, she cajoled, and she rang up sale after sale. And in the lulls when the sales floor was empty, she wandered into the back room to check up on my progress—or reassure herself she wasn't alone.

"How hot is that?" she asked, pointing to the soldering iron I had plugged into an extension cord that allowed me to work on my stained glass at the shipping table. The iron sat in its station while I double- and triple-checked that the foil-edged glass pieces I had tacked together with minimal drops of lead were correctly aligned, with even spaces dividing one piece from the next.

I carefully lifted the tacked piece out of the jig and held it briefly on its edge. Now that the piece was assembled, the image as a whole showed the light passing through, the blues and greens bright and translucent. I nodded approval at my own work, then carefully laid the work flat on the Homasote board. "That regulator keeps the soldering iron at a fixed temperature."

"It keeps it from cooling down?"

I grinned. "It keeps it from getting too hot."

"Really? Why? What happens if it gets too hot?" Carrie's eager fascination struck me as more than somewhat peculiar. True, soldering was one of my favorite parts of the stained glass craft process, but even I would admit it wasn't a riveting topic of conversation.

I laid my palms flat against the table. "What's bugging you?"

"Nothing." She took a half step back and crossed her arms over her belly. "Why would you ask that?"

"Because soldering irons are not that interesting."

"Georgia, all of your stained glass stuff is interesting," she said.

I let my raised eyebrows speak for me.

"Fine. I was . . ." Carrie let out a long, slow sigh. "I know the locks on my apartment are all new and I wouldn't be surprised if Diana intimidated the locksmith into putting in top-of-the-line locks for half the price."

"But?" I prompted.

"But. But what's to stop whoever broke into my apartment from coming back?"

"Why would he or she—"

"Or they."

I shuddered. "Why would you think anyone would come back?"

Carrie leaned a hip against the table. Arms folded across her chest, she rolled her shoulders inward as though hugging herself. She ducked her chin. "I keep thinking about Herb Gallo," she murmured. "Diana said his house was . . . well, she said it was trashed, too. This . . . whoever . . . is looking for something. Who knows what Herb went through before the intruder killed him? What if he was, sort of, tortured?" she asked in a small voice.

Knee-jerk reaction made me want to crack a joke just to pull her up out of the sea of worry she was bobbing in. But the time wasn't right. As much as I thought she was worrying needlessly, I knew nothing I could say was likely to ease her fears, mainly because mine were too close to the edge as well.

Her weekend bag, with toothbrush, hairbrush, and whatever else she deemed essential, was still in the car. All it would take was a swing past her apartment so she could grab a few changes of clothes. And after all, Grandy called it a spare room for a reason.

There was only the one complication.

The bell over the front door jingled. Carrie pushed off the table and hurried out to the sales floor to greet her customer while I stood frozen by the vagaries of luck. Tony was picking me up at seven. After all those weeks I could once again sit down across a table from him, enjoy a good meal with a nice guy. But that wasn't where I needed to be.

With a sigh, I grabbed the bottle of flux and replaced its cap. Heading out of the back room, I stopped at the threshold to the sales floor. "So you'll stay with me and Grandy for a couple days." I leaned a shoulder against the doorway, a casual pose for a casual comment. If she thought I was worried she would worry even more. I couldn't let my concern show. "But I can't promise Friday won't crawl into your purse if you leave it on the kitchen table."

Standing by the register and allowing her customers to browse without pressure, Carrie turned to me. "You have plans," she said. "And I don't want to impose." But her eyes were unmistakably hopeful.

I gave a one-shoulder shrug—the other being busy holding up the doorframe—and grinned. "So you'll buy me dinner instead. Don't worry. I don't eat much."

Carrie took my teasing seriously. While she closed up the shop at the end of the day, I walked across the street to the luncheonette to collect our take-out order.

Pushing the door open, I let a little of the appetizing aromas from inside the luncheonette escape into the humidity of the early evening. A little hint of friend onions, the savory scent of grilled beef, and an appealing mélange of salt and spices wrapped the air around me as I moved inside.

The kitchen would be closing within the half hour, and with Wenwood residents aware of closing time and the last of the tourists having already passed through on their trip back south, only one table was occupied. A dark-haired man sat bent over one of the luncheonette's enormous burgers. He lifted his head a fraction and his eyes met mine.

Out of place as he seemed to be, it took me a moment to recognize him. Curtis. The volunteer fireman who had been so mean to Fifi at Trudy's house. The man who Trudy said "rattles me."

It was too late to look away, pretend I hadn't seen him. I forced myself to smile politely and gave a little wave. He returned the gesture with a hesitant nod.

Niceties completed, I gratefully turned my back on him.

Off to my left, Tom sat in his usual place at the counter, cup of coffee at his elbow and Sunday's plus-sized crossword puzzle open on the counter.

"Georgia," he said as I scooted up beside him. "What's a seven-letter name for a character from *Dynasty*?"

"Um . . . maybe *Crystle*?"

"Georgia, is that you?" Grace's voice carried clearly from the kitchen, so quiet in the luncheonette she had no need to shout.

"It's me," I said.

"That can't be it," Tom said. "There's no *C*."

"I'll be right out with your order," Grace called.

I shouted back my thanks and leaned closer to Tom. Over his shoulder, I reviewed the puzzle. I checked the clue and the empty boxes and shook my head. Nothing else would fit other than *Crystle*.

"What's the down clue?" I asked.

Tom read it out and I shook my head again, a bit more emphatically. "That's where the problem is," I said. "If the down should be *Eureka*, just spell *Crystle* with a *K*."

"That can't be right." Tom leaned in, peering closely at the newspaper. "That's too easy."

"What did I tell you?" Grace asked, bustling out of the kitchen with a pair of Styrofoam containers balanced on one hand. "Sometimes the answer is so simple you dismiss it as impossible. You shouldn't overthink all the time."

"You have to think," Tom said, vocal volume on the rise. "That's what the puzzle is for, to make you think."

Grace rolled her eyes and set the containers on the counter. "How's Carrie making out?" she asked.

"She's okay. Still a little shook." I reached for the wallet at the bottom of my purse. "What do I owe you?"

She gave me the total and pulled a plastic bag from under the counter. Slipping the containers into the bag, she said, "The poor thing. I hate to think of her on her own right now."

"She's not. She's staying with me and Pete until the police can settle things." I dropped a twenty on the counter before scrounging in my pockets for the coin change.

"She's staying with Pete?" Tom repeated.

"And me," I said, triumphantly plunking a quarter down on the counter. "Until the police find the guy who broke into her apartment."

"Terry's gonna stay with me when he comes," Tom announced.

My forehead rumpled, my brain lurched at the sudden change of topic. "That's really nice for you," I managed, as Grace sighed and shook her head.

"Maybe they'll never find him," Tom announced.

"Who? Terry?" I asked, a little lost.

"No, the police," Tom said. "They might never find the guy who burgled the antiques place."

"Hey," Grace snapped. "That's my niece you're talking about."

"What niece?" Tom asked.

I met Grace's gaze across the counter. We shared a sympathetic little smile, and I said good night to both her and Tom before leaving her to explain to Tom, yet again, that her sister's daughter was an officer in the Pace County Police Department. And my good friend.

Sadly, neither one of those facts was sufficient for me to ignore Tom's comment. What if he was right? What if the police never did figure out who was causing all the havoc? Then what?

"All right," I said, dropping my purse on the wingback chair in the living room. "I'll get the plates, you turn on the television. We'll eat in the dining room."

"Deal." Grace's take-out bag in hand, Carrie headed for the television.

I continued on into the kitchen, switching on the light. Ensconced in the middle of the kitchen table, Friday rolled to her feet and arched her back in a stretch. I scratched between her ears, enjoyed the soft fur and the blissful half-mast of her eyes for the brief minutes before she raced away, no doubt to climb inside Carrie's purse and sharpen her claws on her wallet.

I grabbed a pair of plates and the necessary flatware and carried them into the dining room, where Carrie stood at the head of the table, one eye on the television, the other on the stack of photo albums I'd left there.

"Can I move these?" Carrie asked, nodding toward the albums.

Thunder rumbled outside, promising the rain that had threatened all day. "Yeah, be careful with them. They're old."

"Obviously."

Leave it to me to try to tell the antiques expert what was old.

I laid out the plates and cutlery while Carrie carefully shifted the albums to the other end of the table. "Grandy left them out so I could look at pictures of my grandmother when she was my age," I said, dropping into a chair. "Which also means there's pictures of Grandy at my age."

"Really?" Carrie grinned.

"Really. Do you know he used to have a whole head of hair?"

She chuckled. "Do you mind if I take a peek?"

If pictures of my grandparents in their youth were

going to cheer her up, I wasn't about to stop her. "Be my guest." I popped open the lid on the first container. Peering inside, I identified the sandwich as something in the red meat realm, something I might possibly eat once a year. I shoved it in the direction of Carrie's plate and pulled the other container closer. Opening the lid, I inhaled the aroma of melted cheese over tuna and my stomach gurgled in anticipation.

Carrie lifted the top album and set it down next to her plate. She opened the cover and reverently turned to the first page before I could warn her about the pictures falling loose from their pages. "Ooh, you'll have to fix that," she said, running a hand over the empty page, gently lifting the photographs from the album's gutter.

"Oh my gosh." She sank down into her chair and I pushed her food container closer to her. "Will you look at the plaid pants?"

I smiled in agreement, sliding my tuna melt free of the container and onto my plate. As Carrie moved on to the next page, I glanced to the television, assuring myself *Hollywood Hoofers* hadn't yet started. Another rumble of thunder seemed to shake the shingles on the house and for a scant few seconds the picture on the television pixilated. "I hope we don't lose the cable," I said.

Carrie was paying no attention. She was gazing down at the photos in the album, a contented smile softening her face.

Seized with envy, I grabbed the next album from the pile and embarked on my own walk back in time. Careful to keep my food away from the photographs, I eased through the book page-by-page, mindful of the pictures slipping free of their assigned places and sliding into the book's gutter or down into my lap. I squinted at pictures of my grandmother, smiled at pictures of Grandy, and marveled at pictures of my mother. To think she had once been so young.

Yes, Grandy had been younger then, too. But by the time I was grown enough to build memories of him, he had settled into the style and bearing of the man he would always be. In that regard, he was timeless. He stood with people I should have recognized, that I struggled to place as part of his family or Grandma's. Smiling faces, birthday cakes, couples. Always couples.

And there I sat, eating takeout, waiting for *Hollywood Hoofers* to come on the television, and looking at photographs of people I didn't know instead of being out, being part of a—potential—couple.

The sigh slipped out before I could stop myself.

"What is it?" Carrie asked.

I shook my head, not ready to share my thoughts, not prepared to acknowledge much less confess that I might be feeling even the slightest, tiniest, teeniest bit lonely. But apparently, the tears welling in my eyes were enough to give me away.

"Hey, you know," Carrie said overbrightly. "The pictures from the albums in that box I was supposed to give to Russ don't fall off the page like this. What do you think? Better glue or stickier spit?"

Skipping right past rumble, thunder cracked. I took a slow deep breath before a flash of lightning brightened the room.

"Well that doesn't make sense," I muttered, fighting to focus my mind away from my single status and onto a thought that was just out of reach. "The pictures in those albums are older even than these." I recalled blurred faces and sepia tones. Little boys in short pants and women in long dresses. "If these photo corners aren't holding, the others shouldn't either."

Carrie shrugged. "Maybe—what was her name? Heaney? Maybe Mrs. Heaney redid the albums."

My eyebrows crept up my forehead. "Why would she do that?"

"Why not? Preserve memories." She took a bite of her sandwich.

"No." I shook my head. "Why go to all the trouble of resetting old photographs in the same old album? If you're preserving, why not get something new? Something that protects the pictures?"

Her chewing stilled. She raised a hand to cover her mouth and said, "What are you thinking?"

Pushing my chair back, I stood. "I'm thinking there's something important about those pictures. Can we get that box out of your trunk?"

Carrie sprang from her seat. "The keys are in my bag." She hustled out of the dining room and in seconds I heard her dash up the stairs, followed by "Get off my purse, Friday!"

I inverted the Styrofoam containers over each of our plates in case little paws—displaced from the splendor of Carrie's handbag—came seeking. When Carrie returned to the main floor, keys in hand, I waved her ahead of me through the open door.

"What could be special about the pictures?" she asked as we crossed the lawn.

A fat raindrop broke across my nose. "I don't know. Maybe nothing. Maybe it's whatever the arsonist/burglar/murderer is looking for. I figure it's worth finding out, don't you?"

"Oh my gosh, is it raining? Now?" She increased her speed, reaching the car well ahead of me. I was in no rush. For me—and my hair—humidity was far worse than rain.

I looked on as she slipped the key into the lock, and left the key ring in place as the trunk rose. The trunk light burst on, making me blink in discomfort, making me suddenly aware of the encroaching darkness.

Nestled beside the milk crate stocked with automotive necessities in the trunk was the carton and bag Melanie had turned over to Carrie's care. She reached into the trunk and tugged open the flap of the carton. "How many photo albums are there?" she asked, peering inside.

"There's a bunch," I said. "Do you remember which ones had all the pictures still stuck in place?"

She opened her mouth, but nothing more than an *ummm* escaped.

"Maybe take the whole box," I suggested.

Nodding, she wrapped her arms around the carton and lifted it free of the trunk. When she was clear, I reached up and slammed shut the trunk. Raindrops hit forcefully against the top of my head and my shoulders as I tugged the keys free and matched Carrie's quick pace back into the house.

She brought the carton directly into the living room

and set it down atop the coffee table. Wasting no time, she pulled open the remaining flaps keeping the box closed and withdrew a pair of photo albums. "Here." She held one out to me as she sat down on the couch.

Taking the album, I sat down beside her and laid it across my lap. I opened the album and went directly to the first page.

I suppose I expected to see the same pictures I had seen when glancing through the album at Carrie's apartment. Subconsciously I may have been looking for the solemn parents, the restless child, the cascade of lace concealing an infant. So that what I did see registered no deeper than a vague sense of familiarity.

The photos were more recent than those I had previously seen, but still old enough to be thick-papered black-and-white photos, many with deckle-edged borders. I tried to pull one free of the photo corners holding it in place, but the picture came away from the page with its dried-out corners still in place. It came away cleanly and effortlessly, and I knew before I even checked the back that there would be nothing there out of the ordinary.

Memorial Day, 1941.

I sighed, and Carrie looked up from her album.

Seeing what I'd done, she tugged at the picture on the page in front of her.

The photo slipped out of its corners, and left no need to check the back for secrets. The paper that had been tucked behind it fluttered into Carrie's lap.

21

She blew out a breath and began reading. "I, Margaret Mary Heaney, residing at 97 Riverside Drive . . . blah blah . . . declare this to be my last will and testament. I revoke all wills and—" Carrie glanced up at me. "She underlined *revoke* three times."

My fingers itched to take the paper from her hands. I closed the album in my lap and gripped it tightly, keeping my hands to myself. "Guess she changed her mind about something," I muttered.

Carrie's gaze moved rapidly across the page before she gasped. "She's named Herb Gallo as her executor," she said on a breath.

I shifted closer to her, attempting to read for myself the page that she held. "I'm sure a lot of people appoint a lawyer as executor. Of course," I added, "not everyone's lawyers were murdered."

We shared a look between us, the kind that said we understood whatever was in the document was important.

"What else?" I asked, tipping my chin toward the will.

She cleared her throat and returned to the paper. Though her voice remained steady, the paper fluttered from her slight trembling. "Okay, um . . . devise, bequeath, and give the property at 97 Riverside Drive to the SPCA. Oh, that's nice."

I nodded agreement.

"I devise, bequeath and give only"—Carrie glanced at me; "More underlining," she said, before continuing—"the assets in my account at First Federal Savings to my grandson, Curtis Adam Heaney, who has much to learn about the value of money and the importance of making your own way in the world."

"Only?" I repeated, in the split second before the implication fell into place. "'Revised' and 'only.' Curtis was cut out of the will."

"If in the original will he was to inherit the house—"

"On Riverside," I said. "Where Spring and Hamilton are buying up property—"

"He stood to make a lot of money."

"If," I put in, "this revised will stayed hidden." I shifted to the edge of my seat, and lifted my purse from the coffee table. Digging within for my smartphone, I asked, "What are the odds Curtis Heaney is the same Curtis we met that night at town hall?"

"Probably pretty good. How many men are named Curtis these days? And are jackasses."

I pulled my smartphone out and opened a search app. Keying in "Curtis Heaney" and "images," I sat back on the couch and waited for the less than blistering data speed to deliver me content. "What else does it say?"

Carrie shook her head, scanned the page. "That's pretty much it. It—oh no."

"What oh no?"

"The witnesses," she said, turning the paper so I could see. "Adele Chesterton and Trudy Villiers."

"Trudy?" I sat up straight. Memories of Trudy talking about her younger days in Wenwood swirled in mind. "Didn't she mention something about an Adele who died?"

My Internet search completed at the same moment Carrie asked, "What if she didn't die of natural causes?"

On a single breath, I let out every vile curse I knew.

The man on the screen, the one Curtis Heaney, was indeed the same man we'd met at the town hall meeting, the man who was later talking with Melanie. We'd encountered him on the path in front of Trudy's house. And he'd been sitting in Grace's luncheonette not two hours ago. For Pete's sake, I'd *waved* to the slimeball.

I showed the screen to Carrie.

"Oh my God," she said. "It is him."

I sprang from the couch, grabbing my purse and hers as I did so. "We have to get to Trudy," I said.

"What about this?" She held up the will. "What do we do with this?"

283

I handed over her purse. "I don't know. Call your ex? Let's go."

I took a step toward the door, but Carrie stood frozen to the spot, hugging her purse to her chest. "Maybe we should call the police."

Waving my cell phone, I said, "I got it. You just have to drive. Come on."

As if she'd been hit with an electrified prod, Carrie sprang into motion, scurrying to meet me at the door.

I opened my contact list on my phone, found the number for the precinct at the top of my list under "##." Carrie stepped out onto the porch while I pushed "Dial" and followed her, pulling the door shut behind me.

"Why hide the will, though?" I asked. I held the phone to my ear, waiting for the call to connect, and dashed down the steps beside Carrie. "Why not file it with, I don't know, the county clerk or whoever keeps these things?"

"Lawyers keep originals," Carrie said. She raised a hand to her forehead, warding off the rain now falling in steady sheets.

A man's voice stopped us both in our tracks. "How about you stop right there," he said.

We both turned, startled.

Curtis Heaney stood in the middle of Grandy's brick walkway. Rain soaked his dark hair against his head and glinted off his mustache. No bolt of lightning was needed to reveal the gun in his hand.

My body went liquid. Strength drained from my muscles. The arm holding the phone to my ear drifted downward.

"Get rid of the phone and give me the will."

Carrie sidestepped closer to me. Being elbow-to-elbow with her gave my confidence a jolt.

"I really can't afford a new phone and if I drop this one in the rain it—"

"Disconnect it and drop it." Curtis raised the gun. Clearly I had mistaken stupidity for confidence.

I looked down at the phone, at the sound wave icon that told me the phone was ringing on the other end. Reaching to the side, phone in my outstretched hand, I let our connection to help fall into the wet grass.

"Is this where we make a break for it?" Carrie asked, her voice barely audible.

"Can you outrun a gun?" I asked.

"Now give me the will," Curtis said.

"Oh. I don't . . ." Carrie began.

"If the will gets wet, it might be ruined," I said, because of the aforementioned stupidity.

Curtis laughed a great, barking laugh. He stopped just short of letting his head fall back. "You think I want that thing readable? You think I've been following you for days because I wanted that thing to be seen?"

He took a step toward us, as though closing the distance would make the gun more effective. It was with that movement that I realized there was no silencer on the gun. If Curtis fired, the neighborhood would hear.

In fact . . .

"Curtis Heaney!" I shouted. "What are you doing with that gun?"

"Georgia," Carrie cautioned.

"Just put the gun down," I shouted again. "Put the gun down before someone gets hurt."

Curtis took another step closer, and did the same laughing thing. "No one's going to hear you," he said over a slightly amused, mostly manic laugh. "It's hot. It's raining. No one's windows are open except yours. Thanks for that, by the way. I might not have seen where you found that will but I heard enough."

Drat.

"Now hand over the will." He enunciated each word, letting them out one at a time like the bang of a drum.

"Fine. Fine." Carrie shifted her purse around so it covered her belly. Unzipping the main pocket, she looked to me from the corner of her eye. Head down, she asked, "Should I give it to him?"

I narrowed my eyes at Curtis, which, as a bonus, kept the rain out. "Go ahead. Give it to him. You said yourself, lawyers keep originals."

Curtis grinned. "Too bad old man Gallo didn't take better care of them."

The impact of his words sunk in perhaps a little slower than they would have had Curtis not been holding us at gunpoint. "We have the only copy," I said on a breath.

"I'm running out of patience," Curtis snapped.

"Here," Carrie said, shoving her hand in her bag. "Here. Just take it and go."

I wanted to tell her no. I wanted to stop her from pulling the will from her purse and giving it to the man who had very likely been the cause of theft and fire and murder. But I had no idea how.

When no better option sprang to mind, I reached to block her arm with my own. "No," I said. "Don't give it to him."

Again he raised the gun, straightening his arm so his gaze seemed to reach down the barrel. "Do. Now. No more delays."

One deep breath, and I ripped the purse from Carrie's grasp. "Run!" I shouted. "Run for help!"

Roaring like an injured bear, Curtis lurched forward. With his empty hand he reached for the purse I held tucked to my chest.

Carrie, caught unaware by my command to run, stood rooted.

I spun, putting my back to Curtis even as his arm wrapped around me. Anticipating his grab for the purse, I held it tighter. When his arm instead clamped tight around me, he had me pinned.

His breath was hot on my ear. The barrel of the gun pressed to the side of my head surprisingly . . . prickly? But there was no time to focus on mistaken expectations.

"I can shoot you right now," he said, "and your skull will muffle the noise."

"Georgia," Carrie whimpered. Eyes wide and glistening she glanced left and right.

"Go," I managed before the weight of my muscles, the challenge of staying upright while my body melted with fear, became too much.

Somewhere between muscle failure and a swoon, I slid downward. Sinking to the wet ground, the gun barrel slipped against the top of my head, losing contact.

I kept hold of the purse. So did Curtis. He tugged. I held fast. No way was I going to let go of that bag. It's a girl thing.

"Georgia just give him the bag," Carrie pleaded.

"Can't," I said.

"Please," she said.

But Carrie was facing us, her back to the street. She didn't see.

I sunk farther, spine curving, tail tucking. The last thing I saw before my view was blocked by the purse I wouldn't release was the green and gold stripe of the Pace County PD squad car.

The vehicle *shoosh*ed to a stop in the rain. A split second later, my new favorite phrase rang out.

"Freeze! Police!"

"Oh thank God," Carrie said.

"Drop the weapon," the officer commanded. "Drop the weapon!"

The gun fell onto the grass beside me. Literally. The stupid thing sat on top of blades of grass like they were a bed of nails. Two thoughts hit me at once:

The damn thing was plastic. That's why he didn't shoot. Plastic.

And I was going to have to mow the lawn, if it ever stopped raining.

"It would be best, really, if all these squad cars and flashing lights could be gone before my grandfather gets home," I said.

Detective Nolan smirked.

"Really. It's not about you," I said. "He's an old man. I don't want to give him a heart attack or anything."

"First of all, I have no doubt the neighbors have already called him." Standing beside the couch where I sat, the detective folded closed his notebook and slipped it into the back pocket of his worn, frayed jeans. His T-shirt had a faded Captain America logo, and it, along with his hair, was rain soaked. "Second of all, your grandfather is a tough old goat who's going to outlive us all."

He was probably right on both counts.

"What happens to Curtis?" Carrie asked as she set a cup of hot tea down on the coffee table. It seemed wrong, suddenly, to have tea on a coffee table. I giggled quietly. "Tea on a coffee table," I murmured. "Tea. Coffee." I giggled a little more.

"He'll be spending the rest of his night being questioned," Nolan said.

"Don't give him any tea," I said, reaching for my own.

"She might be a little out of it after the stress," Nolan said. I looked up to find him facing Carrie. "You think you could stick around, make sure she's all right?"

"Of course," Carrie said.

I might have been addled after having a gun held to my head, even if it did turn out to be a toy old enough to predate the neon-colored toy-gun law. But I was still aware enough to know Nolan was nice, and Carrie was a good friend.

"Davis—I mean, Diana—will be by after ten to check up on things," he said.

"I'm sure that won't be necessary," Carrie said.

I took a sip of tea, discovered it was very hot, and set it gingerly back on the table.

"It's not about 'necessary,'" Nolan said. He rested a hand against my shoulder, briefly. "We'll be in touch."

He strode from the room, back out into the rainy night. The room, in his absence, seemed somehow emptier.

"He's a nice guy." Carrie dropped to the couch beside me and let her head fall back against the cushions.

I nodded. "He's a cop."

"Yes, he is. And I think he likes you."

"Maybe," I conceded. "But I'm having dinner with Tony next Sunday."

Evidently having decided the coast was clear, Friday raced into the room and catapulted into my lap. I buried my fingers in her warm silky fur and pressed a series of kisses against her head.

"So," Carrie said, "you're having dinner with a construction worker and you've got an admirer who's a cop. If you ever find yourself without a date, I guess you can just pick one of the other Village People."

22

"**I**t's just lovely," Trudy said.

She bent over the long table she had set up in what was once a den but would soon be the breakfast room. Her gaze traced the letters and the blossoms, the whites and pinks, the greens, lavenders, and hints of blue all coming together in a stained glass window that read MAG-NOLIA BED AND BREAKFAST.

"Shame it's raining," she said, looking up at the picture window at the back of the room. Sheets of water struck the pane, relentless.

"I've seen it in sunlight," Carrie said. She formed her fingers into an *okay* sign, half-closed her eyes. "Gorgeous."

Me, I remained crouched close to the floor, rubbing Fifi's exposed belly while she drooled happily into the antique carpet. I was pleased Trudy was happy with her window. Even more, I was pleased Curtis Heaney had been put behind bars before he had a chance to do anything to harm her. In the few weeks since I'd had my life threatened by a plastic gun and been back and forth so Trudy could approve designs and colors, I'd become genuinely fond of her. As yet, though, I haven't agreed to learning mah-jongg.

"I wonder, is there something you can do to bring this motif into the house," Trudy said. Her elegant fingers framed her chin and her eyes narrowed slightly as she gazed around the room.

Carrie mimicked her position right down to the pursed lips. "A mirror, maybe? With the flowers around the edging?"

I gave Fifi one last pat on the tummy and stood. "A mirror would be nice, but—" I paused, uncertain. Of the three of us, Carrie was the expert on decorating. The only expertise I could claim of late was an uncanny ability to alphabetize and a knack for breaking glass.

"But what?" Carrie prompted.

"Yes, do tell us, Georgia. Your opinion counts, you know."

Fifi shoved her cold wet nose against my shin. I smiled. "What if the mirror was old instead of new? What if it had that veining around the edges?"

"Ooh," Carrie said. "I like it. But not too much veining. We still want a functional mirror, right?" She looked to Trudy for confirmation.

The older woman tipped her head, raised her eyes to the ceiling as she considered. "I would suppose that depends on where we put this mirror. If we put it over the mantel in the living room, I'd rather have a new look. It's cleaner, if you understand my meaning."

We nodded. I hoped Carrie knew what Trudy meant, though, because I was faking.

Within my purse—lumped gracelessly atop a wooden travel trunk that served as a coffee table—my smartphone emitted a chime that signaled an incoming text message.

"Sorry, ladies," I said, crossing the room to grab my bag. "That's my ride."

"Georgia." Trudy's brow wrinkled as she scowled at me. "You shouldn't race out the door at the sound of a bell like one of Pavlov's dogs. Your young man should make the effort to get out of the car and come up the walk to meet you."

Carrie bit her bottom lip but could do nothing to quell the mirth in her eyes.

"I'll remember that next time, Trudy," I said.

I looked down at Fifi. "Ready girl?" I asked, taking the leash Trudy held out for me. "You want to come see your new house?"

"Promise me you'll take video of her chasing that creature, okay?" Carrie asked.

Laughing, I snapped the leash onto the dog's collar. Fifi rolled swiftly to her feet and started her full-body wagging. "What if Friday's the one who does the chasing?"

She pursed her lips. "Then I don't want to see it."

Trudy bent and patted Fifi on the head. "You be a good girl for your new mommy. I'm sure she'll take very good care of you."

She sniffled a little as she straightened, then surprised me, and perhaps herself, by pulling me into a hug. "Thank you," she said quietly, her classic perfume scent swirling around us both. "I'm sure Madge would be pleased to have Fifi go to such a good home."

It was my turn to sniffle.

Trudy released me and walked to the kitchen with me and the dog. "Here's her food and her dish and this crazy purple blob of a toy. I don't know what it is," she said, flopping the stuffed toy back and forth, "but she adores it."

Fifi made a little leap and nabbed the purple toy from Trudy. I collected the plastic storage container of food and the ceramic bowl with the black paw print motif and wrapped the leash firmly around my hand.

"Ready for an adventure?" I asked.

Fifi let slide one little string of drool. I sent a silent plea to Margaret Heaney up in heaven, asking that Fifi please not leave too much spit in Tony's Jaguar.

After Trudy gave Fifi one final pat, I said my good-byes and walked out the door, dog at my heels, into the autumn rain.

WELL-CRAFTED MYSTERIES FROM BERKLEY PRIME CRIME

- **Earlene Fowler** Don't miss these Agatha Award–winning quilting mysteries featuring Benni Harper.

- **Monica Ferris** These *USA Today* bestselling Needlecraft Mysteries include free knitting patterns.

- **Laura Childs** Her Scrapbooking Mysteries offer tips to satisfy the most die-hard crafters.

- **Maggie Sefton** These popular Knitting Mysteries come with knitting patterns and recipes.

- **Lucy Lawrence** These brilliant Decoupage Mysteries involve cutouts, glue, and varnish.

- **Elizabeth Lynn Casey** The Southern Sewing Circle Mysteries are filled with friends, southern charm—and murder.